Jaded Moon

by

Laura Landon

Book Two
Ransomed Jewels

PRAIRIE MUSE PUBLISHING
©2016

JADED MOON

Book Two in the RANSOMED JEWELS Series
Copyright © 2016 by Laura Landon
First print edition
ISBN 978-1-937216-70-2

www.prairiemuse.com

With much appreciation
to my readers

Chapter 1

FOR MORE THAN A YEAR, not one soul had been brave enough to darken Ross Bennett's doorstep. The fact that someone had the nerve to disturb him at this late hour flamed the anger that constantly simmered inside him. He'd worked hard to separate himself from the locals and took pleasure in knowing "hospitable" wasn't a term anyone used to describe him.

Ross Bennett, the Marquess of Rainforth, hadn't come to St. Stephen's Hollow because he wanted friends.

He took another swallow of the whiskey in his glass and dropped his head back against the cushion. Whoever had come tonight would discover that soon enough.

He followed the soft padding of his butler's slippers as they scuffed across the floor toward the front door and waited for the persistent banging to cease. Ross had no doubt Benedict would send the unwelcome intruder on his way in a few minutes and Ross would be alone again.

Muffled voices came from beyond the closed door, but instead of a continuation of the familiar silence, Ross heard the solid thudding of boots crossing the tiled entryway. His eyes flew open with a jarring jolt that rocked his whole body. *Bloody hell!* The interloper had entered his home.

Ross bolted to his feet, prepared to confront whoever had barged past Benedict, then throw him out of his house.

There was a single thud as a fist hit wood and the door swung open. A large, familiar shadow filled the entryway and Ross looked again to be sure he hadn't been mistaken. He hadn't.

Ross ground his teeth. "How the hell did you find me?"

The man smiled. "Finding people who don't want to be found is one of my talents."

"I ordered Chambers not to tell anyone where I was."

His cousin, Major Samuel Bennett, stepped into the room and closed the door behind him. "Your solicitor didn't reveal your whereabouts," he said as he walked across the room and poured himself a glass of brandy from a decanter on a small table tucked next to the tapestried wall. "I figured it out on my own."

Ross sat back down in his chair and watched Sam bring his drink to the matching wing chair opposite Ross's and sit down.

Bennett stretched his long legs out in front of him and took a swallow of brandy. "Bloody hell, Ross. It's a long way out here."

"Obviously, not far eno—" Ross started to say, then stopped. Sam didn't deserve the sharp edge of his temper. He owed him far better after what had happened between them. He took a swallow of his brandy and finished with, "It's not so far. Three days from London. Two, if the roads are good."

"Have you looked outside lately?"

Ross cast a glance at the torrents of rain splattering against the windows. "So, how did you find me?"

"Quite by accident, actually. I was going through the yearly reports for each of your estates and stumbled across one I didn't know existed. Imagine my surprise to discover there was at least one property from which you hadn't divorced yourself."

"St. Stephen's Hollow was my mother's. It wasn't connected to the Rainforth name."

"So now you've come here to live out your life in obscurity?"

"If that's how you want to think of it."

Sam rose to his feet and slammed his glass down on the corner of the table. "Dammit, Ross. Don't let them drive you from their clubs and their ballrooms. You can't take the blame for what your father did. It's him they should hate. Not you!"

Ross shrugged. "But Father's not here to hate. I am."

He sucked in a deep breath, the pain of his father's betrayal of England—and of the Rainforth name—cutting as deeply as the day he'd first learned of it two years ago. "They're the ones who lost sons and brothers and husbands in the war because my father sold military secrets to the enemy. They're the ones who are suffering."

Sam stared at him. "And you're not?"

Ross took another long swallow of liquor to mask the wounds Sam's words had ripped raw. He wasn't nearly drunk enough to dull the pain. Not by a damn sight. "Why are you here?"

"I need your help."

Ross stopped with the glass halfway to his mouth. He took in the serious expression on his cousin's face, then burst out laughing. "My help? Haven't you heard a Rainforth can't be trusted?"

"I've trusted you with my life," Sam said, his voice thick.

Ross shook his head. "That was a long time ago. I'm in no position to save anyone now. Not even you."

"Chief McCormick disagrees."

The name caught Ross by surprise. He'd met McCormick the night his father had died. Remembered McCormick's endless questions, as well as the man's attempts to keep his father's traitorous activities a secret. Attempts that had failed miserably. London had learned of the scandal before the funeral. A mob of hecklers greeted him every time he left the house, even following him as he left London to bury his father's body. The memory of the vile words they'd chanted was enough to kill any curiosity he might have about Sam's request for help. "I'm not your man, Major."

"Someone is using a portion of coastline near here to smuggle in opium," Sam continued as if Ross hadn't spoken. "They're supplying the opium dens that are springing up all over London, and the steadily increasing addiction to the drug is at epidemic proportions. Until we discover where it's being brought in and who's behind it, there's little we can do to halt its use."

"And you think it's being brought into England from St. Stephen's?"

Sam sat back down and stared into the fire still burning. "Either here or somewhere close by. One of my agents infiltrated one of London's opium dens and heard bits of information that made us believe the smugglers might be using this area of coastline. It's perfect for smuggling, isolated, and far enough away from London not to attract attention."

Ross turned in his chair and studied the serious expression on Sam's face. "Are you sure?"

"Not positive, but close enough to think it's worth investigating further. Both St. Stephen's and Clythebrook Estate extend to the sea. Every mile of coast on either estate is not only lined with numerous inlets and coves where boats can easily come ashore, but dotted by a catacomb of tunnels where the contraband can be hidden."

Ross didn't want to believe Sam's reasoning but knew it had merit. He rose from his chair and paced a small area. Sam's next question intrigued him further.

"What can you tell me about Clythebrook Estate?"

"Not much. I haven't exactly been the most social of neighbors. I declined the one dinner invitation the Countess of Clythebrook extended and only met her once by accident. We happened to pass on the road bordering our two estates."

"What's she like?"

Ross shrugged. "Pleasant enough, though I'm afraid the conversation was decidedly one-sided. She did most of the talking."

Sam arched his brows. "Why does that not surprise me?"

Ross ignored the sarcasm and continued. "I did learn that she's been a widow for more than ten years. She has no children of her own, but she spoke of someone named—what was it—Josephine I believe it was, whom I gathered she and her late husband rescued from the orphanage. She must be a companion to Lady Clythebrook with connections to Sacred Heart Orphanage. Lady Clythebrook hinted that a great deal of this Miss Josephine's time was spent running the orphanage and seeing to the children's needs."

Ross stared into the flames in the grate and pictured the person about whom Lady Clythebrook had spoken. "No doubt she's a mousy little thing so grateful to have been rescued from a life in an orphanage she is eager to do anything to please."

"Perhaps she has some information that might be valuable."

Ross was quiet for a moment as he considered Sam's line of thinking. "Surely you don't suspect Lady Clythebrook or her companion of being involved in the smuggling?"

"I don't suspect anyone. I only know the little information we've been able to gather leads us here." He was quiet a moment longer, then sat forward in his chair. "The queen has taken a special interest in this, Ross. One of her closest advisors has a son who is wasting away because of his addiction to the opiate and Her Majesty has vowed not to rest until every one of the blackguards responsible for bringing the drug into the country is hanged as an example. I'm also confident that those involved with stopping its availability will be richly rewarded."

"And you thought the queen's recognition would be of interest to me? Well, you thought wrong. The answer is no."

Sam continued as if Ross hadn't just turned him down. "I'd come here myself if I thought I could investigate without being found out, but we both know I wouldn't go unnoticed even one day. A stranger snooping around draws too much attention. Just stopping at a nearby inn earlier tonight caused more notice than I would have preferred. That's why we need someone local to gather information for us."

"What's happening in London is no longer my concern. I've made a life for myself at St. Stephen's. I can't help you."

"Can't, or—"

"Leave it be, Sam."

Ross heard Sam's labored sigh. No doubt there were several

more reasons his cousin could give to convince Ross to help, but Sam didn't argue further. Instead, he silently finished the last of the liquor in his glass and stood. If there was one facet of Ross's character that had become more firmly engrained since the night he'd fired the gun that had killed his father, it was his deep conviction to forge his own way without a care for Society or their approval.

"Will you think about it, Ross? You don't have to give me your final answer now, but sleep on it. Perhaps—"

"Let me find you a bed," Ross interrupted. "You can get at least a few hours' sleep before dawn. You'll want to be on your way before anyone notices you were here."

Ross rose from his chair and showed Sam to an empty bedroom. "I'll wake you before dawn," he said, then stepped out into the hallway. He turned back when Sam called to him.

"Ross. Here. I almost forgot."

Ross focused on a letter in Sam's outstretched hand.

"Your solicitor forwarded this to me on the chance I might be able to deliver it. He seemed to think it might be important."

Ross stared at the letter in Sam's hand, then took it. "Thank you. I'm sure it's nothing. Probably just papers I need to sign."

"If anything needs to be returned, have it ready and I'll take it when I leave."

Ross nodded and stepped out of the room. He closed the door behind him and walked down the stairs to his study. He'd just as well stay awake until Sam left. He was already too tired to fight the demons he knew were standing ready to attack the moment he closed his eyes.

Ross took the envelope and sat down behind his massive oak desk. He pulled the lamp closer, then broke the note's seal. The letter was dated a few months earlier. It was from his solicitor and from the condition of the missive, numerous attempts to deliver it had obviously been made with no success.

Ross opened the folded paper and reached for a small slip of paper that floated to the desk top. He picked it up and glanced at it, his brows furrowing in confusion. It was a bank draft in the amount of five hundred pounds, made out to Mrs. Carrie Gardner. It had obviously never reached her.

Ross dropped the draft onto the desktop and picked up the letter.

19 January, 1858

> *My dear Lord Rainforth,*
> *As per your instructions, for the past four years an annual draft of five hundred pounds has been sent to Mrs. Carrie Gardner residing in the dower house at St. Stephen's Hollow.*

Carrie Gardner. Hearing her name forced him back to his past—a past he had no desire to relive.

He turned back to the letter in his hands and read on.

> *Upon the return of the enclosed draft, I sent a trusted employee to investigate. My representative found Mrs. Gardner's residence vacated and upon inquiry discovered the details as I know them. It is with the utmost regret that I inform you that Mrs. Gardner has met with a most unfortunate accident which has claimed her life.*
> *Even though the details are still quite sketchy, it seems Mrs. Gardner was a passenger in a carriage that overturned. The lady did not survive the mishap. The representative sent on your behalf checked as to the whereabouts of your child—*

Ross's breath caught and he stopped.

His child.

He read the words again.

> *…the whereabouts of your child but was unable to locate it. Since Mrs. Gardner was not known to have any family, my assumption is that the child was placed at Sacred Heart Orphanage*

*located nearby. Inquiries have so far yielded no
information.*

Ross's heart beat faster as he skimmed the words, eager to find out everything.

> *I have followed to the letter the demands
> Mrs. Gardner stipulated more than four years
> ago, before she left London. It was during our last
> meeting that she informed me she was carrying
> your child and assured me that you were in complete
> agreement with her request to use a portion of the
> money to provide for the child. Since you'd already
> gifted her with the dower house on St. Stephen's
> and provided her with a more-than-generous
> allowance, I saw no reason to bother you with such
> minor details. Therefore, one half of every year's
> allowance has been put into a trust, to be released to
> the child when said child reaches its majority.*
>
> *Please advise if you want to send Mrs. Gardner's
> portion of the money to the orphanage to see to the
> child's immediate needs, or if you want the entire
> amount put into the trust.*
>
> *At present the trust is still in Mrs. Gardner's
> name since I do not have any other information
> concerning the child, such as its name, the date of its
> birth, or whether the child was a boy or a girl. If I
> might please prevail upon you to provide me with
> the above information I will see that the money
> already accrued in Mrs. Gardner's name is put into
> a proper account.*
>
> *I await your instruction.*
>
> > *Your most devoted servant,*
> > *Elvin Chambers, Esq.*

Ross stared at the letter for several long minutes. There was a child. The woman who'd been his mistress for more than a year was dead. And had left behind a child. *His* child.

Ross stared down at the words in the letter again. *It was during our last meeting that she informed me she was carrying your child and assured me that you were in complete agreement with her request to provide for the child.* He read the words again, thinking that this time they'd seem more real.

He had a child.

Ross placed the letter on the desk and rose to his feet. His legs felt unsteady beneath him and his mind wanted to doubt that the child was his. But deep inside him he knew it was not only possible he had a child, but probable. He had been acquainted with Carrie long enough to know she'd never take another lover while sleeping with him.

Why hadn't she told him?

He wanted to laugh. The reason was obvious. What difference would it have made even if he'd been aware? She was his mistress. What male of the peerage married his mistress?

Ross wrapped his fingers around the brass handles on the multi-paned double doors that led out onto the patio and threw them back. A cold gust of air rushed into the room and struck him full force. He breathed in deeply and opened his mind to think more clearly.

A picture of Carrie as he'd last seen her appeared in his mind. She'd been stunningly beautiful with a pleasing personality and a certain talent in bed. She'd been interesting to talk to, and as long as he remembered her with several new gowns a season and an expensive piece of jewelry every now and then, she expected nothing more from him than an infrequent afternoon of his time or a ride in the park. He'd never loved her but neither had she loved him. It had been the perfect arrangement. Until she'd decided she didn't wish to continue as they had any longer.

Their parting had been amicable and he'd gifted her with a modest annual income as well as the home in the country she'd asked for. In return, she'd promised to sever their relationship. And she had. Now, he regretted to admit that in the more-than-four years that she'd been gone, he hadn't given her more than an occasional thought.

Ross closed the door that led outdoors and walked back into the study. The fire was still aglow with a few larger pieces of wood that burned bright and he sat back in his chair and stared at the flickering flames.

He'd offered her the dower house at St. Stephen's because he'd had no intention of ever returning here. Then, after he'd come, he'd gone to see her that one time, but had found the house empty. He'd assumed she'd tired of the country and had returned to Town. Now he knew that wasn't what had happened.

Why hadn't he asked after her? Why hadn't he been curious enough to wonder where she'd gone?

But he hadn't given her a second thought.

He dropped his head back against the cushion and closed his eyes. Carrie Gardner was dead and his child was out there—alone.

Ross squeezed his fingers around the arms of the chair. Perhaps that might be best. Perhaps the child would rather grow up thinking he had no family than having to admit Rainforth blood ran through his veins. Perhaps he would be doing the child a favor by leaving him or her in the orphanage. But…

Perhaps by leaving the child in the orphanage he would be condemning his son or daughter to a horrible existence.

Ross sat in front of the fire until the embers grew cold and lifeless, then paced the floor hour after endless hour, debating the course he should take. What did he know about raising a child? He had no experience with children. At least if he left the child in the orphanage…

He remembered what Carrie had told him when she'd revealed that she'd grown up in an orphanage. If the child were a boy he would be sold to a farmer the minute he was old enough to hold a sickle in his hand and expected to work long and hard with no chance to ever improve his lot in life.

And if the child were a girl it would be worse. She would be given over as a maid or servant like Carrie had been. And if she was pretty as Carrie had been, she'd be at the mercy of every lecherous male in the house. When she found herself with child, she'd be thrown out on the street to fend for herself. Or forced to live the life Carrie had chosen, as some nobility's mistress.

Even though there was a trust set up for the child, what good would it do the child if no one knew who to give the money to? What good would it do unless his child were identified and provided for?

A rush of determination raged through him. This was *his* child. Flesh of his flesh. How could he abandon it? Yet…

What child would grow up proud to claim the name of a traitor?

The sun hadn't yet begun its ascent in the sky, but Ross knew it wouldn't be long before the blackness turned a lighter shade of dark. He'd have to wake Sam soon if he intended to be gone before first light.

Ross crossed the foyer and took the stairs one by one as if weighing the options he'd struggled with all night.

What child would grow up proud to claim the name of a traitor?

But if he did something to make his son proud of him…

When he reached the door to Sam's room, he paused to give his decision one final evaluation, then turned the knob.

Sam bolted upright, his years in the military having trained him well. He stared wide-eyed at Ross, then swung his feet over the side of the bed and dropped his head into his hands. "You're lucky I didn't have a gun handy," he said, raking his fingers through his hair.

Ross handed him a cup filled with coffee Cook had made before retiring the night before.

Sam reached for it with an inaudible grunt Ross took for thanks, then walked to the window and stared out into the darkness. He waited until Sam's cup was half empty before he spoke.

"If I agreed to help you, what would I have to do?"

Sam rose and reached for the trousers he'd tossed over a chair the night before. "Find out the exact location where they bring the opium ashore and where they store the contraband. If you can, try to discover if there's any set schedule to its arrival."

A strange thrumming raced through Ross's blood. Gathering information about a band of smugglers didn't come close to making up for what his father had done, but it was something.

"And if I discover anything useful?"

"McCormick and I will handle it from there. The government intends to make an example of everyone involved. They'll be put on trial and hanged as a lesson to other smugglers. We need them to realize bringing in illegal drugs comes with a very high price."

A lump formed in Ross's throat and he felt an unexpected surge of self-worth. This was his chance to do something to make up for what his father had done. To offer his child a name he could wear with pride.

Sam stared at Ross for a few seconds as if trying to understand the reason for his reversal. Steel-gray eyes that were a Bennett trait narrowed, then honed in more keenly.

"Why the change?"

"This is what you wanted me to do, isn't it?"

"Yes, but—"

"Then leave it at that."

Sam nodded. "No heroics, Ross."

Ross smiled. "You know me, Sam. I'm the least likely person to do anything risky."

"I don't think you have the faintest idea what qualities you have inside you."

Ross sobered. But he did. He knew better than anyone what he was capable of, and it turned his blood cold.

Chapter 2

JOSEPHINE FOLEY CLOSED THE DORMITORY DOOR with a soft click and tiptoed down the hallway, careful not to make any noise.

"Did you finally get them to sleep?" Mrs. Lambert asked when Josie reached the stairs. Mrs. Lambert lowered her silver-gray head and wiped her hands on the corner of her worn apron. She was obviously on her way to the nursery, which was where one almost always found her, caring for the smallest babes who'd been left at Sacred Heart.

Josie chuckled. "Finally. Robbie and Ben insisted now that Charlie had turned four, they were too old to take naps in the afternoon."

Mrs. Lambert smiled. "I knew that was coming. I heard them planning over breakfast. So what did you tell them?"

"Oh, I agreed."

"You didn't."

"Yes. I told them that now that they had all turned the ripe old age of four, they were old enough to put all their childish pastimes behind them. From now on they would no longer be expected to take afternoon naps, or suffer through morning biscuits and milk, or put in extra time in the afternoon to play on the swings. I told them I was glad to hear they were now grown up and I'd inform Master Graham to expect them for additional time in the classroom with the older boys."

Mrs. Lambert covered her mouth to stifle her giggles.

"What'd the little rapscallions say to that?"

"They suddenly decided perhaps they weren't so terribly old after all. Charlie told me his birthday was just yesterday and so far he didn't feel any older than he had the day before."

"They'll be glad they aren't so old this afternoon at tea time. Cook was taking cookies out of the oven when I left the kitchen."

Josie smiled. "Charlie will be especially glad. Just before he fell off to sleep he told me he missed the cookies his mama used to bake for him."

"Did he now?" Mrs. Lambert asked, her surprised expression obvious. "That's the first he's spoken about his mother since the accident. That's a big step for the little tyke, I'm thinking."

"Yes, it is."

Josie tried to hide how difficult it had been to watch the little boy struggle with his mother's death. It was hard each time another child was brought to them because they'd lost a parent. Especially their mother.

"He'll be all right," Mrs. Lambert said, patting Josie's arm affectionately. "He's got you to guide him. And no one knows what he's going through better."

"It's still a rough road he'll have to travel. Losing the only parent you've ever known is very frightening."

"Look how well you survived."

"Yes. But I had Lady Clythebrook."

"And little Charlie will have you."

"I hope I'm enough," she said with a smile intended to hide her fears. "But I think it's different for a boy. They need a father, and I haven't had much experience there."

"You'll do fine, Miss Josie." Mrs. Lambert gave her arm another pat before she bustled down the hallway toward the nursery, her plump body moving at a remarkable speed. "I'd best make sure Sophie got all the wee ones down for their naps before I think of resting these tired feet o' mine," she said over her shoulder, then stopped to ask another question. "I know winter hasn't given up its hold on us yet, but have you decided when we're going to start taking inventory of the summer clothes?"

"I'm going to talk to Vicar Chadwick about it right now. He was scheduled to return today and promised to come here as soon as he arrived. Hopefully, he's in his office waiting for me."

"Did he say what he had to go to London for this time?" Mrs. Lambert asked. The vicar's frequent trips had long been a subject of curiosity. Especially to the eligible women in the parish who considered the vicar a prime matrimonial candidate and worried they had competition in London.

Josie shook her head and smiled, refusing to encourage any speculation.

"Well," Mrs. Lambert said, shifting the clean laundry from one arm to the other, "tell him we have to have summer clothes for the children. They're growing like weeds. Especially Howie Gifford. I'm afraid when we go to outfit him for the warmer weather, we're going to be in for a shock. My granny always said it was the full moon that made the young ones grow so much."

"Then we'd best put Howie in the cellar to sleep. We're running out of hand-me-downs to fit him."

"Don't worry, Miss Josie. You'll find something. You always do." With a deep chuckle, Mrs. Lambert bustled off down the hall.

Don't worry, Miss Josie. You'll find something. You always do.

A knot formed in Josie's stomach. Oh, yes. She'd beg if she had to as she'd done often enough in the past. But what demands would Lady Lindville put on her donations of food and hand-me-down clothes this time? If ever God could pick a more unlikely benefactress to be responsible for the scores of orphaned children living at Sacred Heart, Josie didn't know who it could be.

Lady Lindville controlled the area's wealthiest family with an iron hand, the same as she did Sacred Heart, often asking the impossible. From the accounting she demanded of every pound she donated, to the rationing of the food that went into the children's stomachs, she was a strict and exacting benefactress who enjoyed the power she wielded over Josie as well as every person in the parish. Only Vicar Chadwick seemed able to side-step her authority, which still puzzled her. She wasn't sure how he managed to do what no one else could.

Perhaps he would offer to go to Lady Lindville himself. Or better yet, perhaps Lady Clythebrook could—

Josie shook her head. No. Lady Clythebrook wouldn't be able to help the children this time. Josie had spent all week going over the books and she knew only too well their lack of funds.

She sighed. If only it were time for another shipment of goods to come in, but she estimated it would be another two weeks yet for sure. And in the meantime…

Josie fought the worry that wouldn't leave as she made her way down the long flight of stairs, searching for another way to provide for the children. Oh, what she wouldn't give for an extra pig or cow to butcher to fill the stomachs of the growing Howie Gifford and little Charlie and Robbie and Ben.

At least she could be thankful it was springtime that was nearly upon them and not the dead of winter. In a few months the gardens would be ready to plant, and it didn't take near the clothing to outfit the children in the warm summer months as it did the winter. Until then, she would pray for a miracle so the children wouldn't have to do without.

Josie walked across the stone foyer, then to the second door on the far side of the room to a small office the vicar used when he came to go over the accounts once every month. She knocked, then turned the knob and entered at his friendly bidding.

"Josie," Vicar Chadwick said, lifting his gaze from the stack of papers in front of him. "Cook just brought tea and I was hoping you'd get here before it got cold."

"That sounds wonderful."

Josie smiled at the vicar, a man she'd known for nearly ten

years. He was a handsome man who'd escaped any sign of aging. He wasn't overly tall, but his body looked more like that of a thirty-year-old than a man nearing fifty. Silver streaks tinged his dark hair which gave him an even more stately look. Josie knew in his youth he must have been terribly handsome and had wondered more than once why he'd never married—why he didn't marry even now. She knew from working with him at the orphanage he'd be a perfect husband and father and it was almost comical to watch the widows after church every Sunday morning make fools of themselves vying for his attention. There were at least a half dozen of them who would jump at the chance to be the vicar's wife.

"Is there a problem with one of the children?" he said, taking a gumdrop from the jar that always sat within easy reach on the corner of his desk.

Josie refused his offer of one of the candies and walked to the tea tray. She put two lumps of sugar in Vicar Chadwick's like always, then poured. "No. Just three little boys anxious to be older than their years."

"But of course, you encouraged them to stay young as long as possible."

Josie felt the familiar tug pulling at the edges of some unknown emotion. Her determination to protect them from the outside world was a point the vicar often brought up. "They grow up fast enough as it is. If we don't hold onto them, they're forced to be adults before most of them have even had time to be children."

"Do you know how much less it would take to run Sacred Heart if you'd just place the children earlier?"

"Not so much that it would be worth it."

"Ah, Josie. That soft heart of yours is going to be your undoing."

Josie sank into a chair and took a sip of tea. "Perhaps. But until it is, I'll keep each and every one of them here where they're safe as long as I can."

Josie pushed the nightmares that motivated everything she did for the children back into the far recesses of her mind and reached out to set down her tea cup.

"Cook informed me the larder is drastically empty of supplies and we need to take inventory of the summer clothes. We are desperately low of some of the staples, especially meat, and in another month or so the weather will be too warm to wear the heavy clothes the children are still in."

"Do you anticipate needing much in the way of clothing?"

"Unfortunately, yes. We gained six new children during the last year and—"

"And didn't lose any," the vicar finished for her.

"We had none who were old enough to be sent out."

"Amy and Sarah and Mary-"

She shook her head. "They're not old enough. They're not ready."

"You can't keep them here forever, Josie. We must prepare the children to find a place in the world."

"But not until they're able to fend for themselves."

"Amy is ready now. As is Sarah. They'll be sent to good Christian homes where someone will see to their everyday needs."

Josie bolted to her feet and walked to the window at the far side of the room. "Not every home is as it seems. Some only portray a perfect picture of goodness to hide the rot that resides inside."

Josie looked over her shoulder to find the vicar studying her even more intently. She turned back to watch a group of children toss a ball back and forth and was fortunately saved from continuing the conversation when Amy, the oldest of the girls still at Sacred Heart, interrupted with a knock on the door.

"Excuse me, Vicar Chadwick, but a man who says he's the Marquess of Rainforth is here to see you. He says it's quite important."

"Send him right in, Amy."

"Yes, Vicar Chadwick."

Josie stayed in the shadows and leaned against the wall beside the window. A place of obscurity suited her just fine.

"This is a surprise," the vicar said, turning to her. "Are you acquainted with the marquess?"

Josie shook her head. "Lady Clythebrook met him on her way to visit the widow Milton. She said he introduced himself. Nothing more."

"I wonder what he wants."

Josie didn't have time to answer that she didn't have the faintest idea, before the door opened and the Marquess of Rainforth entered the room.

From what Lady Clythebrook said, she knew he was not a small man, but she wasn't prepared for a man of his stature. He stood several inches taller than Howie Gifford and Howie was nearly six feet tall. His carriage was regal and the well-tailored cut of his expensive jacket allowed it to fit his broad shoulders to perfection. He was a prime example of what the nobility had to offer. But there was something else about him Josie couldn't put her finger on. An uneasy agitation that surrounded him. A tumultuous thunderstorm whose forces were building to a dangerous level.

He entered the room with long determined steps and stopped before the worn desk. His focus didn't leave the vicar sitting behind it.

Josie knew he hadn't seen her, a fact in which she took great satisfaction. It gave her time to study him: his thick, dark hair, brushed back from his face and noticeably longer than fashion dictated, even in the country; the hunter-green suede jacket that stretched tautly over his broad shoulders; rich buff pants that molded to his muscled thighs, showing off a strength Josie hadn't ever seen in a man before. She sucked in a quiet breath and looked closer, wondering if she could see through to the black soul he was reported to have.

Nowhere, however, did she see any semblance of the demon he was rumored to be. If only half the gossip that had circulated about the man were true, Josie knew she was looking at one of the most disreputable members of London's social elite. And now one of the most spurned.

She tried to pull her gaze away from him but couldn't. The longer she stared, the more she had to battle the intense wariness that spread through her chest, then traveled downward into her stomach, then lower, until it consumed every part of her. He represented everything she despised. Everything she'd grown up hating. She clamped down on the anger that raced through her and pressed her back deeper into the corner, glad he hadn't noticed she was there.

"Lord Rainforth," Vicar Chadwick said, rising from behind his desk. "Allow me to introduce myself. I am Vicar Chadwick. And this is—"

"Are you in charge of the orphanage?"

Vicar Chadwick cleared his throat. "In a manner of speaking. I am one of many who see to its needs."

"I am searching for a child."

"A child? We have many children here. What is the child's name?"

"I don't know."

There was a slight lift to the marquess's shoulders, putting more height to his bold stance and rigid demeanor.

"I see. Then perhaps you can tell me the age of this child."

"I'm not exactly sure. Three. Perhaps four."

There was a hesitation in the vicar's voice when he asked his next question. "And is the child you're seeking a boy or a girl?"

From her vantage point, Josie watched Rainforth clench his hands at his side, an indication that he was noticeably more ill at ease than she'd first realized.

"I don't know that either."

"What, exactly, do you know concerning this child?"

"Nothing, except there is a chance he or she was brought here perhaps six months ago when the child's mother was killed in a carriage accident. The mother's name was Mrs. Carrie Gardner."

A sudden jolt knocked inside Josie's chest. Of course. She

should have known. Carrie Gardner had been living in the dower house on St. Stephen's, an estate owned by the Marquess of Rainforth. Of course.

Damn him!

Vicar Chadwick waved to a chair in front of the desk. "Please, sit down, Lord Rainforth."

Vicar Chadwick waited until the man sat, then took his seat behind the desk. He folded his hands atop a stack of papers on which he'd been working, then continued in a low, calming voice. "If by chance we know the whereabouts of the child, what is it you want with it?"

"I intend to take the child with me."

Josie bristled. "By whose authority?"

The Marquess of Rainforth spun around in his chair at the sound of her voice, then stood, his towering height emphasizing his formidable presence. The steel-gray of his eyes locked with hers and Josie found the intensity of his gaze difficult to escape.

Vicar Chadwick stepped around the corner of his desk. "Allow me to present Miss Josephine Foley, Lord Rainforth. I don't believe you've met. She works with the children here at Sacred Heart and is in charge of their placement when they leave."

He stared at her, his gaze traveling over her in an assessing glance that hinted her interruption didn't meet with his approval. The slight arch of his brows was the only indication that her appearance might have surprised him.

"Then you are obviously the one to whom I wish to speak."

Josie stepped into the open, closing the gap that separated them. She prepared herself to battle him, sensing that his presence here posed a threat to one of her children.

"I'm not sure I can help you, my lord."

"You can tell me if Mrs. Gardner's child was brought here after her death."

"To what purpose?"

He frowned at her question. "I want the child."

She met his frown with one of her own. "What right do you have? Are you a relative of Mrs. Gardner?"

Josie noticed a slight hesitation before the marquess answered.

"Not a relative exactly. Mrs. Gardner and I were friends."

Josie smiled. "I'm sure Mrs. Gardner had many friends. I certainly wouldn't consider giving her child to just any of them."

The marquess's eyes narrowed. "Of course you wouldn't. But Mrs. Gardner and I were very…*close* friends. The child's welfare is important to me."

"As it is to me."

Josie felt an undeniable anger burn deep inside her. An anger fueled by resolve to do whatever was necessary to protect Carrie Gardner's child from this man. Unfortunately, if the look on his face was any indication of the determination lurking beneath the surface, the marquess was equally as resolved to have his way.

"I'm not sure I understand your hesitation, Miss Foley. One would think Sacred Heart would be more than pleased to find homes for their children."

"We are always most eager to see our children be part of a family. It is what we pray for. Unfortunately, not every family who is willing to take one of the children can provide a good home."

"And you are questioning the home I would provide for the child?"

"Of course not, my lord. How presumptuous that would be of me. I am merely trying to explain why every detail of a person's lifestyle is considered before we place one of our children into someone's care. What I am having a certain degree of difficulty understanding, is why Mrs. Gardner's child should be of any concern to you…*now*."

From the slight rise of his shoulders, the openness of her question had at least surprised him. Josie steeled herself as she waited for his answer.

"Is it not enough that I am offering to take Mrs. Gardner's child and provide for it?"

"A man of your reputation?"

The words had spilled out of her mouth before she could stop them. Words she honestly meant but sincerely wished she hadn't said.

"Ah," he answered, his voice brimming with a subtle hostility that came through with blatant clarity. The muscle at the side of his jaw knotted as evidence to his building anger and his steely glare didn't leave her face for a second. "I see my father's indiscretions have even reached your delicate ears."

Josie couldn't hide her surprise. "It's not your father's indiscretions we're talking about, Lord Rainforth. He's not the one who wants to take one of the children out of my reach. It's *your* reputation that's in question. I could never in good conscience release one of the children into your care knowing what I do about your character. What I cannot understand, is why you want the child?

"My reasons are no one's concern but my own."

"I'm sure they would be of great concern to Mrs. Gardner. May I suggest that your relationship to Mrs. Gardner was far more than friendship? And unless I'm in error concerning the…ah, circumstances surrounding the child's birth, I'm sure you also provided the lady with a modest income so she could live in relative comfort in some remote area of England where you would never have to lay eyes on her again. That's what the nobility does to their castoff mistresses, is it not?"

The air held a dangerous tension as the two stood locked in battle. Only the nervous clearing of the vicar's throat penetrated the silence.

"Miss Foley," Vicar Chadwick interrupted, clearly embarrassed by her outright accusations. "I think—"

"It's all right, Vicar Chadwick," Josie said, barely able to contain her anger. "We're all adults. We're all acquainted with the ways of the world. Especially the habits of the nobility. And the marquess's reputation certainly speaks for itself on this matter. Have you come to dispose of the child, sir? Are you suddenly concerned that if not dealt with now, the child might be a future embarrassment to you?"

Another long, uncomfortable silence filled the room. It was several tense seconds before the Marquess of Rainforth answered. When he did, his voice contained a deadly tautness that sent a chill racing down Josie's spine.

"I hardly have to answer to you, Miss Foley. Suffice it to say, the child *is* important to me."

"How can it be? It hasn't been from the day it was born. Besides, it can never be a legal heir."

"The child's birthright is not at issue. Only the child's welfare." With hands tight into fists at his side, he took one more step closer until he towered over her. "I'll repeat my question. A question you'd be wise to answer. Is this where Mrs. Gardner's child was brought after the accident?"

Josie couldn't mistake the fury in his eyes. Couldn't ignore the tension so thick it nearly suffocated her.

"I expect an answer," he said, his voice not a loud demand that would have fueled her anger even more, but a soft, deadly command that sent a wave of apprehension racing through her.

With an act of defiance much braver than she felt, Josie stepped so close to the marquess that the hem of her worn cotton gown rested on the tips of his black leather boots. She was so near him she had to lift her chin to look him in the eyes, and when she did, she nearly stumbled backward. But she didn't. Couldn't. She couldn't show any weakness. Not if she wanted to protect another child from the cruel whims of the nobility.

"Well, Miss Foley?

"No, my lord. The child was *not* brought here after the accident."

Josie could not mistake the angry rush of air from his lungs. It took a long minute more before he asked his next question.

"Do you know what happened to the child, then?"

Josie lifted her chin even higher. "I know what happens to every child. It's my responsibility to make sure none of them are placed in harm's way."

"The child would hardly be put in harm's way."

"Really? Explain to me how a man who claims to want only what is best for the child does not know the child's name. Or whether it is a boy or a girl. Or even when it was born. Hardly a reassuring recommendation."

"You would be wise not to cross me, Miss Foley."

"I'm not trying to cross you, Lord Rainforth. I'm simply protecting one of my children from a questionable fate."

Vicar Chadwick stepped out from behind his desk. "Enough, Miss Foley. Lord Rainforth, please, sit down."

The marquess didn't sit as he'd been asked, just as he didn't release her from his piercing gaze. Finally, the vicar's soft voice sifted through the hostile tension.

"If it's any consolation," the vicar said, clearing his throat, "I will promise to look into the matter personally. If I discover anything, I'll let you know."

"I'll hold you to that."

The marquess gave a sharp nod in farewell then left the room. The door slammed against the frame with a loud thud and for a long time there was only silence in his wake.

Josie sank down onto a chair, her knees trembling. Damn him! How dare he march into her orphanage and demand one of her children.

"Ah, Josie," Vicar Chadwick said, clicking his tongue as he was wont to do. "I can't condone what you just did."

"I saved a child from being torn from the only stability he's known since his mother was taken from him."

"With a lie."

"It wasn't a lie," she whispered. "Exactly."

"Wasn't it? The boy is here and you know it."

"But that isn't what the marquess asked. He asked if the child was brought here after the accident. And he wasn't. I took him home with me first. For more than a month. Until his nightmares lessened."

"I don't think that's what Rainforth meant."

Josie bolted to her feet. "What would you have had me do?

Hand the boy over to one of the worst rakes in all of England? You know his reputation as well as I. His name has been linked to more scandals than anyone can keep track of. Tales of his debauchery and wild living have made it all the way across England. And those are only the escapades that can be mentioned in polite company. There are worse ones to be sure."

"Such as the fact that his father was a traitor?"

Josie swiped her hand in dismissal. "That is certainly a black mark on the Rainforth name, but not of his doing. It was his father who betrayed his country and the blame for that can't be placed on the son's head. The marquess has enough to answer for on his own."

"But the child is undoubtedly his. The eyes are the same. The face. His coloring." The vicar shook his head. "You can't keep the boy from him."

Josie lifted her chin a little higher. "I won't hand the child over to a man with Rainforth's reputation. You don't believe he really wants him, do you?"

The vicar furrowed his brows in contemplation. "You can't know he doesn't," he said softly. Firmly. "And he won't give up. He seemed a very determined young man."

"Well, I'm a very determined young woman. Besides, the child can't mean that much to him. If he did, he'd have been here long before now."

With a swish of her skirt, Josie left the room, heady with the realization that she'd just stood up to a member of the nobility and won. She'd savor her victory, since something told her the marquess wouldn't surrender the battle easily. He had too many weapons at his disposal. Money. Property. A title. Not to mention those indescribable gray eyes and that powerful physique—which had no doubt slain many a female heart.

But she would not be conquered so easily.

Chapter 3

THE FULL MOON ROSE in the cloudy night sky, sending down hundreds of long, silvery fingers that reflected in shimmering splendor as the waves rolled to shore. Ross pulled his heavy woolen cloak tighter and leaned back against a boulder near the edge of the jagged cliff where, for the past several hours, he'd kept watch.

Tonight was the third night he'd come to the cliffs. The third night he'd stayed hidden near the coastline to watch for any movement below.

From here, he could see miles in either direction and had a clear view of the water's edge and any boats that might come ashore.

His view to every inlet and cove that dotted the coastline where St. Stephen's stretched to the north and Clythebrook stretched to the south was perfect. If opium was being smuggled into England as Sam suspected, it had to be from somewhere near here. It was the logical spot. The shoreline on this part of St. Stephen's and Clythebrook was dotted with a multitude of caverns and ideal hiding places.

Ross lifted his head to look around, then, after he was assured the coastline was still clear, he pulled his collar tighter around his neck and sank back down into the tall grass that concealed his hiding place. The hours spent in the chilly, early spring air cleared his head and gave him time to decide what action he had to take to discover the whereabouts of Carrie's child—of *his* child. A child whose whereabouts Miss Foley knew considerably more clearly than she was telling.

Well, he'd be damned if he'd let his son or daughter be foisted off onto some poor tenant farmer to be slave labor as he knew was all too common. He'd find his child if it was the last thing he did.

Ross tried to relax the taut muscles that bunched across his shoulders every time he remembered his conversation at the orphanage. She wasn't at all like he thought she'd be. He envisioned her somewhat older and more severe looking. Instead, he guessed she couldn't be much more than twenty-seven or twenty-eight, and she was far from ugly. In fact, she was—

Ross turned his attention back to the shoreline. He refused to remember the delicate frown that deepened at the bridge of her pert little nose, or the mass of golden blond hair that framed her heart-shaped face, or the unfathomable depth of her deep blue eyes and how they turned even bluer when she became angry. He couldn't think of any of that. He could only remember that she had his child and refused to give it over. She said the reason was because she objected to his reputation, but he didn't believe her.

Children and kittens. There always seemed to be a never-ending supply of both. One would think she'd be glad to rid herself of one more mouth to feed and another growing body to clothe. Instead, she placed herself in the middle as if his child needed protection from *him*.

He sucked in a harsh breath. He'd be damned if he'd let his child go to bed each night tired and hungry and frightened. Damned if he'd let her keep his child away from him. Waves of angry desperation slashed through him and he slammed his fist against the ground in frustration.

With a sigh that exemplified his helplessness, he brushed the thoughts of Josephine Foley to the back of his mind and lifted his head. His gaze froze on a spot in the distance. One skiff, at first a small dot on the water, then growing larger, skimmed toward shore several yards to the south. The craft seemed to move effortlessly as two burly men rowed through the rolling waves. The boat didn't sit terribly low in the water, and by peering through the eyeglasses he'd brought with him, he could see the boat was otherwise empty.

Keeping low to the ground, Ross made his way southward until he was directly above where they'd pulled ashore, then crawled closer to the cliff's edge. He watched as the two sailors secured their boat then moved up the beach. Suddenly, a tall third man wearing a hat and long overcoat stepped out from the shadows. Ross strained to get a glimpse of the man but his face was hidden by the rim of his hat and his up-turned collar.

The three talked for a few seconds, then the tall man handed over a packet. One of the sailors checked the contents of the envelope then stuck it in his jacket pocket. After a few more seconds, the two sailors stepped back into their skiff while the third man disappeared into one of the caves. Ross knew in that short span of time arrangements had been made concerning the next shipment of opium.

His heart beat in anticipation. This was the first concrete piece of evidence he'd been able to gather. He knew now there would be another shipment. And he knew where it would come ashore. That was something.

He watched until the small boat was out of sight and the shore below him deserted, then rose to leave. He looked around, memorizing the landmarks so he knew precisely where to return. With a start, he realized he wasn't on St. Stephen's property any longer. He was on Clythebrook land and the caves the smugglers were using to hide their contraband weren't that far from the orphanage.

Ross tried to formulate a plan, realizing he'd have to investigate this area closer later. He'd find a reason to come back tomorrow after he'd had a few hours' sleep and his mind wasn't so muddled. For now, he'd have to be satisfied with what he'd discovered.

Ross took one last look over the edge of the cliff to make sure he hadn't missed anything, then retraced his steps to the north until he was certain he was back on St. Stephen's property. When he was safely out of sight, he stopped to catch his breath. He'd finally learned at least something that would be useful. Not enough, but at least something.

A feeling of satisfaction washed through him as he continued on his way home. He'd just entered a grove of trees when something to his left caught his eye. He stopped short.

He wasn't sure exactly what it was for a few seconds because the darting figure stayed mostly in the shadows as it rushed through the woods, but he knew eventually it would have to come out into the open. As quietly as he could, he circled behind a large tree and waited.

For several long, tense moments, time seemed to stand still. The only sound he heard was the gentle slapping of the waves in the distance and the hollow hoot of an owl in the trees. But he knew the fleeting figure was out there, steadily moving closer. He could feel it.

Leaves rustled to his left and Ross followed the sound. He tried to imagine where the intruder had come from, especially at this hour. The only building near here was the cottage he'd passed not too far back. And, of course, the orphanage.

Ross stepped further behind the tree and waited. He'd been a fool to leave St. Stephen's without a weapon to defend himself and swore he'd remember next time.

He took another breath, then caught it when he heard the sharp snap of a twig close by. The muffled sounds indicated that the midnight traveler was close. All he needed was a glimpse and if the prowler was one of the smugglers, hopefully he'd recognize him and have another part of the puzzle to piece together.

The intruder was almost on top of him and Ross pressed

further into the shadows. The first things he saw were small, booted feet—too small to be a man's. Then, he saw as well as heard the hushed swish of skirts swirling the leaves. He tried to get a glimpse of the woman's face but a dark, hooded cloak covered all but a few wisps of the stranger's light hair. He stepped out to block her escape.

"It's a little late for a stroll, isn't it?"

The moonlit shadows exposed no more than her outline, but Ross took great satisfaction in watching her hand fly to her mouth and hearing her startled squeal of fright.

Before she could recover, he stepped even closer. From the corner of his eye, he saw her gather handfuls of her skirt in her fists and knew her instinct was to run. He clamped his fingers around her upper arms and pinned her firmly against the tree.

"Are you often in the habit of running through the woods at three o'clock in the morning?" he asked softly.

Ross could feel her tremble beneath him, and even though he had no intention of hurting her, he knew this was an excellent opportunity to get information. Perhaps even about the smugglers. Who better than from one of the locals?

"Release me. This instant."

"I don't think so," he said, bracketing her legs with his. It was impossible for her to escape now. His entire body was mere inches from hers, and he could tell from the way she pulled herself away from him, she had no intention of leaning forward even a fraction.

"I think I'd like to know what you're doing out here all alone."

She turned her face away from him as a denial to his request and Ross placed his finger to the side of her narrow jaw to bring her back. In one swift movement, he turned her face forward, then brought his hand upward to push aside the hood of her cloak.

The clouds took that moment to slide away from the full moon, illumining the spot where they stood. Brilliant streams of moonlight floated around the girl, surrounding her in an ethereal halo. Her hair glowed like shimmering gold, and wide, expressive eyes stared back at him from her heart-shaped face. She had high cheekbones, a pert little nose, and full lips she pressed tightly together. There was something very intriguing in her features, not beautiful exactly, but attractive nonetheless. And for some unexplainable reason, he didn't want to step away from her.

It wasn't light enough to tell the color of her eyes but he didn't need a light. He remembered from when he'd seen her before. And it was bright enough to see an emergence of the same anger he'd witnessed three days ago when he met her at the orphanage.

"Well, Miss Foley. What a surprise."

Josie lifted her chin and forced herself to put on a brave front. "Stand aside, Lord Rainforth. I wish to pass."

"Not until you tell me what you're doing out here all by yourself."

Josie wasn't about to tell him she'd been sitting with his son because he'd had another nightmare. She'd promised little Charlie she'd stay with him until he fell asleep and she'd held him until he'd fallen asleep a little while ago.

"I was taking a walk."

Josie couldn't tell for sure but she swore he was smiling at her.

Her first thought was that she must be mistaken. From the little she'd been around him, she doubted Lord Rainforth knew how to smile. But here he was, staring down at her with a condescending grin on his face.

Although she was usually quite adept at controlling her anger, she felt her temper raise another notch. And her fear, although she'd never let him see it. When he spoke, his voice wrapped around her like filigree netting, holding her, confining her.

"This far from home?"

"It's not so very far from Clythebrook. It's only—"

"You're on St. Stephen's property."

Josie often cut through the woods when she left by Sacred Heart's south gate. It was shorter than going around to the front. She ground her teeth and glared at him.

"What are you doing out here, Miss Foley?"

The air caught in her lungs. She pulled to escape his grasp but he wouldn't let her go.

"You obviously have some reason for being out at this hour. And I doubt it's to take a moonlight stroll. A midnight rendezvous perhaps? Who is he?"

Josie felt an intense desire to kick him. In a swift move, she picked up her skirts and darted to the side. But before she could take her first step toward freedom, he flattened both hands against the trunk of the tree behind her and trapped her between his outstretched arms.

Josie fought the emotions racing through her. Her heart thundered in her breast and she was suddenly so warm she thought she must be standing very near a blazing fire. She wanted to pull away from him. Knew his presence was the cause of the heat that consumed her. And yet…

"You haven't answered my questions."

"And I don't intend to."

He smiled, but instead of backing away and letting her go, he leaned closer as if he knew his towering height would intimidate her. It did.

"I haven't lived in this area long, Miss Foley, but since I've arrived I've heard your praises sung every time your name comes up. What do you think everyone would say if they knew about your midnight rendezvous?

Josie wasn't about to give him the satisfaction of a response.

"Such behavior is not at all what I expected from such an outstanding example of propriety. It makes one quite curious as to who or what is so important that you venture out at such a strange hour."

"I'm simply taking a walk," she bit out.

He broadened his grin. "You make a terrible liar. Perhaps you'd like to try again with more conviction."

"What I'd like, is for you to step aside and let me pass."

Josie followed her demand by placing her hand against one of his arms and pushing. The nighttime sky was dark again as a puffy cloud skittered in front of the moon. But she didn't need light to point out what her other senses already knew. Touching his muscled forearm was like pushing against a stone wall. The feel of him beneath her fingers was rock solid.

"What secrets are you keeping, Miss Foley?" he whispered, then ran one long, graceful finger down her cheek and across her jaw. Josie sucked in a gasp of air and tried to ignore the way her heart thundered in her breast. Damn him. Damn him!

"I have no secrets."

"Don't you?"

He moved his hand to the other side of her face and cupped her cheek. His thumb gently stroked the contour of her jaw and she shivered.

"Please, take your hand away from me." She gritted her teeth and pressed her head against the bark of the tree until her scalp hurt. She wanted to blame her reaction on fear but she knew that wasn't the only reason her blood pounded against her ears and her skin tingled as if on fire. It was him. "I don't want you to touch me."

His brows shot up as if he questioned her words, then rubbed his thumb across her jaw once more. She prayed he'd let her go, but instead he anchored his hand against the tree again to keep her from escaping.

"Why won't you tell me where I can find Carrie Gardner's child?"

His abrupt switch of subject caught her off guard. A small gasp caught in her throat at the same moment a cloud slid away from the moon to expose his face in vivid clarity. It was then that she remembered in detail the steel gray of his eyes, the dark, haunting boldness. The promise of danger.

"You're lying when you say you don't know what happened to the child. From what I've gathered, there isn't anything about a child in the whole area to which you are not privy."

"I don't know what you've heard, Lord Rainforth, but—"

"I've heard that you're the first person on the spot when a child is left unprotected. I've heard you steal them away before the authorities have a chance to decide what's to be done with them."

"Steal them? You make it sound as if I'm a bigger threat to the children than if they were left alone in the world to fend for themselves."

"Do I?"

Josie bristled. "Just what are you implying?" She shoved hard against his chest, trying to move him. He didn't budge.

"I'm not implying anything. I'm simply stating a fact as I see it."

"As you see it?" Josie gritted her teeth. "Then you are either blind or your mind is so warped it's left with no option but to create answers as you wish to see them."

"I don't think there's anything warped about being concerned for children who have no one else to protect them. Especially from someone like you."

"Like me? Just what nefarious plan do you assume I have in mind for any child unfortunate enough to be left alone in the world?"

"Perhaps sell them to anyone willing to pay a price."

The air rushed from her lungs and her hands balled into fists at her sides. "What did you say?"

"Don't tell me there aren't plenty of tenant farmers searching for cheap labor. What better place to supply that labor force than an orphanage."

Josie battled a wave of fury unlike anything she'd ever experienced.

"What is the going price for a child, Miss Foley?"

"You think I sell the children? You think I take money…"

"I think it takes a sizable amount to run an orphanage. The money has to come from somewhere. How better than to—"

Before Josie could think better of her action, she reached out her hand and slapped him hard across the face. His reaction was equally as swift.

In a movement so fast she didn't see coming, he clamped his fingers around her wrists and pinned her hands against the tree on either side of her face. The bark bit into her flesh, but she barely felt it. The look in his eyes caused her more concern than a little pain. She kept her gaze focused on his anger, but refused to let him think she was afraid of him.

"I would advise you to never do that again," he whispered in a voice so deadly soft it sent shivers down her spine.

"As I would advise you to have a care with your accusations."

The next few seconds stretched headlong into eternity while she stood still as stone. If she could have found the courage to risk his wrath, she would have turned her head to the side in defiance. But she couldn't move. In that one second she realized what a formidable force he presented. And she knew without a doubt that if she backed down now, he would destroy her. As well as the children.

She clenched her hands into tighter fists and locked her gaze with his. "Release me," she said, her voice sounding remarkably steady considering how violently every part of her seemed to tremble.

He held her a fraction longer, then loosened his fingers from around her wrists and pulled away. Josie dropped her hands to her sides. But he didn't step away from her.

"I won't give up, Miss Foley. If you refuse to help me locate Mrs. Gardner's child, I'll simply have to find another way."

"And I'll simply have to do everything in my power to keep you from succeeding."

There was enough space between them now for Josie to escape his overpowering presence, but she didn't move. Pride wouldn't let her run away from him. She'd had to stand up to insurmountable odds her whole life. From the moment she'd been left alone in the world. This was no different. No matter how hard he glared at her; no matter how much he tried to intimidate her, she refused to buckle beneath his domineering ways. No one would ever have that control over her again. Never again.

"Don't involve yourself in what doesn't concern you, Lord Rainforth," she said, unsettled by the silver gleam in his gray eyes.

"Is that a warning, Miss Foley?"

"Yes. Stay away. From here. From the orphanage."

"From you?" he asked huskily.

She swallowed. "Yes. From me."

His sensual gaze moved along the length of her body. "And if I don't?"

She stepped back into the shadows where he couldn't see the hot blush on her face. "You've been warned."

He arched a brow and opened his mouth to reply but she didn't give him a chance. She turned around and walked away before he could utter a retort.

Josie expected to hear his footsteps crashing behind her. Dreaded hearing them…yet inexplicably hoped for them as well. The flush of heat inside her signaled a warning of its own, making the Marquess of Rainforth more dangerous than she'd ever imagined.

Chapter 4

R OSS FOLLOWED THE NARROW LANE that wound through St. Stephen's, then across the border onto Clythebrook Estate. If he continued onto the main thoroughfare, the lane would go east through neighboring Lindville Grange, then onward until it merged with a more well-traveled road that would eventually find its way to London.

It had been nearly a week since his confrontation with Miss Foley. Six days and nine hours to be exact. And during that time, he'd spent every minute going over the estate books. He had a child now, a child that—because of its illegitimacy—could never inherit any of the entailed Rainforth property. But that child could inherit St. Stephen's Hollow.

Ross knew what the books indicated and if he wanted to ensure St. Stephen's would always be profitable, he needed to make improvements to accomplish it.

He'd come up with a plan that would not only make St. Stephen's more financially rewarding, but would also give him access to the land overlooking the caves used by the smugglers. The idea had merit, but if there was a drawback, it was that it would be necessary to include a rather large section of Clythebrook Estate.

After considering every aspect of the venture, then talking it over with Virgil Thompkins, his steward, Ross was more convinced than ever that his plan would work. Not only would his venture make St. Stephen's and Clythebrook independently wealthy, but it would also, as Thompkins pointed out, provide an abundant bounty for the orphanage—a benefit to which Miss Foley could hardly object.

He remembered his confrontation with the children's caretaker a few days earlier and was certain she wouldn't refuse anything that would help the children. This understanding of her very complex and confusing personality led him to map out his plan very carefully.

He'd already discovered making demands of her didn't accomplish anything. The more he tried to intimidate her with the power and influence afforded those of his station, the more determined she was to keep his child from falling into his lecherous hands.

She'd already figured out that Carrie had been his mistress, and that she'd had a child by him. It was his character she objected to and his most damning black mark was that she assumed he'd banished Carrie to St. Stephen's to get rid of her. This was why Miss Foley considered him the worst rake in all of England. Well, he thought with a wry sense of humor, he hardly cared what she thought about him. The child was his and he wasn't about to let her keep it from him.

Ross considered his idea with renewed determination. His plan was good and as he traveled across Clythebrook Estate, he noticed several other glaring facts that told him the added income from the venture he intended to propose would be more than welcome.

Although the tenants' cottages seemed in relatively good repair, the same could not be said of the outbuildings on the small plots of land where they lived. Neither could it be said of the crumbling stones on the bridge that spanned the dry creek or the condition of the lanes and byways leading to and from Clythebrook Manor. Even the stone wall once built to keep the earth on the hillsides from eroding stood riddled with huge, gaping holes.

Ross urged his mount forward. The road in front of him, if a road you could call it, was no wider than the span of a wagon in spots and in desperate need of repairs in others. He made a mental note to hire a crew to see to its improvement. The ruts were so deep from the last rain it was barely passable now, and would be a quagmire of sticky mud if nothing was done before the next downpour. Perhaps once he explained how his venture would bring in enough capital to make several necessary improvements, Lady Clythebrook would agree without hesitation.

Ross smiled. It would be worth it to see the frustration on Miss Foley's face when she realized Lady Clythebrook supported him. Even more worth it to watch her torn between her determination to keep him as far away from her and the orphanage as possible, and her desperation to provide for the children.

He wanted to smile at his sudden sense of satisfaction, but the reality of what he intended sliced through him as a double edged sword. For some reason he couldn't explain, she affected him like no other woman ever had. She appeared to him at the most unlikely moments and infiltrating her world would only make it that much more difficult to banish her from his thoughts. That was already happening. He'd had a devil of a time trying to do just that since the night he'd found her running through the woods.

For six sleepless nights he'd tried to pretend the heat that had seared his body when he'd pressed himself against her hadn't really happened. But he knew it had.

He shifted uncomfortably in his saddle and pushed his mount toward Clythebrook Manor. He knew what his problem was. He'd been without a woman too long. That was the only logical explanation for the turmoil caused by just thinking about her. A turmoil he was determined to ignore—which was why he'd chosen this time of day to pay a call on Lady Clythebrook.

If Josie Foley kept to her schedule, she would be at the foundling home now like she was every afternoon, and he could discuss his idea with Lady Clythebrook without her there to put down every item he proposed. Because somehow he knew she would. At first, at least. Until she found out about the added income for the orphanage.

Ross turned his mount down the long tree-lined lane that led to Clythebrook Manor. The ancient, three-story stone country house still stood majestically on the top of a small rise, but the once carefully-tended lawns and gardens were now threatened with weeds and scraggly bushes. A double row of spreading linden trees flanked the manor house on two sides, yet beneath the lush branches, dozens of saplings sprouted in wild abandon. Ross looked, but there wasn't a single gardener tending what must have once been a well-landscaped lawn.

He rode his horse to the apex of the semi-circular drive and dismounted. At Rainforth Park, where he'd spent a month or so during every summer in a life he seldom let himself remember, one of a dozen or more stable hands would have been standing ready to take charge of a horse or carriage before any guest could even dismount. The lack of even one servant to care for his horse sent a distinct message. Ross looped his reins through a ringed brass pole and made his way to the front door and lifted the ornate knocker.

After several long minutes, a very distinguished-looking elderly gentleman in faded maroon and black livery greeted him. Although well past his prime, the butler exhibited an austere demeanor Ross was accustomed to from the well-trained, professional staff his father had employed.

"Good day," Ross said, remaining on the pillared portico. "I'd like to speak with Lady Clythebrook."

"And who may I say is calling?"

"The Marquess of Rainforth, from St. Stephen's Hollow."

The butler gave a curt nod and stepped back to allow Ross to enter the circular foyer. "Won't you please come in?" he said, taking Ross's hat and placing it on a table beside the door. "I'll see if Lady Clythebrook is receiving."

Ross watched the butler climb the winding staircase, then let his gaze move over the interior of Lady Clythebrook's home. The vestibule was bright and cheery with radiant streams of sunlight that poured in from the four wide, floor-to-ceiling windows that bracketed the entrance. Ross could imagine Josephine Foley standing in this hall, her golden hair bathed in sunlight. An uncomfortable weight settled low in his gut and he pushed the unwelcome image away.

The furniture was of exquisite taste and quality, although the few pieces that dotted the room were far from new. An ornate receiving table sat in the center of the vestibule atop a round Turkish carpet. Ross could only imagine how vibrantly beautiful the colors had been before the carpet had lost its battle to the constant abuse of the sun.

He looked from one side of the room to the other. Everything shone as if routinely polished with loving care. Even the crystal chandelier hanging high from the two-story ceiling gleamed from recent attention. If he were forced to search for a word to describe the feelings he perceived standing here it would be— comfortable.

Even though he was a stranger to this house, he felt welcome here. The walls were a pale yellow that he guessed hadn't seen a fresh coat of paint for years, but there was an inviting homey air that even the threadbare carpet leading up the curved staircase couldn't diminish. Ross smiled. His father would have been appalled. But strangely, to Ross it didn't seem to matter. It only made the house more inviting.

He clasped his hands behind his back and made a complete circle of his surroundings. Several doors led off the foyer, but only one stood open. Before he could amble over to see what room it might be, the butler returned.

"Lady Clythebrook will see you. If you'll please follow me."

Instead of showing Ross up the stairs as was customary, the butler led the way across the vestibule to the open doorway he'd noticed before.

"Lady Clythebrook will be down momentarily," he said, stepping aside to let Ross enter.

"Thank you."

With a slight nod, the butler backed from the room, leaving Ross alone.

This room held the same inviting warmth he'd felt upon entering the house. A huge fireplace took up most of the opposite wall, but there was no fire burning in the grate.

Two burgundy chairs with matching ottomans flanked the fireplace, while a matching settee and small table sat off to the side. An ornate writing desk sat in front of a large multi-paned window on the opposite side of the room and another cluster of chairs was positioned close to a curtained French door that led out onto a patio.

Ross stepped to the opening and noticed there was a surprisingly well-tended garden beyond the paned door. Someone had obviously taken great care to tend this one spot near the house. Lady Clythebrook, perhaps. Or even Miss Foley. He could imagine her kneeling in the soft black earth with her hands in the loose, moist soil. He shook his head, not at all comfortable with where his thoughts were leading. With a raspy clearing of his throat, he turned his attention back to his surroundings.

A large portrait of a very distinguished-looking gentleman with silver hair and eyes that shone with a sparkle of intelligence hung above the mantel on the opposite side of the room. Ross was drawn to his infectious smile and thought the man would have been someone he would have enjoyed knowing.

"That was my husband. The Earl of Clythebrook."

Ross spun around as the Countess of Clythebrook stepped into the room. Her butler walked close to her side in case she needed assistance, but she didn't reach out to him. She relied instead on the ivory-handled cane in her hand.

"I gathered as much," he said, stepping forward to offer her his arm. She took it with a smile.

Her step was hesitant as she leaned with aging grace against him, and Ross noticed the butler stayed at his post until she waved him away. Then he closed the door behind him and they were left alone, staring at the portrait.

"He was a remarkable man with a good sense for business as well as a humorous outlook on life."

The longing in her eyes when she stared at her late husband's portrait spoke volumes. "You were very fortunate then."

"Yes, I was. I'm reluctant to admit, however, I haven't done nearly so well at managing since he died."

"Running an estate is not easy," he said, standing next to her. "I haven't met your steward but I'm sure my man, Mr. Thompkins, knows him."

The open smile on her face when she lifted her gaze stopped his words.

"I'm afraid you are looking at the only steward Clythebrook Estates has."

"You, my lady?"

She laughed. "Yes. Although, in actuality, it's Josephine who sees to everything."

"Miss Foley?"

"Yes. She took over the daily running of the estate even before my husband died nearly ten years ago."

"Before? But that means she was scarcely—"

"She was seventeen when Walter died."

Lady Clythebrook turned so she faced him, then breathed a deep sigh. "Josephine grew up in the orphanage, you know, and was always Walter's favorite. Walter's grandfather had built Sacred Heart nearly a century ago and Walter was expected to care for it as his father had before him. Every time he visited, he took something special for his little tag-along, as he always called her. When he returned, he would have some little gift tucked in his pocket that she'd given him. Sometimes a swatch of embroidery she'd stitched herself. Other times, a doll she'd made from hollyhock flowers."

Lady Clythebrook leaned more heavily against her cane and looked up at the portrait on the wall. "From the day she came to live with us, she rarely left his side. She rode with him wherever he went and sat in a chair at his side while he worked on the books, sometimes late into the night. She was such an avid learner it was only natural that she absorb everything there was to know about running the estate.

"When Walter became ill, Josephine assumed even more of the responsibility. She was seventeen when he died and she took over. She visited the tenants the same as Walter had, and made sure none of them went without."

"But?" Ross asked, knowing there was more.

"It's been difficult. Clythebrook Estate is not a profitable piece of land and there were many ways Walter found to make ends meet that are not available to a woman."

"Such as?"

Lady Clythebrook smiled. "Walter made a point of spending time in London periodically. Not that he enjoyed going there. He was much more content here in the country running his estate and overseeing the land. But he said it was the only way he could find out what ventures to invest in and which ones to avoid. He didn't always make a great deal of money, but enough added income to get us by until the fall harvest. It seems as if the money doesn't go as far as it did before. And it isn't that Josephine doesn't spend endless hours trying to make it stretch."

Ross fought an emotion he wasn't sure he understood, suddenly realizing he was eager to learn everything he could about Josephine Foley. It also occurred to him that Lady Clythebrook was sharing the details of Miss Foley's life as well as her involvement in running the estate for a purpose. Ross turned to face the older woman as he waited for her to continue.

She smiled, her bright eyes twinkling. "Ah, you see through me, don't you?"

"Let's just say I think it's possible you told me all this for a reason other than to satisfy my natural curiosity."

"Yes, well…"

Lady Clythebrook turned to face him. "Josephine tells me you've been to the orphanage to inquire after Mrs. Gardner's child and that she refused to tell you the child's whereabouts."

Ross lifted his eyebrows.

"I can see you are a man who does not give up easily once you've set your path. I could tell that the first time we met. But I want you to understand there is a reason why Josephine is equally as firm in her resolve. The children are very dear to her and she sees herself more as a guardian and protector than someone to simply see to their physical needs. They have no one else, you see."

"And that explains why she won't tell me where she's taken Mrs. Gardner's child?"

"Perhaps she fears the consequences of handing the child over to you." Lady Clythebrook paused before continuing. "I haven't shared all of Josephine's past with you, some of which I don't have the right to divulge. She didn't come here first, you see. She went to live with a local merchant named Foster, and his wife, but something…happened while she was there and she ran away. Perhaps she fears giving Mrs. Gardner's child to you will be as disastrous as when she was handed over to strangers."

"Except I mean the child no harm."

"No one meant to harm Josephine either, but that wasn't the end result."

Ross felt an uncomfortable gnawing deep in his gut. "So Miss Foley has set herself up as protector and defender for all the children?" He paused. "That's quite an undertaking for one person, especially someone so young."

"Yes. There are times I have to admit I worry over her."

"There's no need to worry, my lady," a voice tinged with an icy edge said from behind them. "I am more than capable of taking care of myself."

Both Ross and Lady Clythebrook turned to see Josephine Foley standing in the doorway.

Ross didn't know how much of their conversation she'd overheard but couldn't help but smile at the cold, determined look on her face. It was almost as if she were giving him fair warning that they were on a more level playing field today and she wouldn't allow him to use brute strength or physical intimacy to intimidate her as he had that night in the woods.

"Josephine, dear. Come in and sit down. Lord Rainforth has come to call."

"So I see," she said, walking across the room.

She wore a green striped day-dress that—even though it was not quite what Ross remembered as being in fashion—was still very attractive. *She* was very attractive.

"And what is the purpose of your visit, Lord Rainforth?"

"You don't think I came just to make Lady Clythebrook's acquaintance?"

"No."

Her answer was short and clipped, and Lady Clythebrook cleared her throat as if trying to cover Miss Foley's veiled rudeness.

"Josephine," Lady Clythebrook interrupted. "Banks is bringing tea. Perhaps we could have refreshments before Lord Rainforth brings up any business he might wish to discuss?"

"I doubt Lord Rainforth intends to stay that long. Do you, my lord?"

"On the contrary, Miss Foley. I'd be delighted to stay for tea."

The look she gave him was murderous. He fanned the flame of her fury even further when he offered Lady Clythebrook his arm and escorted her to one of the chairs flanking the fireplace. Without looking to see Miss Foley's reaction, Ross lifted a nearby chair and carried it closer. He didn't place it next to Lady Clythebrook's chair, but close to the chair in which he intended to sit.

"Please, Miss Foley. Won't you join us?"

He saw the fire in her eyes, but in perfect timing, the door opened and Banks carried in a tea tray and set it on the small table in front of Miss Foley. She had no choice but to sit down in the chair closest to him and pour tea.

"Please try a pastry," Lady Clythebrook said after Miss Foley had handed each of them a cup and saucer. "Mrs. Downey makes the best pastries in all of England."

"Thank you." He reached over to take a frosted crust filled with fruit and tucked it onto his floral china saucer. "Miss Foley?" He lifted the plate and offered it to Miss Foley, more for an excuse to look at her than to be polite. He wouldn't exactly call her expression a scowl, but it was close enough to make him wary. If he wanted to change her mind about him, he'd best begin right now.

"No," she said, her voice unnaturally forced. "Thank you."

"Lady Clythebrook?"

Lady Clythebrook gave Miss Foley a curious look, then took a small square of yellow cake with white frosting.

Miss Foley, he noticed, took one swallow of her tea as if that was all politeness required, then set down her cup and saucer and turned her attention to him.

"Now, Lord Rainforth. Perhaps you'd care to tell us why you're here."

Lady Clythebrook looked at Josephine with a disapproving frown on her face but she didn't say anything.

"Very well. I've come to propose a venture that I think will benefit both Clythebrook Estate and St. Stephen's."

"I'm sure we're not interested," she began, but stopped when he continued to speak over her interruption.

"As well as the orphanage."

Her gaze narrowed. "What venture?"

"A venture that will hopefully increase profits for both estates as well as increase the value of the land, while at the same time provide added income for the orphanage."

"And that would be?"

"Cattle."

Both Lady Clythebrook and Miss Foley stared at him as if he'd uttered a foreign word neither of them understood.

"Yes, cattle." Ross set down his cup and moved in his chair so he could face them both. "As you know, St. Stephen's is blessed with an abundant reservoir of underground water. It is, however, lacking in adequate grazing land near enough to that water to sustain a sufficient number of cattle to be profitable. Clythebrook Estate has acres of unused grazing land, but because there is little water, those acres are going to waste. I'm sure your husband realized long ago it would be too costly and time consuming to haul in a sufficient amount of water needed by a herd of cattle the size to which I'm referring."

"He did. So how do you intend to solve that problem?" Lady Clythebrook asked, interest sparking in her eyes.

"With a minimal amount of digging into an aquifer located on St. Stephen's, I'm positive we can create our own natural springs. If we ignore the border between St. Stephen's and Clythebrook, there will be both sufficient water as well as more than enough grazing area to support a sizable herd. We can double, perhaps even triple the amount of cattle that are currently being raised on either estate now and, if the market remains steady, double or triple our current yearly profits."

"We would go into this venture together, then?" Lady Clythebrook asked, clearly interested.

Ross smiled. "We would be equal partners, of course. In time, we should see a profit from the sale of our cattle that will meet all our needs."

Ross glanced at the excitement in Miss Foley's eyes. "Where do you anticipate the added cattle will graze?" Lady Clythebrook asked.

"On the unused parcel of land that makes up the border between Clythebrook and St. Stephen's. The land nearest the cliffs."

Ross watched the color leave Miss Foley's face. "No," she said, rising from her chair. "There will be no joint venture. Nor will you and Lady Clythebrook form any working partnership."

Ross took note of the firm set of her jaw. Her reaction wasn't exactly a surprise and yet, the vehemence in her voice was. Ross let Lady Clythebrook try to soothe the turbulent emotions while he leaned back in his chair and studied her.

"Josephine, I don't understand. Surely we can hear Lord Rainforth out? I'm certain he's given this a great deal of thought and if it would help the people of Clythebrook—"

"We don't need Lord Rainforth's help. We don't need—"

"Yes, you do." Ross sat forward in his chair. "Look around you. How long has it been since you did any general upkeep to the manor house? How much longer before something major happens and you're forced to?" Ross set down his cup and saucer and turned to face just her. "How long has it been since you've had an adequate staff to see to your needs? Or a new dress? Or—"

"Enough!" The glare in her eyes shot daggers. "How we live is none of your concern."

"I would like to make it my concern. I would like to do something that would not only benefit the tenants who live and work on St. Stephen's, but those who live on Clythebrook as well."

"Lady Clythebrook's tenants have never gone without."

"No. They haven't. But Lady Clythebrook has. As have you."

Ross rose from his chair and turned his back to her mutinous glare. He stood facing the lifeless fireplace for a moment. When he turned, he aimed his words as well as his penetrating gaze directly at her. "If you won't do it for yourself or Lady Clythebrook, then think about the children."

"How dare you."

"Who supports Sacred Heart Orphanage?"

For a brief second, no one answered. Finally Lady Clythebrook spoke. "Lady Lindville often gives to the orphanage."

"And does she provide for all of their needs?"

"She does what she can."

"And you…?"

"I do what I can as well." She lifted her chin and faced him with an inborn regal pride. "Josephine somehow finds enough to meet the children's needs. We manage on what is left."

"Now I am offering you an opportunity to be assured there

will always be money left. At no cost to you whatsoever."

Miss Foley lifted her chin and looked at Lady Clythebrook. "We'll get by. We always have."

"But the land Lord Rainforth is talking about is of little use, Josephine. What would it hurt if—"

"No!"

Ross arched his eyebrows in question. "Is there a reason why that particular land cannot be used, Miss Foley?"

"It's not just *that* land. It's all of it. We don't want you on any of it."

"Is that true, Lady Clythebrook?"

Ross stared at the small, fragile woman and waited. Confusion was written plainly on her face and Ross knew she was torn between the thought of doing what might be best for the people of Clythebrook, and Josephine Foley's determination not to even consider his idea. She exhibited another slight hesitation then looked directly at him.

"Can you guarantee that this venture will realize a profit?"

"Not immediately, of course. But in a year at most—"

"The children can't wait a year," Miss Foley argued even more emphatically. "They need food and clothing every day."

There was another long pause, then Lady Clythebrook set her cup and saucer on the small round table and looked at him.

"I will consider it, Lord Rainforth. In the meantime, I want you to take Miss Foley out at your earliest convenience—"

Lady Clythebrook held up her hand when Miss Foley started to object.

"…and explain to her in detail everything you propose to do."

"Of course," Ross said, nodding in respectful compliance.

"If there's anything with which she doesn't agree, she'll be free to voice her opposition, and an agreement will be reached before I make my final decision."

"That's fair enough. I'm free tomorrow. Does that meet with your approval?" he asked, turning to where Miss Foley was standing rigidly beside her chair.

Her look held a blatant warning and Ross knew there would be more than one item upon which the two of them disagreed.

"Until tomorrow then," he said, saying his farewell, then taking his leave.

Tomorrow promised to be a very interesting day.

Chapter 5

"He's here!" Jenny, one of the older girls, yelled as she ran down the footpath to where Josie sat on a blanket beneath a chestnut tree, reading to the younger children. The sun was out and the temperature was more reminiscent of late May than early March. The day had been perfect—until now.

Josie rose to her feet, then cast a quick glance up the path that led to the orphanage to make sure they were still safe. "Robbie. Charlie. Would you go with Jenny, please?"

"But Miss Josie. You're not done with the story yet," Robbie said, looking at her with a confused frown on his face.

"And you're getting to the best part," Charlie echoed, equally disappointed. "The baby bear's gonna say, 'Who's been eating my porridge?'"

"I know, but this is important."

Josie dropped the book onto the grass and rushed to where the two little boys stood. She put an arm around each small shoulder and turned them toward the path that led to the apple orchard. She was desperate to get them away before he saw them.

"But we don't want to go," Charlie said, speaking for both of them. He was usually the one who took control. The one who spoke for Robbie even though Robbie was the older of the two.

"I know you don't, Charlie. But…" Josie knelt in front of them so she was eye level with the two four-year-olds. "If you go with Jenny now and mind everything she says, tonight when the rest of the children have to go to bed the three of us will stay up. We'll sit in front of the fire in the study and I'll read you the story."

"From the beginning?" Robbie asked.

"From the beginning," she agreed.

"And can we have some hot chocolate?" Charlie asked, bobbing his head enthusiastically.

"If you are very good and obey everything Jenny tells you to do."

"We will, Miss Josie!" they both chorused in unison. "We'll be very good."

"Come on, Jenny," Charlie said. "Miss Josie wants us to go down to the orchard and you're to come with us."

"Mrs. Lambert will come to get you in a little while," she told Jenny as the girl led the two little boys away. "And hurry."

Josie watched the two little boys until they were out of sight, then sat back down on the blanket to finish reading the story. She'd known he would come today. He'd said as much yesterday when he left Lady Clythebrook's. And if she couldn't keep him away, she might as well use his presence to her advantage. She'd let him see all the children who were approximately the age of the child he'd come to find; all of them *except* the one for whom he was searching. She'd never let him see that one. She'd never let one of her children go to someone with his reputation. It would be like throwing Charlie to the devil.

Josie looked at the children sitting at her feet, many of them with backgrounds no different than the child the marquess sought. A nagging question ate away at her. Why did he want to remove Charlie from Sacred Heart? What better place was there for an unwanted child than an orphanage? That was the solution most commonly adhered to by members of the nobility.

Bastard children were unfortunate mistakes that needed to

be dispensed with. Well, she'd take care of his mistake for him. Little Charlie didn't need to spend his whole life waiting for his father to come back to get him like she had. It was better if the boy thought his father was dead. Better if he didn't have a face to put with the name of the man who would never love him.

She focused again on her story, saying the words with no thought to what she was reading. After every sentence, she cast a glance toward the orphanage and felt an intense sense of relief when the path remained empty. But she knew it wouldn't be long. Mrs. Lambert promised to keep him occupied long enough to get the boys safely hidden, then bring him where she had the children gathered so he could inspect them. Maybe when he was satisfied the child he was looking for wasn't here, he'd leave them alone and continue his search elsewhere.

Josie looked up the path again then back to the words on her page. Not only did she have to keep him away from the orphanage, but from Clythebrook as well. For at least a month. He could ruin everything if she didn't.

Her last thought came to an abrupt halt. He was close. The tingle at the back of her neck told her he was. She read on, keeping her voice normal as she concentrated on the words that swam before her. One by one every small pair of eyes moved to a spot high above her right shoulder. But still she read on. She would give him adequate time to take note of each child. To wonder if the child he was searching for was here.

She waited a few more agonizing seconds, then closed the book and placed it in her lap. She steadied herself, then lifted her gaze.

He stepped in front of her to block the sunlight and she had a perfect view of his features. He was magnificently handsome, but the somber look on his face indicated he didn't particularly care if anyone noticed.

"Allow me," he said, reaching out his hand to help her to her feet. His deep, resonating voice wrapped around her as he issued his invitation and a shiver raced down her spine.

He stood with his feet braced wide, his back rigid and straight, and it was all she could do to tear her gaze from his face to his large, solid hand extended toward her.

She glanced back to his face but his features remained an unreadable mask. Josie focused on the subtle nuances concealed behind the slight curve of his mouth and the gleam in his eyes in an effort to read his expression. When she couldn't, she glanced back at his extended hand and considered ignoring his offer. Then realized refusing would be cowardice.

"Thank you." She placed her hand in his and let him help her to her feet.

The feel of his flesh against hers jolted her with more awareness than she thought possible and as soon as she could, she pulled her hand free. She wasn't sure if he noticed; couldn't tell from his expression.

"I see you've brought the children outside," he said, his words innocuous enough while his intense gaze moved to study each and every child as she knew he would.

"Yes. We take the children out whenever the weather permits."

"Are these just the younger children, then?"

He didn't wait for her to answer, but stepped closer to the group of youngsters.

If circumstances had been different, Josie would have laughed at the expressions on the children's faces. Every one of them stared with open mouths and wide eyes at the giant standing before them. She had to admit he was an impressive figure even to an adult. She couldn't begin to imagine how intimidating he must seem to a child.

"All the children here are between the ages of three and five."

His eyebrows shot upward. "This was planned?"

"I assumed you would not give up until your curiosity had been satisfied."

He cast her an amused glance. "I'm impressed."

"Don't be. This just seemed the most expeditious method of satisfying your curiosity. It's preferable to having you return to

Sacred Heart and frighten the children."

The Marquess of Rainforth crossed his arms over his chest and leaned against the tree she'd been sitting beneath. "You don't have a very favorable opinion of me, do you. May I ask why?"

"Your reputation has preceded you, my lord."

"*My* reputation, Miss Foley? Or my fath—"

"*Your* reputation," she repeated. "Your riotous lifestyle and extravagant spending have always been of interest to everyone at St. Stephen's. So were the scandals in which you were involved."

"And you believed everything you heard?"

"Are you saying the rumors that made their way to St. Stephen's were unfounded? Nothing more than vicious gossip?"

She saw his hesitation as if he realized a lie would have served his purpose better. She felt a sense of admiration when he admitted what everyone knew.

"No. There was probably more truth to them than I would like to admit."

"Yet now you want me to hand over a child into your care and keeping."

She saw his eyes flash but she reinforced her stand with another accusation. "The fact that you are searching for a child you've never seen or made an effort to find until now is hardly to your advantage."

"Yet, here I am."

Josie swung her arm out to encompass the small group of children still sitting on the grass. "And I can see you won't give up until you've met the children. So, I have assembled them for you."

Josie didn't give the marquess time to respond, but turned to the children and called out, "Richie, please come here."

A little boy at the back of the circle slowly rose to his feet and came forward.

"Richie, I'd like you to meet the Marquess of Rainforth. Lord Rainforth, Richard Carruthers."

Josie took immense satisfaction from the surprised expression on Rainforth's face. She knew this wasn't what he expected but he recovered quickly.

"How do you do, Richard," he said, holding out his hand in greeting.

With a little prodding, Richie extended his small, trembling hand. "How do you do, sir."

"Richie is four years old, aren't you, Richie?"

"Yes, Miss Josie. But I'll be five next month."

"Oh, yes. How could I have forgotten? Richie is getting very old on us."

Josie gave the youngster's shoulder a gentle squeeze and pulled him close to her while she continued. "Richie's parents were killed in a fire that destroyed their home when Richie was only a babe. Richie survived and came to live with us because we wanted him so very much. Isn't that right, Richie?"

"Yes, Miss Josie," Richie answered with a smile so wide it brought tears to her eyes. "And Miss Josie takes me to the cemmary—"

"Cemetery," Josie corrected.

"Yes. The cemtatary every Sunday so I can talk to my mama."

"That's very nice of her," the marquess said, his face an unreadable mask.

"Glenda," Josie said, calling for the next child.

"Lord Rainforth. Miss Glenda Johnson."

Glenda curtsied a wobbly bob that the marquess answered with a bow as regal as any Josie had ever seen. But Glenda wasn't brave enough to face the intimidating stranger and quickly buried her face in Josie's skirts. "Glenda's mama came back to Clythebrook from London. She worked in a beautiful mansion there, didn't she, Glenda?"

"Yes, Miss Josie. All the walls in the house where my mama lived were painted gold."

Josie gave the little girl a loving hug. "Glenda's mother was an upstairs maid for the Duke of Shakely. Perhaps you are acquainted with him?"

Josie could tell from the harsh rush of air Rainforth sucked into his lungs he was familiar with Shakely's reputation. From the rumors that had made their way this far in the country, she doubted if there were many with close ties to London who weren't.

She kept her level gaze locked with his so he could not misunderstand the meaning to her next words. "Glenda's mama came back to Clythebrook to live with her parents when…her services were no longer required."

"She went to heaven, though, when I was born," Glenda added quietly. "And I don't have a father like Richie. But I have a granny and granda who come to see me sometimes."

"Glenda's grandparents aren't well enough to care for Glenda yet. Maybe someday they will be."

Josie didn't want to admit that the day would probably never come when Glenda's grandparents would take her. It had been almost five years and neither one of them had recovered from the guilt that plagued them. They were the ones who'd sent their daughter to London to give her a better opportunity to find some nice young man to marry and settle down with. Instead, she'd come back carrying Shakely's bastard child and had died birthing it.

"And this is Jeremy Black," Josie said, placing her hand atop the curly blond head of the nearest youngster still sitting on the grass. "He's just three and very special to us. Jeremy, say hello to Lord Rainforth."

Jeremy stood and Josie saw him swallow hard. "lo, Lord Rainforth," the little boy said softly, then held out his hand like he'd seen Richie do.

"How do you do, Jeremy," Rainforth said, taking Jeremy's tiny hand in his massive one.

"You're very big," Jeremy said, craning his neck and tilting his head way back to look into the marquess' face.

"Yes, I am. Perhaps one day you will be, too."

Jeremy couldn't come up with an answer so he just smiled a baby-faced grin.

"Jeremy's mother left him with us when he was just a babe. She needed to go away to London to earn a living, and because she knew we wanted him, she left him in our care."

"But she sends me letters on my birthday and at Christmas," Jeremy said enthusiastically. "Miss Josie reads them to me."

"She never forgets, does she?" Josie said, giving the child a gentle pat before letting him sit down.

Josie glanced up and noticed the bleak expression on Rainforth's face turn even darker. He was astute enough to at least guess at the truth to the letters. She lowered her gaze and walked over to the next child.

Before she could ask him to stand so she could introduce him to Rainforth, a little boy with a riot of curly red hair and a face filled with freckles jumped to his feet and held out his hand.

"Hello. My name is Frankie Hawkins and I'm five."

"How do you do, Frankie," Rainforth greeted, carefully observing the boy as if looking for any clue as to his identity.

"Frankie's mother also comes to us from London. She had a home in London for some time before her services were no longer required. She moved back right before Frank was born and lived close by until a fever took her when Frank was three."

"I went to live with my uncle Clyde first but he didn't want me. He used to hit me and he even hit Miss Josie once. The day she came to get me. Uncle Clyde was terribly mad at her."

"That's enough, Frankie."

"But I don't ever have to go back there, do I, Miss Josie?"

"No, Frankie. You never have to go back."

Josie made the mistake of looking at the Marquess of Rainforth's face.

"Is this man a tenant on your estate or mine?" he growled softly.

"No. He's from a neighboring estate quite a ways from here."

"That's fortunate for him."

Josie thought it best if she moved along. The fury she saw in his gaze showed a side of him she'd never glimpsed before.

Josie stepped to the next child and helped her up. "And this is Amanda, my lord."

"How do you do, Amanda," the marquess said, bowing again.

"Hello. I'm four and I'm special."

Josie couldn't help but smile. Lord Rainforth opened his mouth to speak then closed it.

"Don't you want to know why I'm special?" Amanda asked her eyes wide with expectancy.

"Why…of course."

"I'm special because Miss Josie said the angels brought me. Didn't they, Miss Josie?"

"That's right, Amanda. The angels left you on our doorstep so you could live with us."

Amanda looked up at Lord Rainforth with an expression so angelic Josie had to hold herself to keep from hugging the child to her.

"And this," she said moving to the next child, "is—"

"Enough."

He'd said the word so softly Josie wasn't sure she'd heard him. "What?"

"You've made your point, Miss Foley. The child is obviously not here or you wouldn't be making such an effort."

Josie kept her gaze locked with his. A myriad of accusations lay exposed within the piercing steel-gray of his eyes. She waited, not wanting to be the first to look away. But as each heartbeat stretched on, she realized he would not allow her the victory, no matter how minor. His next words proved it.

"That doesn't, however, mean you don't know where the child is. Nor does it mean I intend to give up my efforts to find it."

"I didn't for a moment believe you would. We couldn't have been so fortunate."

She smiled innocently, refusing to let him intimidate her. He wouldn't force her to tell him where Carrie Gardner's child was. The Marquess of Rainforth may be a nobleman by birth, but none of his actions since he'd gotten Carrie pregnant with his child had been noble. And he would not trick her into betraying the child.

She took a deep breath and walked away from him. "Children, go with Mrs. Lambert now. I think Cook has a treat for you."

There was an enthusiastic cheer as the children scampered to their feet and raced toward the orphanage. "I must go with them," Josie said, walking past him and up the path. She hoped she could somehow escape him, but she'd only taken a few steps before she realized he was walking beside her. She cast a glance over her shoulder and met his open smile.

"I have my carriage waiting. When you've taken care of the children we'll take a ride and I will attempt to answer any questions you might have concerning the cattle venture I'm proposing. Unless you've already changed your mind?"

She shot him a sideways glance. "No. I haven't changed my mind. And never will. You can't expect me to agree that your plan is a good one when it isn't."

"You already know the plan is good. So does Lady Clythebrook. There must be another reason you are so adamantly opposed to it."

She stopped in the middle of the path. He stopped beside her. "There is, sir. I am *adamantly opposed*, as you put it, because you are asking me to trust that you will provide for the children when you haven't stepped foot on St. Stephen's to see to its running for the last twenty years and more. How can I in good conscience give over the care of nearly sixty children to you?"

"There were reasons—"

"I'm sure there were. There always are, but they don't seem very important when you are four years old and your mother has just died and you go to bed alone and frightened every night."

Without giving him a chance to counter her attack, she spun away from him and watched the children scamper ahead of her.

She only had to keep him from going forward with his plan for one more month. There would be a shipment arriving in a matter of weeks with enough goods to provide for the children through the summer months and into the fall.

She thought of all their needs. Just the amount of food it took every day to feed them was daunting. As well as the clothing the children were always outgrowing. She couldn't give such a responsibility over to anyone else. Especially the Marquess of Rainforth, who might decide to abandon them tomorrow to go back to London.

Nothing was more important than caring for the children.

Why else would she align herself with a band of smugglers?

Chapter 6

IF EVER IN HER LIFE Josie'd felt as if she were being pulled in opposite directions, it was now. For the past hour, she'd sat rigidly straight in the carriage seat next to a man she vowed to dislike and felt her resolve to fight him shatter into a million pieces. He was such an antithesis. He was a member of the nobility, one of Society's elite. This alone should be enough to solidify her resolve to dislike him. But it wasn't.

He wasn't at all like she'd anticipated he'd be. He wasn't the least bit arrogant or conceited like most of the titled men she'd met through Lady Clythebrook. He wasn't rude or toplofty like she was certain he'd be. It would have been so much easier to dislike him if he were. Instead, he included her in his conversation even though she tried to portray disinterest. He was jovial in an almost teasing manner and before they'd reached the crest overlooking the ocean, she'd nearly forgotten how great a threat his plan was to the children.

He asked questions about everything imaginable. Who were the people who lived closest to the area where he intended to put the cattle? How long had they lived there? He was concerned about anyone who might be affected by his proposal as well as anyone who might benefit. And if she were any judge, his curiosity was genuine. Or he was the most accomplished liar she'd ever met.

She talked with him while he drove along the rough, rutted lane that led from Clythebrook Manor toward the cliffs that overlooked the ocean below. More than once, she forgot the difference in their stations. Then, she'd hear a certain turn of phrase or watch him take command of the horses and realize they were oceans apart.

His long, competent fingers held the reins to the carriage as if he'd been born with ribbons in his hands. His control over the team was both gentle and masterful, reflecting hours of training by an expert. His words were elegant and refined, and his voice as he explained every detail of his proposal, cultured. She was mesmerized by him as if he had the ability to cast spells. And to her chagrin, the plan he'd formulated was, if not brilliant, at least remarkable enough that she could envision its success without question.

If only he were someone she could trust. If only he weren't a member of the nobility. If only he weren't just like her father. No. She could never give up that much control to someone with his reputation.

She was left with no choice but to keep coming up with road blocks to deter his enthusiasm. And he was, if not enthusiastic, at least confident. She could hear it in his voice. See it in the gleam of his steel-gray eyes. Feel it as if his determination were a palpable thing that had a will of its own.

But stop it she must.

Josie stiffened with new resolve. How could she even consider agreeing with him? This was a man who hadn't cared enough for St. Stephen's to take a personal interest in anything that had happened here his entire life. What guarantee did she have that before he put his plan into motion he wouldn't tire of the country and go back to his wild and carefree life in London? What guarantee that before anyone saw even one pound of profit from the sale of the cattle, he'd decide to use his money elsewhere and leave them without notice? What guarantee did she have he even had enough capital to fund such a venture? She certainly hadn't seen any indication of abundant wealth.

Oh, no. She couldn't chance putting the children's lives in his hand. At least now she had control over the provisions that came into the orphanage. Going along with his plan would change all that. The shipments would have to end. No one would dare bring anything into the coves if there was a risk they might be seen and arrested. And if his plan failed? What then?

She looked over at him and threw out another obstacle. "And just where do you intend to find the knowledgeable manpower you'll need to care for the number of cattle you intend to raise?"

"The number of out-of-work soldiers returning from the Crimea is staggering. Not all of them are city-bred. I venture a great many young men were raised on a farm and know a great deal about cattle."

"But who will contact them and where will they live?"

As if he found humor in her attempt to erect another barrier, he looked down at her and smiled. The broad upturn of his lips caused matching creases to indent on either side of his mouth. They turned his handsome features from simply arresting to magnificent and Josie's stomach somersaulted.

"I have the means at my disposal to hire as many men as we'll need. And there's an old hunting lodge on St. Stephen's not far from here that can be used as a barracks of sorts. After the conditions most of the soldiers endured in the Crimea, a roof over their heads, a warm fire, and plenty of food to fill their bellies will seem like heaven."

Josie clamped her mouth shut. He was right. She knew he was. Yet, every clop of the horses' hooves took them closer to the border that separated St. Stephen's and Clythebrook. Closer to the broad patch of land near the cliffs where she couldn't allow him to venture. How long would it be before he discovered what the cove was being used for? How long before the authorities were summoned and they were all arrested?

"This scheme of yours will never work, Lord Rainforth. There are no—"

"Miss Foley."

He pulled on the reins and the carriage came to an abrupt halt. She had to grab onto the seat to keep from falling against him.

"Before long you will run out of reasons why my proposal won't work and you will have to admit I'm right. If you can for one minute stop thinking of me as some dangerous villain out to destroy everyone in my path, you will be able to see that bringing in cattle will help not only the tenants of both estates, but the children of the orphanage as well."

"Can you guarantee without a doubt there is a profit to be made?" she countered.

"My every instinct tells me there will be a handsome profit."

"And if you're wrong?"

"I'm not."

Josie stopped arguing long enough to hear the growing sound of an approaching rider. They both turned.

"Someone you know?"

Josie lifted her head. "Yes. It's Baron Lindville. He must have recently returned from London."

The man sitting beside her changed. Gone was her relaxed companion who'd found humor in her objections. In his place was a wooden replica, complete with his defenses firmly in place.

"Are you acquainted with Baron Lindville?"

"No, I haven't had the honor," he answered, but Josie thought from the tone of his voice he didn't consider meeting Baron Lindville an honor at all.

Before she had time to wonder more, Baron Lindville had stopped and was smiling at her.

"Miss Foley. What a delightful surprise."

Geoffrey Lindville removed his hat and bowed slightly in the saddle. His golden hair was brushed back to expose a high forehead and sharp, striking features. While his thick eyebrows were not terribly dark, they did serve to draw attention to the piercing blue of his eyes. Lindville graced her with a smile that spoke of a long-standing friendship and years of acquaintance. The smile on his face hardened, however, when his eyes took in the man sitting beside her.

Josie felt the need to speak first. "Baron Lindville. I didn't know you'd returned from London. Have you been here long?"

"No. Just a few days. I see you're out enjoying this fine day."

"Yes. Baron Lindville, allow me to present the Marquess of Rainforth. Lord Rainforth, Baron Lindville of Lindville Grange."

"Lindville," Rainforth said, his voice containing a hint of iciness she hadn't heard since the first time she'd met him.

"Rainforth." Lindville's brows arched. "My, what a surprise. Did you…*tire* of London?"

The Marquess of Rainforth shifted the reins from one hand to the other in a most casual gesture. But casualness was not what Josie felt sitting next to him. There was a tension that sifted through the layers of her skirt and rasped against her skin. When he spoke, his acidic tone only heightened the uncomfortable wariness that settled about her.

"Actually, I did," Rainforth said. "The drawing room topics were becoming extremely tedious."

"I'm sure you found them less than palatable, at least the comments that were said to your face."

Josie felt the blow of Lindville's words as if his attack had been aimed at her and couldn't stifle a shocked gasp. Lord Rainforth, however, buffered the assault with nothing more noticeable than the slight lift of a brow. For the first time, Josie wondered how often he'd had to endure such condemnation since the rumor of his father's traitorous activities had been uncovered. And how many times he'd been unjustly blamed for his father's crimes.

"I can't imagine Lady Clythebrook approved of your accompanying Rainforth, Miss Foley. Let alone without a chaperone."

Josie bristled, unable to let Lindville's insult go unchallenged.

"It's been several years since I've required a chaperone, sir. And even longer since the company I keep has been questioned."

"Perhaps Miss Foley is not familiar with the reason your presence is not welcomed in London's social circles," Lindville said, leaning forward in his saddle. He kept his glaring gaze focused accusingly on Rainforth and didn't lift it.

The Marquess of Rainforth smiled. At least the corners of his mouth lifted in an outward indication that he was smiling. Nothing else in his features suggested that. "Oh, I think the lady has heard. Have you not, Miss Foley? Are you familiar with the fact that my father sold military secrets to the Russian government during the Crimean War? And that he was an English traitor?"

Josie glimpsed briefly at a raw, torturous hurt Rainforth quickly masked with a blasé look of inconsequence. She didn't answer. She couldn't. The pain she felt was too acute. A pain she understood all too well.

But when he slowly turned his head to face her, she made sure there was no softness in her eyes. No trace of sympathy. He was too proud a man to accept such a sentiment and every instinct told her he would hate the slightest hint of pity even more than she did. If there was one fact she understood more than any other, it was that the Marquess of Rainforth was no more accountable for his father's sins than she was for hers. She looked at him with a commanding firmness as if the accusations were inconsequential.

"Did you assist your father in his crime?"

His first reaction was anger. She could see it in his eyes. But when that wore away, there was only surprise at the boldness of her question.

"No."

"Then I hardly see where your father's indiscretions have bearing on what you are proposing here."

She saw an appreciativeness in his eyes before he quickly hid it. Then, he challenged her support as if he wasn't sure he'd read her right. "I think she knows, Lord Lindville, and has survived under the weight of my father's sins, horrendous though they be. Does my presence distress you terribly much, Miss Foley?"

"I've told you before. It's *your* reputation I'm concerned with. Not your father's." Josie leveled Baron Lindville a harsh look to indicate her displeasure. She'd always known he considered himself in a class far above tenants and small landholders, which was a result of his mother's constant pampering and elevating. But he more than anyone should know not to cross the line of proper conduct. To be so overtly rude to Lord Rainforth, a fellow peer of the realm was far beyond intolerable.

Lindville ignored her condemnation. "What brings you to this part of Clythebrook, Miss Foley? Hardly anyone comes this far."

"Actually, I came with Lord Rainforth to discuss a venture he and Lady Clythebrook are considering."

"A venture?"

"Yes. Cattle."

There was a shocked look on Lindville's face, then he threw his head back on his shoulders and laughed. His laughter died when he realized she hadn't been joking. "You're serious!"

"Actually, I am."

Josie watched the grin from Lindville's face flatten as his face paled. "Tell me Lady Clythebrook isn't seriously considering something so foolhardy."

"Yes, she is."

Lindville glared at the marquess with a warning that Josie read all too clearly. Rainforth answered the challenge with an attack of his own.

"Perhaps Lady Clythebrook doesn't consider the idea foolhardy. Perhaps she looks on a venture which could double or perhaps triple her profits as wise. As I was explaining to Miss Foley, St. Stephen's has a more-than-adequate supply of underground water, and the land on this part of Clythebrook Estate is ideal for grazing."

The baron's expression turned serious. "And Lady Clythebrook agrees with this?"

"Nothing's been decided," Josie answered, watching the look in Lindville's eyes turn more threatening.

"Then perhaps I might suggest you explain the drawbacks of such a scheme to Lady Clythebrook."

"And what would those be?" Rainforth asked, his voice low and questioning.

"Clythebrook and Lindville inhabitants have always had an amicable relationship. Lady Clythebrook's generosity provides the entire area with easy access to the north and west. Lindville generosity allows access to the east. Without such an alliance, both Clythebrook Estate and St. Stephen's would be virtually cut off from the rest of the world. The inhabitants of both estates would be forced to go miles out of their way to reach London."

Rainforth's reaction was tangible. "Are you suggesting that permission to cross Lindville Grange may no longer be granted?"

Baron Lindville gave out a sinister laugh. "Of course not. I can't imagine matters going so far. Can you, Miss Foley?"

Josie couldn't answer. She knew exactly how much was at stake and it had nothing to do with access roads.

"I am only warning you because this area is not always the safest," Lindville continued, his glare shifting from her to Rainforth.

"Are you warning me of highwaymen in the area?" the marquess said, leaning back in his carriage seat as if he were enjoying the conversation.

Lindville smiled again and Josie couldn't stop the shiver that raced down her spine. Or ignore the uncomfortable tension that sparked between the two men.

"There are all manner of dangers, Rainforth. I would hate for something to happen to you and realize I'd been remiss in my obligation to give fair warning to anyone venturing where they didn't belong."

Josie clutched her hands in her lap to keep from reaching out to cover the fist Lord Rainforth had clenched on the seat beside her. Geoffrey Lindville was generally the most good-natured of men, but she knew why his reaction to Rainforth's venture had elicited such a strong response. Geoffrey had just as much at stake as she did.

"Thank you for the warning," the marquess said sitting forward. "I'll keep it in mind."

"Well, I've done my duty, then. If you will excuse me." Lindville turned his mount as if preparing to leave, then stopped. "Oh, and Miss Foley," he said, glancing over his shoulder. "If you're ever in need of an escort, don't hesitate to call upon me. I'm always at your service."

Josie stared at Geoffrey Lindville's retreating back as he cantered off down the narrow path toward Lindville Grange. She felt the need to apologize for Lindville's rudeness but couldn't find the words. Rainforth's voice stopped her.

"Is there some reason Baron Lindville thinks he has the right to tell you with whom you may or may not associate?"

She lifted her chin. "Of course not. I alone decide with whom I associate."

"And do you associate often with Baron Lindville?"

"Baron Lindville and I have known each other since the Earl and Countess of Clythebrook took me into their home. Lord Clythebrook and Baron Lindville's father were boyhood friends and had attended Eton together. It was only natural that the two families associate when they were both in the country."

Josie saw the taut lines etched on either side of Rainforth's mouth. The confrontation with Geoffrey had obviously affected him even though he was trying to give the impression it hadn't. She wondered how many times he'd had to face the same demeaning accusations and knew it was probably often from the tight grip he still had on the reins. He was as primed as a powder keg near a burning flame and she thought of what to do to ease his anger. She placed her hand atop his arm before he could snap the reins and begin their journey home.

"Would you mind if we got out and walked?"

She almost heard his sigh of relief as he answered, "Of course not."

She thought he might need to walk off his frustration and anger, just as she always needed a brisk walk when the concerns of the orphanage weighed too heavily.

The marquess stepped down and turned around to lift her out. His hands came around her waist and she stepped into his arms with a confidence she felt with very few people. A warm rush spread to every inch of her, from her cheeks that a moment ago had felt the chill of the air, to the tips of her fingers, tingling where her hands rested on his broad shoulders.

She couldn't let herself feel this way. Couldn't let his nearness affect her like it did. Yet it did. A shiver of awareness ran up and down her spine.

"Are you cold?"

She shook her head, not able to tell him it wasn't the cold that affected her, but a blazing heat inside her she couldn't explain.

He held her gaze and her body for a long moment while a riot of unfamiliar sensations battled to be acknowledged. A frown made a deep furrow on his forehead as if he were asking himself the same questions as she. With a rush of breath he released her, then took off his jacket and placed it around her shoulders.

The sturdy wool was still warm with the heat from his body, and the backs of his fingers brushed against her flesh as he slowly brought the material together beneath her chin.

Josie knew she should step away from him. Knew she should insist he remove his hands, but she didn't. She wanted to stand here just a little while longer and let the unfamiliar emotions he brought out surge through her. She wanted to absorb the pulsing heat that raced down her arms and legs and settled low in her belly.

She drank in the warm gray of his eyes that today seemed soft and inviting, then lowered her head until her gaze rested on the top bone button that fastened his shirt. He was close to her, closer than she'd ever let a man stand to her before and yet…

A small voice deep inside her wanted him to step even closer. Wanted him to take one small step forward until their bodies touched.

As if he'd read her thoughts, he clutched both lapels of the jacket he'd placed around her shoulders and held it securely beneath her chin with one hand. Then, he inched his other hand upward, following the narrow column of her throat, then upward further until the long, slender fingers that had handled the carriage reins so deftly skimmed her face. His hands were not soft, but not roughly callused either. They felt incredibly perfect against her skin.

He cupped her cheek, his hand cradling her face. Then his index finger slid beneath her chin and raised upward, forcing her to meet his gaze.

She didn't speak; couldn't speak. Her mouth was too dry to form any words, even if her mind had the ability to function enough to find them. She stood frozen, her gaze locked with his, her heart a runaway train that thundered in her chest.

He didn't smile and she didn't know why she thought he might. Perhaps to make light of the intensity that enveloped them. Instead, the expression on his face seemed to darken, the gray of his eyes deepening even more. Then his gaze moved down to her lips and she knew he was going to kiss her.

Time seemed to stand still and race ahead at the same time. Sunlight exploded through the clouds that billowed in the sky. The breeze that a moment ago had been damp and chilly was suddenly warm and balmy. Without a word, he lowered his head and pressed his lips to hers.

Josie had never been kissed before. She was not so naïve she didn't know what happened between a man and a woman, nor was it that she'd never seen two people kiss. But she'd never imagined that the feel of a man's lips against hers would cause the eruption of fiery heat to spread like a burning wildfire as it ignited every part of her body.

In her confusion, she wrapped her arms around his neck and

leaned forward to answer his kiss. She didn't want him to stop. Didn't want him to break the captivating contact of his mouth against hers. And just when she thought it was impossible for her blood to rush through her head any faster, he deepened his kiss and she soared to a place even more amazing than where she'd been.

He gently pressed downward on her chin and she opened her mouth for him.

Someone moaned. Perhaps it was her. She wasn't sure. Then the moan came again and Josie tightened her hold around his neck. He deepened his kiss. And her world bloomed around her.

For an eternity they remained locked in each other's embrace, absorbed in each other's warmth, reveling in the feel and touch and taste of the other. He kissed her long and deep, with an intensity that startled and consumed her. Then, with a low growl, he lifted his mouth from hers and ended the kiss.

As if he knew the effect his kiss would have on her, he wrapped his arms around her and pulled her to him. With her arms clamped tightly around his waist, she rested her cheek against his chest and listened to the violent thundering of his heart beneath her ear.

For several long moments Josie didn't move. She knew when she did she'd be forced to face what she'd done. It was as if she'd traveled too far down the wrong path and now it was too late to turn back. As if he'd shown her something it was impossible to forget.

She took a shuddering breath and dropped her hands from around him. Waves of anger built inside her, anger at herself for being such a fool. And anger at him for forcing her to give in to an emotion to which she had no intention of ever succumbing. On legs that were still not steady, she turned away from him.

"Stay away from here, Lord Rainforth. Nothing good can come from you being where you don't belong."

"This is where I belong. It's maybe the only place I truly belong."

Josie sucked in a breath and held it, then turned to go back to the carriage. She didn't look at him. Not because she didn't want to. Oh, she did. She wanted to study his strong, noble features, and memorize the rigid cut of his high cheekbones and angular jaw. And she wanted to drown in the pewter-gray of his eyes, eyes that drew her in like a lush, secret hideaway. And most of all, she wanted to sit close to him and let his quiet strength envelope her. It was this strength she both admired and feared. A strength that had the ability to both save and destroy. And she was so afraid she knew the direction his path would take him.

They rode back in silence and when they reached the front of Clythebrook House, he jumped down and tied the reins to the brass pole. Before he could return to help her dismount, Josie stepped down from the carriage unassisted. They hadn't spoken during their journey back from the cliffs. Maybe the marquess was trying to understand why he'd been so foolish and had kissed her. Maybe his silence indicated his regret. Whatever the reason, Josie was glad he hadn't felt the need to talk.

As if he realized she wouldn't accept, he didn't offer to escort her up the walk. Instead, he nodded politely and let her pass him. Josie was only a few steps away from him when she met Banks coming down the walk.

"My lord," he said, stopping before the carriage. "Lady Clythebrook is hosting a small dinner party tomorrow night and would enjoy the pleasure of your company. She has invited several landholders and local merchants from Clytheborough and thinks perhaps the gathering might give you an opportunity to discuss your idea."

Josie's heart thundered in her chest. This couldn't be happening. Didn't Lady Clythebrook realize how opposed Josie was to this?

"Tell Lady Clythebrook I shall be honored," the marquess answered, the confident tone of his voice sending a shiver down her spine.

"Very good," Banks answered and returned to the house.

A blinding flash of fury raged through her. She spun around to face him and was met by a blinding smile. "You haven't won. I still intend to stop you from proceeding with a venture I consider fanciful, even dangerous for Lady Clythebrook to become involved in."

"As you intend to stop me from finding Carrie Gardner's child?"

"Yes. The child is happy and content where he is, and I intend for him to remain that way. It will be a cold day in hell before I divulge any information concerning his whereabouts. And a colder day still before you lay eyes on him."

Before he could reply, Josie spun on her heels and stormed to the house. With a loud crack, she slammed the door behind her.

Her head throbbed, her chest ached. And her lips burned from his kiss.

She'd never been more miserable.

Chapter 7

HIM.

He had a son. She'd confirmed it when she'd said *a colder day still before you lay eyes on "him".*

Ross stared absently out his study window, then turned his attention back to the papers scattered across his desk. They were filled with words he'd written to present to Lady Clythebrook when they talked, but for the life of him, he couldn't recall what he'd put down. Since Josephine Foley had let slip that the child Carrie had given him was a son, he'd found it impossible to concentrate. And Miss Foley probably didn't even realize she'd given away such a telling detail.

He dipped his pen in the ink well and started to write, then placed his pen back on the desk. How could he possibly keep his mind focused on such insignificant details as grazing acres, water estimates, and the market value for a few hundred cattle when he'd just discovered he had a son? How could he do the figures for well depths, manpower needs, and initial outlay expenses, when for nearly four years he'd had a son and he didn't even know his name? Or if the child was well or sick? Or blond-haired like Carrie, or dark like him?

Ross shoved his chair back and bolted to his feet. He thought he knew every nuance of living with the heavy burden of guilt:

the racing heart; overwhelming fear; shortness of breath; cold, clammy flesh; sleepless nights; terrifying nightmares; the ringing in his ears, and blood rushing through his head. That he'd killed his father was secondary to knowing that his child was out there somewhere, alone. Perhaps frightened and hungry. Perhaps being mistreated.

He raked his fingers through his hair and fought a fresh wave of guilt that attacked him. How could he have gone more than four years without realizing Carrie might have been carrying his child when she left? Oh, theirs was no great love match. Neither of them had ever considered it so. But they had both genuinely cared for the other.

At the time, she'd explained she was weary of being someone's mistress and asked him to provide her a modest yearly income and a home someplace a safe distance from London. He'd thought it a reasonable request. It even seemed a welcome solution. Breaking off with a mistress was always unpleasant. He remembered thinking how easy Carrie had made it for him. He'd escaped their relationship virtually unscathed.

Bloody hell. What kind of bastard had he been? What kind of fool? To not consider there'd been another reason that she'd left him. To not give the woman he'd lived with for more than a year a second thought and to continue his high living without skipping a beat. No wonder his father had stooped to selling military secrets so the son he'd always doted on could continue his extravagant lifestyle.

Ross almost ran to the small side-table to pour himself a drink. For months, the numbing effects of gallons of liquor had been the only panacea to forgetting that he'd been the one who'd caused his father to betray his country. That to save Sam's life, Ross had been the one who'd pulled the trigger that had put a bullet through his father's heart. But drinking hadn't softened what he'd done; only made the nightmares worse. So he'd given up his goal to drown his past and faced it headlong.

If discovering who was behind the smuggling ring was the

only way he could redeem the Rainforth name, then he'd move heaven and hell to accomplish it. And nothing Josephine Foley could say or do would stop him.

Ross looked back down at the papers on his desk then stopped when Benedict knocked softly and opened the door.

"You have guests, sir."

"Guests?"

"Yes, sir. Lady Lindville, and her son, Baron Lindville."

Ross hesitated. After his confrontation with Lindville yesterday, his first inclination was to have Benedict tell them he was from home. Curiosity finally got the better of him and he placed his pen on the stack of papers he'd been reading and stood.

"Show them to the morning room, Benedict. I'll be with them directly."

"Very good, sir."

Ross tied a hasty knot in the cravat he'd pulled loose and grabbed his jacket from the back of the chair. Lindville had all but spit in his face yesterday. He couldn't imagine what could be important enough to bring him here today. And the fellow's mother, as well.

Ross shrugged into his jacket and prepared himself for what promised to be an interesting meeting. A part of him welcomed the interruption. At least it stopped him from thinking about Josephine Foley or trying to figure out why he'd kissed her. And why the hell that kiss had stolen the air from his lungs.

Bloody hell! He'd kissed hundreds of women. Had even had a child with one of them, and no one's kisses had affected him like hers had.

He walked down the hall and gripped the door to his study, thankful he had something else on which to concentrate.

"Lady Lindville. Lindville," he said, entering the room. "What a pleasant surprise."

He looked to Lady Lindville first. The regal-looking matriarch of the Lindville dynasty was exactly as he imagined she'd be.

She sat on the velvet settee in the center of the room with her chin high, her back ramrod straight—and a scowl on her face.

She wore a gown of rich emerald green velvet that was as fashionable as the gowns worn in London at the height of the Season. When he entered the room she slowly turned her head and greeted him with a slight nod and an unsuccessful attempt at a smile.

Her son stood on the other side of the room, staring out one of the two ceiling-to-floor windows that overlooked a flower garden not yet flush with the blooms that would be a riot of colors in late spring and all through the summer. Baron Lindville turned to face him when Ross entered the room.

Lindville wore the same superior expression Ross had noted the day before, and the glassy look in his eyes wasn't any clearer. Nor any friendlier. Ross supposed the man might be considered handsome in a soft sort of way, and no one could fault his perfectly tailored attire, even though it was a bit overdone for a casual country call. In London, the expensive cut of his clothing would speak clearly of his wealth. Here in the country, it stood out in a condescending way, as if to make a point of his elevated place in rural society.

Ross took Lady Lindville's hand in greeting. "I see you are taking advantage of this beautiful spring morning."

"There is a reason we've come," the baroness said, shifting to sit even straighter.

Ross sat opposite Lady Lindville. "I see. Might I interest you in some tea first?" He pointed to the tea cart Benedict had rolled into the room but she stopped him with a shake of her head.

"No. I prefer to get right to the point." She pulled her lace handkerchief through her fingers with the same finesse as he imagined a farmer wringing the neck of a chicken, then dropped her hands to her lap. "Geoffrey and I have come to make you an offer for St. Stephen's Hollow."

Ross swallowed. "I beg your pardon?"

While walking down the hallway Ross had anticipated many

possibilities for why his wealthiest neighbors had come to pay their respects to a man who'd been shunned by all of England. But never had he considered this. He leaned back in his chair and waited for Lady Lindville to continue.

"I've been interested in purchasing St. Stephen's for several years, but until now haven't seen the necessity to act upon my wishes."

"But now you do?"

"Yes. My son has indicated a desire to marry and I know it would be advantageous to add St. Stephen's Hollow to Lindville Grange. It's common knowledge that St. Stephen's isn't entailed, nor has it been of any importance to you since you haven't stepped foot here since you were a youngster and your mother was still alive. Until recently, we thought you'd forgotten you owned St. Stephen's."

"But now that I've returned, you suddenly see the need to acquire it?"

"Yes. I wish to leave my son with a substantial inheritance and the acquisition of St. Stephen's will ensure his security as well as that of his children."

"How noble," Ross said, taking note of the brandy Geoffrey Lindville eyed so enviously. "Unfortunately, St. Stephen's is not for sale."

"You haven't heard the amount we're offering," Lindville said, his tone of voice as condescending as his mother's.

"The amount is irrelevant. Selling St. Stephen's is not a possibility."

"But why ever not," Lindville countered, his voice rising in intensity. "You haven't given this isolated little corner of England a second thought until now."

"As you can see, that has changed."

"Perhaps if we give you time to consider our offer…"

"Time will not alter my decision. I couldn't accept your offer even if I wanted to—which I don't. St. Stephen's belonged to my mother and there is a stipulation that prevents it from ever being sold."

Tension-filled silence seeped into the room.

"I see," Lady Lindville said, her voice dripping with icy hauteur.

Lindville stepped forward. "And you still intend to use the land overlooking the cove to graze cattle?"

"The opportunities for both St. Stephen's and Clythebrook are well worth the risks."

Lindville paused then slowly lifted the corners of his mouth. "I doubt you'll find that to be so," he said, leveling Ross a hostile glare. "Come, mother. We've stayed long enough."

Without bidding Ross farewell, Baron Lindville escorted his mother from the room. Ross wanted to leave them to find their own way out of his home, but years of training forced him to escort them out. He stood beneath the marble portico and watched until their carriage was out of sight.

Lindville and his mother were suddenly very hungry for land. Land Ross knew was being used by the smugglers.

Ross made his way back to his study and looked down at the map spread out on top of his desk. St. Stephen's wasn't the only land to which the smugglers needed access. They also needed to get their hands on a large portion of Clythebrook Estate.

Ross sat down behind his desk and wondered if Clythebrook Estate was entailed. If not, he suddenly wondered to what lengths Geoffrey Lindville would go to get it.

Josie sped across the meadow at an easy run on her way to Clythebrook Manor. Tonight was Lady Clythebrook's dinner and Josie wanted a chance to speak with her again before the guests arrived. She'd spent hours last night trying to convince Lady Clythebrook not to go along with Rainforth's venture. When she'd been unable to get a firm answer one way or the other, she'd bargained for her second option—at least one month of grace time before she let Rainforth start his project.

Lady Clythebrook had listened to her request but hadn't agreed to anything yet. She said she'd give her answer when the evening was over; after she'd heard any objections from the guests she'd invited tonight.

Josie cut across a dry ravine and had only gone a few more steps before she heard the pounding of horses' hooves behind her. She glanced over her shoulder and stopped. Geoffrey Lindville was racing toward her so quickly she had to step out of the way until he got his horse under control.

"Good afternoon, Lord Lindville," she said after he'd jumped to the ground.

"Miss Foley. I was afraid I'd missed you. I went to the orphanage but they said you'd already left."

"Yes, I wanted to—"

"We need to stop him."

Josie didn't need to ask who Lindville was talking about, she knew. And she knew why it was important to stop him.

"Nothing has been decided yet. Lady Clythebrook hasn't given her approval for the project."

"Lady Clythebrook *can't* give her approval," he said, slapping his hand against his thigh. "You obviously don't realize what's at stake here."

"I'm just as aware of what we could lose as you."

"No! I don't think you are. All you think about is that damned orphanage and making sure the children have what they need. We're not talking about the frivolous little extras the children could do without. We're talking about what *I* could lose. It's *my* future that's about to be destroyed!"

Josie stared in dumbstruck disbelief as Geoffrey Lindville paced a small area in front of her. She'd never see him like this. The two of them had been partners for almost two years and not once had she seen such a display of temper from him. But never had their venture been tested as it was being tested now.

"I know what you think you will sacrifice if the money we make from the smuggling is lost." She tried to keep her voice calm. "You will lose—"

"Everything! Until I'm thirty my mother controls my spending. You know how generous she is to the orphanage." His sardonic laughter sent out a spine-chilling sound. "Well, she's no more giving to her own son. It's how she remains in control."

Josie pulled the thin shawl she wore closer around her shoulders and fought the niggling voice that whispered a warning. "Rainforth can't do anything without Lady Clythebrook's approval. And she hasn't made a final decision."

"Then you have to make sure she refuses to give him permission to use the land."

"I'm almost certain she will. I've pointed out every reason I can think of to convince her. She promised she wouldn't make a decision until after the dinner tonight and I have every belief she'll refuse him."

"Are you sure?"

"I'm fairly confident she will."

Lindville visibly relaxed. "I should have known you had everything under control. If you see Lady Clythebrook wavering, you can always use your charms to convince Rainforth to abandon his plan."

"My charms?"

Lindville laughed. "Really, Miss Foley. You act as though you've never realized with your looks you could wrap any man around your finger. And you know what they say about catching flies with honey."

Josie remembered the kiss she and the Marquess of Rainforth had shared and her cheeks blazed. "I have no intention of being any nicer to Rainforth than I must."

His brows furrowed. "There's a lot at stake here, Miss Foley. It might be worth removing that icy exterior of yours just this once to stop Rainforth. Perhaps you can force yourself to endure a man's attentions for just a little while for the children's sake."

Josie knew what Lindville thought of her. She knew what

everyone thought. Well, let them think she was a cold fish. Let them whisper behind her back that she thought she was better than everyone because she'd been raised by the Earl and Countess of Clythebrook. She knew most of their objections stemmed from the fact that she'd soundly rejected every attempt to court her.

But she'd never give in to a man like her mother had. Nor would she be fooled by the blatant efforts of the local gentry to pretend the circumstances surrounding her birth didn't matter to them when she knew they did. She knew every attempt to court her had been for one purpose only—to gain the property they knew she would inherit when Lady Clythebrook died. Baron Lindville had been the only one who hadn't offered her that lie. Not because her illegitimacy didn't matter to him because it did. The fact that she was a bastard child offended him equally as much as it repulsed his mother. But he was forced to overlook her tainted birth because she played such a vital role in the smuggling operation.

"I have to go," she said, shaking off the qualms of unease she suddenly felt.

"Don't forget what I said. If you want to keep the orphanage open and the children fed and clothed, you'll do whatever you must to stop Rainforth."

Josie clutched her hands within the folds of her skirts and tried to ignore the threat she heard in Lindville's voice. He was mistaken if he thought she would ever throw herself at any man, especially the Marquess of Rainforth. And even more mistaken if he thought it might do any good. She would never give in to any man. Especially a man with the Marquess of Rainforth's reputation.

Her mother had done that and died regretting it.

Chapter 8

Josie stood in the drawing room near the fireplace, waiting for the first of the guests to arrive. It was early yet—too early for Rainforth to make an appearance. He would be the last to come.

She didn't know why she thought that, except she'd seen firsthand the reaction the marquess had received from Baron Lindville when they'd met the day before. This may not be London, and the guests Lady Clythebrook had invited tonight might not be the cream of Society, but she doubted his reception would be any different. Rainforth's father had been accused of treason, after all, and the people of Clytheborough had been just as affected by what he'd done as the rest of England had.

Josie didn't know why it was so easy for people to transfer the sins of a father to his children. Perhaps because it gave them someone to blame. But she thought she knew the Marquess of Rainforth well enough to know he wouldn't back down from the assault. Nor would he take the easiest route. He would arrive late to face Lady Clythebrook's guests en masse rather than coming early to dilute the unpleasant task into bite-sized pieces.

"Is something wrong, Josephine?"

Josie turned as Lady Clythebrook entered the room. The countess looked lovely tonight. The gown she wore was her very finest, a silver brocade with an overskirt of shimmering filigree netting. Her cheeks were flushed pink and her eyes held a glow that Josie remembered from a time long ago. Tonight she did not seem nearly so fragile. She seemed…hopeful. And they had the Marquess of Rainforth to credit—or blame—for such optimism.

"You look stunning," Josie said with a smile on her face. "Still the most elegant woman in England."

"You've stolen Lord Clythebrook's line."

Lady Clythebrook smiled then lifted her chin slightly at the fond memory. "And you look…worried."

Josie walked across the room to help Lady Clythebrook to the place of honor in the center of the room. She'd chosen not to use her cane tonight and walked a little unsteadily. But if she was in pain, she hid it well. "Are you sure this dinner party is a good idea?"

"Are you worried it isn't?"

Josie hesitated, then voiced her concerns. "I saw the way Baron Lindville reacted to the Marquess of Rainforth yesterday. Tonight he'll have to face Lindville's mother and the other guests. You know as well as I that Squire Pearsons lost a nephew in the Crimea."

"What would you suggest Rainforth do? Hide away for the rest of his life?"

"No, of course not, but…"

"If he intends for his venture to succeed, these are the people he's going to have to convince of the worthiness of his plan. Don't you think it's better that he face them now while there's still a chance they feel included in his final decision than after the cattle are already here and they feel as though they've been forced to go along with him?"

"Are you saying you've decided to allow Rainforth to put cattle on Clythebrook Estate?"

"I haven't decided anything yet. I told you I'd consider your objections. Much will depend on what happens tonight."

"And if he's rejected out of hand?"

"Then my decision will be more difficult."

"All I ask," Josie said, carefully choosing her words, "is that you trust me enough to know I wouldn't oppose Rainforth's plan without good cause."

Lady Clythebrook smiled. "And if I decide to agree to Lord Rainforth's plan?"

"Then give me a month."

A frown deepened on Lady Clythebrook's forehead. "Is it Rainforth to whom you object, Josephine? Has he done something to offend you?"

Josie shook her head.

"I was hoping not. He's an exceptional man. Quite your match."

Josie jerked her head to face Lady Clythebrook. "He's not my match. He's a marquess. A nobleman."

"And your match." She smiled, then added, "It must be his plan, then. Why are you so opposed to it?"

"Because he cannot guarantee that it will work. And even if it does, it will be more than a year before we will see any profits. The children cannot wait a year."

"Oh, Josephine. When will you give in just a little and trust someone else to shoulder some of the burden for the children?"

"Never. I'll never give the children over to someone else's care and that's what would happen by encouraging Lord Rainforth."

"It seems you aren't the only one who feels this way."

Josie put the small figurine she'd been holding back on the elegantly carved table. "What do you mean?"

"Lady Lindville paid me a call earlier today to suggest I use my dinner tonight to dissuade Lord Rainforth of continuing his plan."

"What did you say?"

"That I intended to do just the opposite. That the reason for my dinner was to give Lord Rainforth the opportunity to answer any questions anyone might have."

"Do you think that was wise?"

A frown deepened on Lady Clythebrook's face. "And why wouldn't it be?"

"Because…"

Because Lady Lindville and her son are the last people on earth you should alienate.

Because there's so much more going on than you realize.

Because…

But Josie was spared having to answer. Before she could gather the right words, Banks announced the arrival of their first guests.

In attendance were Baroness Lindville and her son, Baron Lindville, Vicar Chadwick, and Mr. and Mrs. Sharpe, one of the wealthiest merchants in Clytheborough. Squire Pearsons, the local magistrate and his wife, had also been invited, along with the Pottsworth sisters, Miss Evangeline and Miss Eustacia— spinster sisters whose father had been the vicar before Vicar Chadwick. Their inclusion was mandatory at all functions of importance. And this was indeed important.

All of them had been specifically chosen because of the effect the Marquess of Rainforth's venture would have on them. It was a known fact that any proposal would run smoother with their support. But if the wary undercurrent Josie sensed as the guests mingled remained, the evening promised to be anything but ordinary.

Josie walked around the room, making sure conversations flowed smoothly and that each guest had a glass of the special wine Lady Clythebrook had brought up for the occasion. Everything progressed perfectly, except for a halt now and then as one or another of them paused to check the doorway to see if he was here yet.

Josie knew the exact moment he arrived. And saw the impact of his presence.

He stood in the empty doorway for several seconds after Banks ushered him into the room, letting them all study him.

There was not a hint of reticence or self-consciousness, but a boldness in the way he faced them. His stature was tall and erect with his shoulders back and his head high. His demeanor contained an air of arrogance that he wore as casually as he wore his perfectly tailored clothing. Josie tried to pull her gaze away from him but couldn't. He was dark and bronzed and magnificently handsome, and every ounce of his breeding rose to the forefront, from the proud lift of his sharply defined chin to his noble countenance.

The stony silence echoed in her ears as every eye in the room remained riveted on where he stood.

He didn't lower his gaze but let them drink their fill, then walked through the room with long, confident strides that ate up the space between the doorway and the sofa where Lady Clythebrook sat. He was an imposing figure on the most ordinary of days, but tonight he was even more impressive as he crossed the room to lift Lady Clythebrook's hand to his lips in greeting.

She'd told herself she wouldn't be affected by him—by the warmth in his pewter-gray eyes or the inviting pull of his smile or how elegant he looked in his black evening clothes. But none of her lectures had done the least bit of good. A slow, tumultuous churning commenced inside her the moment she realized he was there.

From the smile on his face and elegant grace of his movements, no one would have guessed that he noticed the sudden stillness that swept through the room.

Josie watched him for as long as was considered polite, then forced her gaze to move to the other guests who stood in rigid stillness. How she survived the uncomfortable tension his arrival caused she didn't know. How *he* survived it, she couldn't imagine.

Josie would have liked to have continued her conversation

with the Pottsworth sisters and Mrs. Sharpe, but didn't want to give the impression she was avoiding him. No matter what tragedy happened tonight, she didn't want any hint of blame placed at her feet. She excused herself and selected a glass from the tray Banks had just brought into the room.

"Lord Rainforth."

"Miss Foley. How lovely you look tonight. If Lady Clythebrook were not in attendance, no one would compare to your beauty."

"I'm sure Lady Clythebrook thanks you."

"Indeed I do," Lady Clythebrook said with a broad smile.

"But you do not?"

Josie met his gaze. "Let's just say I'm much too realistic to believe such flattery."

"Or perhaps you have just not heard a compliment often enough to believe its accuracy."

She lifted her brows, hoping he would realize his accolades didn't affect her. "Would you care for a glass of wine? The vintage was Lord Clythebrook's favorite."

He smiled a smile so natural and at ease she wondered how he managed, then he reached out to take the glass.

Their fingers touched. A spark ignited her flesh that stunned her and held her. She felt her cheeks warm and looked again at his fingers wrapped around the glass. How could just a touch cause such a reaction? Lady Clythebrook's voice caught her attention.

"Josephine, come. We must introduce Lord Rainforth to our guests."

Josie nodded, cast a glance at the intimidating gathering, then looked up. The expression on Rainforth's face was unreadable, an impenetrable mask hiding any hint as to what he might really be feeling.

The room was deathly quiet, the lack of a smile on anyone's face a grim indication of the reception the marquess was about to receive.

Had he known it would be this way? Had he gone through

this before? So often he was immune to people's reaction? His voice did not give away what he might be feeling.

"Yes, Lady Clythebrook. I've been quite anxious to meet the good people of Clytheborough."

Josie stepped to the side as he held out his arm for Lady Clythebrook to take, then followed as the countess led him to the far side of the room where Lady Lindville stood with her son and Vicar Chadwick.

"Baroness Lindville. Baron Lindville. Vicar Chadwick. May I present the Marquess of Rainforth?"

"Yes, we've met," Lady Lindville said in a tight voice that held no warmth.

"Wonderful," Lady Clythebrook responded as if she hadn't noticed the strain.

The marquess didn't reach out to take Lady Lindville's hand as he might have done, perhaps to avoid the embarrassment of her refusal to offer it. Instead, he returned the greeting with a polite bow to the baroness and a formal nod to both Baron Lindville and Vicar Chadwick.

The moment was uncomfortable enough but would have been worse if Lady Clythebrook had waited for Lady Lindville or her son to return the greeting. But she didn't. Nor did she pause long enough to give Lady Lindville or her son the opportunity for a direct cut, but proceeded into a conversation about how pleased she was that the weather had cooperated and that even though the night was chilly, it was clear and the moon full, which made it so much brighter to see.

Both Baron Lindville and the vicar had no choice but to agree, which at least gave the impression of cordiality. Lady Lindville, however, took the first opportunity to separate herself from their small group and join the Pottsworth sisters, who were standing nearby, paying close attention to every word spoken.

Although there hadn't been any open hostility in the meeting, the dye was cast the minute Baroness Lindville turned her back on the Marquess of Rainforth.

Taking their cue from the wealthiest and most influential land-owners in the area, the other guests followed suite. Their actions were not perhaps as blatant, and some even carried on an enjoyable conversation with Lady Clythebrook and Josie, but it was impossible to miss the cold reception the Marquess of Rainforth received.

Josie had known this was a possibility but had prayed it wouldn't be a reality. The uncomfortable tension that filled the room was so thick she could cut it with a knife. Her cheeks burned in embarrassment, yet the marquess acted as if nothing were amiss. As they made their way across the room, he even seemed eager to meet the next guest, knowing his reception would not be friendlier.

A knot formed just inside Josie's ribcage and gnawed uncomfortably. She looked about, searching for a way to undo what was happening, but unable to find the answer. After nearly a quarter hour of stilted conversations and unfriendly encounters, Josie felt her nerves stretched to the breaking point. How did he do it? She felt as if she couldn't endure the scrutiny another second and was never so glad of anything as when dinner was announced and they were able to escape the confines of the drawing room. At least at the table she could pretend to be enjoying her food.

The meal, however, didn't turn out to be the respite she'd hoped for. Lady Lindville and her son made sure of that.

"Have you organized the spring drive yet, Miss Foley?" Lady Lindville asked, intentionally interrupting the question Lady Clythebrook had just asked the marquess. The cut was obvious.

Josie cast the marquess an apologetic look and felt a deeper rawness when he answered her with a smile. He held her gaze for a brief second then she turned her attention back to Lady Lindville's question.

"No, we haven't started the drive yet," Josie answered, lifting her spoon out of the soup she'd barely touched and placing it on the table.

"Father always said the spring drive was the event he anticipated most during the year, as well as the one he was the most relieved to see come to an end," Miss Eustacia Pottsworth added, looking at her sister for confirmation. The two nodded in unison.

"Have no fear, Miss Evangeline. Both you and Miss Eustacia will be the first I call upon for help."

Demure smiles brightened both women's faces and warm flushes darkened their cheeks. Conversation flowed smoothly through the various courses of the meal, from the fish, to the roast duckling, then the lightly creamed vegetables and candied fruit. It wasn't until the footman served the dessert Mrs. Downey had specially prepared for the dinner party that Lady Lindville chose to make her move.

"Squire Pearsons," Lady Lindville said, speaking at the precise moment when there was a lull in the conversation. "I wanted to ask after your sister. The death of a child is indeed tragic, but to lose your only son. Well, I cannot imagine her bereavement."

Josie's heart skipped a beat. She knew Lady Lindville's intent with this line of conversation. So did Lady Clythebrook and everyone else at the table. Only the Marquess of Rainforth was oblivious. He cut into the thick piece of Mrs. Downey's layered cake and put it in his mouth with only a cursory glance in the speaker's direction.

Pearsons cleared his throat. "It is indeed difficult for her, even after this length of time."

Josie looked to Lady Clythebrook for help but realized the older lady had already anticipated this turn and intended to let it take its course. Josie couldn't. She looked around, frantic to find something that might distract. The only thing in reach was a plate of candied fruit. She held it out to Vicar Chadwick. "Would you care for another—"

Lady Lindville cut off her attempt.

"I can't imagine the grief of every mother who lost a son during the war. Especially when their loved one was cut down in the prime of life."

The eerie silence seemed suffocating and Josie noticed a slight pause in the marquess's movements. He knew.

"All those hundreds of precious lives so needlessly sacrificed because of one man's—" She paused for effect. "Well…"

Lady Lindville's sentence went unfinished, but there was no need. Her words had been intentional and malicious.

The Marquess of Rainforth barely reacted. But he'd heard. And he understood.

He took a deep breath, then slowly placed his fork down beside his plate and lifted his head. His features seemed no different, as if he'd gone through situations similar to this so often he was adept at controlling his reaction. With deliberate slowness he placed his linen napkin on the table and turned to face Squire Pearsons.

"Your sister lost a son in the war, sir?" he said, his voice thick. The look in his eyes dark with an emotion too intense for her to read.

"Yes, during the siege of Sebastopol."

"You have my most heartfelt sympathies."

The room was deathly silent.

Everyone waited for a reaction. Lady Lindville had laid her trap well. Her intent had been to kill, not just wound. If the squire refused to accept Rainforth's apology, he would make plain how he and the other guests felt about Rainforth, regardless of the improvements the marquess intended to make. And Rainforth would have to give up his plan. Which was what Josie had been hoping for. The means to keep him away from the caves.

Oh, but not like this. Not to have Rainforth brought to his knees so cruelly. Not if it meant destroying his pride.

Not like this.

She waited, praying the final blow wouldn't come.

Chapter 9

SQUIRE PEARSONS SAT UNMOVING in his chair, his intelligent gaze locked with the marquess's. Josie fought the painful gnawing that ate away at her. A voice inside her wanted to cry out that Rainforth wasn't responsible for what his father had done, but she knew the marquess would resent her intrusion. So she sat as immobile as the other guests, locked in the drama unfolding around her without being able to do anything to stop it.

She swiped her damp palms against the linen napkin in her lap while the mantel clock ticked away one uncomfortable second after another. Josie knew Squire Pearsons was weighing the earnestness of Rainforth's words and prayed he read them as she did—filled with genuine sincerity.

The squire finally shifted his round bulk in the chair and gave a short nod, his decision made.

"Thank you, my lord. I will extend your condolences to my sister. They will mean a great deal to her."

There was another uncomfortable moment of silence, followed by a variety of inane movements. The Pottsworth sisters both meticulously straightened their napkins in their laps. Several of the guests developed a sudden thirst and lifted their wine or water glasses to their mouths. And some just sat, intently studying the food that remained uneaten on their plates.

Only Lady Lindville reacted in an expected manner, with hostility and anger. The scorching glare she sent in Rainforth's direction frightened Josie. Her son didn't look at anyone, but gave an irate wave of his hand as he motioned for the footman to refill his wine glass. He drank it in record time then motioned for the footman to fill it again.

Cornelius Sharpe made the next conciliatory attempt by directing his question at the Marquess of Rainforth.

"Lady Clythebrook has informed us that you have an idea to propose she believes will benefit everyone in the area."

Cornelius Sharpe owned several shops in Clytheborough and was always interested in anything that would affect what the people had to spend.

"Yes. With Lady Clythebrook's involvement, I intend to increase the number of cattle on Clythebrook Estate and St. Stephen's by several hundred head."

A collective gasp echoed in the room, every eye now focused on the man speaking.

Mr. Sharpe was the first to recover. "Several hundred?"

"Yes, for a start."

"But how can you manage such a large number?"

"Clythebrook Estate is lush with grazing land and St. Stephen's has an abundant underground water supply at its disposal. By utilizing both estates, we will be more than able to raise a substantial herd."

"What part of the estates do you intend to utilize?" Vicar Chadwick asked, clearly interested.

"The strip of land bordering St. Stephen's eastern edge and Clythebrook's western."

"The land closest to the sea? Above the caves?"

"Yes. It's not ideal for anything else. And other than the orphanage located inland from the cove, the rest of the land is not being used at present to its full potential."

Squire Pearsons's eyes brightened. "Oh, my. What a remarkable idea."

Mr. Sharpe leaned forward, his attention focused on Rainforth. "And do you anticipate an influx of workers?"

"I do, Mr. Sharpe. First, we'll take advantage of what local manpower is available. Then, we'll have to bring in extra workers to fill our needs. It will, of course, mean a substantial increase in goods required to provide for the added tenants and their families but I've been assured you are capable of making such goods available."

He beamed. "Oh, yes. Of course."

"Lady Clythebrook, surely you don't intend to go along with this foolhardy proposition?"

There was an accusatory tone to Lady Lindville's voice and everyone turned to Lady Clythebrook, the person on the receiving end of Lady Lindville's glaring look.

"I don't consider it foolhardy at all. Quite the opposite. And Lord Rainforth assures me the profits from such a venture will provide everyone in the area with added income. This will not only benefit the tenants on both estates, but the children in the orphanage and every shop in Clytheborough. How can I not at least consider such an endeavor?"

Josie couldn't remain quiet any longer. "Can you guarantee such a profit, Lord Rainforth?"

He smiled. "I can. Not immediately, of course. I have already explained that it will take at least a year before the first cattle will be ready to take to market."

"How do you intend to get the cattle to market?" Squire Pearsons asked, his interest as evident as everyone else's.

"By rail. And the nearest stop is Lythesborough. Which means we will have to cross Pearsons Grange."

Squire Pearsons sat straighter and the marquess focused his steel-gray gaze down the table to where the squire sat across from her.

"I'm hoping to convince you of the advantages to this venture so you will want to become involved."

Pearsons was engrossed in every word. "As you can tell, I'm

already interested. I would, however, want to discuss everything in greater detail."

Josie couldn't keep her temper from rising. Everything was slipping away before her very eyes and if she didn't stop it now, she'd lose control of the only means she had to provide for the children.

"Even though we'd all like to believe your idea will be lucrative," she said, trying to keep her voice soft and steady, "surely you have to admit there's a possibility what you're proposing will not be profitable?"

The corners of his mouth lifted into a heart-stopping smile. "I refuse to admit any such thing, Miss Foley. Even if the market remains stable, there will still be a profit. The only point I am willing to concede is that the profit will not be immediate. It will take at least a year before the first cattle are ready to go to market."

"And in the meantime?"

He frowned. "In the meantime you will go on as you always have."

But we won't be able to!

She wanted to scream at him. His plan would ruin everything. How could they risk continuing their smuggling operation with scores of workers watching from above? And without the goods that were smuggled in every quarter, the children would be forced to go without.

She remembered the days before Geoffrey Lindville had come to her with his plan. Days when there was not enough to feed the children and they went to bed hungry. Or when winter came and there were not enough coats, and even the donation drive the Misses Pottsworths were so proud of running didn't bring in nearly what the children needed. Now, Rainforth's plan would ruin everything.

She felt her anger mounting from deep inside her. She couldn't allow him to take away the little control she had over what came into the orphanage without a fight. Baron Lindville hadn't made her a part of the smuggling operation because he cared about the children, but because he needed access to the tunnels that ran beneath the orphanage. He'd had no choice but to include her. Without her help he had no way to bring the goods inland.

She opened her mouth to voice another objection but didn't have an opportunity to get the words out. Everyone was too interested in the details of his plan to interrupt.

"Have you anyone in mind to oversee such a project?" Squire Pearsons asked, even more excited than before.

"Yes, the man I've chosen is—"

"Lord Rainforth," Lady Clythebrook interrupted, stopping the conversation. "Perhaps you and the other gentlemen would like to retire to the study to further discuss this venture over a glass of port, and we ladies can talk of more pleasant things than cattle and grazing."

The men heartily agreed and slid back their chairs and left the room, still discussing the economic possibilities Lord Rainforth's venture would provide.

Josie sat rigid in her chair while the footman poured coffee and set around small plates of chocolates. The same flush of excitement she'd noticed in Lady Clythebrook's cheeks earlier was back. So was the gleam in her eyes.

"Constance," Lady Lindville said, addressing Lady Clythebrook by her given name. "How could you!"

Lady Clythebrook nodded to Banks, then waited until all the servants had quit the room. "How could I what, Lavinia?"

"Don't be obtuse. You know exactly what I'm speaking of. *Him*. How could you align yourself with a traitor?"

Everyone at the table found a spot in their laps on which to focus. There was a momentary silence before Lady Clythebrook answered. "If you are referring to the Marquess of Rainforth, then you had best be very careful what you imply. The marquess is not now, nor has he ever been accused of being a traitor. There was some evidence that his father, the late marquess, committed the grievous crime of betraying his country, but the young man seated at my table tonight talking about a plan to improve the living conditions for all of us, had nothing to do with the travesty you'd like to lay at his doorstep. My question to you is, what possible objection could you have to Rainforth's cattle venture?"

All eyes lifted to where Lady Lindville sat.

"It's not the venture. It's the man. You're not so isolated here in the country that you don't know his reputation."

Lady Clythebrook chuckled, then reached for a chocolate on a plate in front of her. "Oh, Lavinia. Every young buck with a title has a reputation before he settles down. He'd be a dull fellow indeed if he didn't."

There was a chorus of twitters from all the ladies, even the Pottsworth sisters.

Lady Lindville, of course, didn't find anything humorous in Lady Clythebrook's statement. She placed her napkin on the table with a snap and leaned forward. "That's not what I mean and you know it, Constance. The marquess' reputation has left behind it a dead woman whom he abandoned when he realized she was carrying his bastard and a child of no more than four to find his own way in the world. And the man has not even made an effort to find the boy. Has he, Josephine?"

All eyes darted to where she was sitting.

Josie cleared her voice then answered. "The marquess has inquired after the child, but—"

"And you let him see him?"

Lady Lindville was aghast and so were the other women at the table. In unison, they stared at her, waiting for an answer.

"No."

"Your reason for refusing him was…?"

"Because…Well, because…"

"I'll tell you why," Lady Lindville finished for her. "Because Josephine knows how disreputable he is. She knows to keep the boy as far away from him as possible."

Josie couldn't admit Lady Lindville was right. It would sound much more damning coming from her. She was spared having to lie when Lady Clythebrook interrupted.

"That's enough, Lavinia. You don't have to like the Marquess of Rainforth, but I won't allow you to blacken his name with lies and accusations."

"Well!"

Lady Lindville rose from the table. There was a venomous look in her eyes that no one missed. They all lowered their gazes, everyone except Josie and Lady Clythebrook.

"You'll regret this, Constance. Mark my words. The marquess cannot be trusted any more than his father could. If word ever reaches London that you've aligned yourself with him, you'll be ruined."

"Society thrives on shocking revelations," Lady Clythebrook answered.

"Society swallows such offenders whole. If you believe that won't be your fate, then you are a fool."

With that, she shot Lady Clythebrook a frigid glare that sent chills down Josie's spine. "Please tell my son I am ready to leave."

The order was directed at Josie and there was a condescending tone to Lady Lindville's voice that was always there when she spoke to her. As if she needed to remind Josie that even though she'd been raised in Lord Clythebrook's house and given privileges she was lucky to have been given, she would never be more than a bastard daughter of little consequence.

"I'll send for Banks—" Lady Clythebrook started to say but Josie rose to her feet.

"No need. I saw Lord Lindville remove himself to the patio." She nodded toward the double French doors. A terrace ran along both the dining room and the study where the men had gone and Josie had seen Lindville pass the window. "I'll tell him he's wanted."

"He probably went outside to escape the undesirable company in the study."

Josie ignored the snide comment and went through the doors

that led outside. She was grateful to escape Lady Lindville's spiteful insinuations and inhaled the crisp, cleansing nighttime air the minute she closed the door behind her.

At first she didn't see Baron Lindville. The flagstone terrace ran the length of the house and he'd stepped over to the far side where he would be out of view. She watched him lift a glass to his mouth and empty the contents, then tip a half-full bottle he must have taken from the study and fill his glass again. If he wasn't already drunk, he soon would be. He slowly turned when she took her first step toward him.

"Your mother wishes to leave, sir."

He lifted his glass again and drank. "I imagine she does." He took a faltering step and reached out his arm to steady himself. "You'll extend my heartfelt thanks to Lady Clythebrook for a most enlightening evening."

"Yes. Of course." Baron Lindville gave her a stiff bow and started to leave. Josie stepped closer to the cement railing that surrounded the patio and leaned against it. "What are we going to do?" she said, not asking really, just voicing her question out loud.

"Do?" Lindville looked at her over his shoulder. He smiled. "Nothing, Miss Foley. We aren't going to do anything."

"But—"

He held up a hand to stop her words, then looked out into the moonlit darkness. "It's too late to do anything, and from the reaction of our esteemed neighbors, there's nothing to be done."

"But the children?"

He dropped his head back on his shoulders and laughed. The sound was a low and sinister echo that matched his voice when he spoke. "Yes, the children. It's always the children with you, isn't it?"

He reached for the bottle he'd set down earlier and poured some of the liquid into the glass and drank it. "Now, if you'll excuse me. I'll see to Mother."

Josie watched him walk back into the house by the door off the dining room but she didn't follow him. She needed time to sort through what was happening. Even Cornelius Sharpe seemed to approve of Rainforth's venture, and it was to his shops the smuggled goods were sold. Surely he realized that the cloth goods and wines and tobaccos he bought at such a reasonable rate had questionable origins? But of course he didn't realize that the goods that arrived every quarter came ashore directly below the pasture where the Marquess of Rainforth wanted to put his cattle. Or that once the area was inhabited, the risk would be too great and all deliveries would cease.

Josie thought of all that would be lost and shuddered. She wrapped her arms around her middle and hugged herself, both for support and to ward off the cold that seeped thought her. She spun around when the door behind her opened and closed. It was the Marquess of Rainforth.

"I met a maid Lady Clythebrook had sent with this," he said, walking toward her with a shawl. "I said I'd deliver it."

"Thank you."

He stepped behind her and placed the shawl around her shoulders. It wasn't her imagination that he let his hands linger on her shoulders. Nor was it her imagination that her entire body warmed from his touch. She hated the way her body betrayed her.

"Have the guests gone home?" she said, turning around to face him. She used the motion as an excuse to put some distance between them.

"Lady Lindville and her son left a few minutes ago. The rest are preparing to leave now."

"I should go in then." She started to leave but his words stopped her.

"Lady Clythebrook is doing fine. Stay."

Josie turned back to look out into the darkness. Even though the cold was going through her, she stayed because she didn't want to go inside and offer pleasant farewells when her mind was consumed with concerns for the children. She breathed a deep breath and pulled the shawl closer around her.

"You're cold."

He stepped up behind her and placed his jacket around her shoulders.

"Just a little," she said on a sigh.

He didn't remove his hands right away, but kept them clasped around her upper arms. For a brief moment, they stood immobile, his body so close he touched her. Then he stepped away and Josie clutched the lapels of his jacket to bring the fabric tighter around her.

The velvet was still warm from his body and Josie brushed her face against the lush material. It smelled a mixture of clean soap and the pungent odor of tobacco.

"This is the second time you've suffered the cold to keep me warm," she said, lifting her gaze. He stood close beside her, his nearness creating as much warmth as the jacket.

"The pleasure is mine."

She took a deep breath. "I'd be lying if I tried to assure you Lady Lindville's intent was not to cause harm."

He didn't answer, but turned to look up at the stars.

"Is her reaction so common then?" she continued.

She saw the slight smile that curved his mouth. He leaned one hip against the stone balustrade and crossed his arms over his chest. That put him eye level with her and when his deep gray eyes locked with hers, her heart began a slow, steady race that picked up speed with each breath.

"Everyone who was affected by what my father did feels justified in their condemnation. Lady Lindville's reaction tonight was no different than her son's was yesterday."

Josie could no longer hold his gaze. "I'm sure Baron Lindville was just overreacting."

"Was he? In what regard? In his condemning comments concerning my father? Or his insinuations of danger? Or in the warning he issued to stay away from you?"

She turned toward him. "Baron Lindville wasn't warning you to stay away from me."

Unable to stay so close to him, she took one step away. "He has no reason to care who I associate with. Nor does he have the right. We're neighbors, and if he feels any closeness it's only because he knows someday I will inherit Clythebrook Estate and there will always be an association between us."

"You will inherit Clythebrook Estate?"

She looked over her shoulder and smiled at the incredulity she saw on his face. "Now who is surprised?"

"Forgive me."

"That's quite all right. Who would ever imagine Lady Clythebrook would leave her estate to an orphan? And a female at that?"

Josie ran her fingers over the soft lapel of his jacket. This was not a topic she enjoyed talking about. "Clythebrook Estate isn't entailed. I knew even before the Earl of Clythebrook died that the estate would be mine someday."

"Does Baron Lindville know this?"

"I'm sure he does. Lady Clythebrook hasn't kept it a secret."

"I can see where your friendship would be in his best interest."

"A friendship between neighboring estates is always in everyone's best interest."

"Yes, it is."

From the corner of her eye, Josie saw him rise from where he'd been sitting. Her heart raced when he closed the distance between them and she knew she couldn't allow him to stand that close to her if she wanted to keep a clear head. She had to make one more attempt to convince him to give up his scheme.

"How old are you, Lord Rainforth?"

She looked over her shoulder to see his dark eyebrows arch. Her question had surprised him.

"I will be thirty on my next birthday."

"And how old were you when you last stepped foot on St. Stephen's?"

"I believe I was eight or nine."

She pivoted to face him. His eyes were dark and he cocked his head a fraction to one side, which gave him a roguish appearance.

"And during that time, where did you live?"

"In London mostly, although I spent a month or two each year at one of the Rainforth estates." He paused, then asked, "Is there a reason you are interested?"

"Yes, there is. Why did you spend so little time away from London?"

His lips curved upward to form a smile that changed his features from breathtakingly handsome to dangerously magnificent.

"Because I was young and carefree and didn't want to rusticate in the country when there was so much to see and do in London."

"But you do now? Want to…rusticate at the ripe old age of nine and twenty? And you have chosen St. Stephen's as the place where you wish to rusticate?"

"Do you find that so improbable?"

"Yes, I do. You'll excuse me if I have a hard time believing that after an absence of more than twenty years, you have all of the sudden developed a deep love for country living. Your appreciation for all that London has to offer is well known. So is your reputation. Tales of your youthful peccadilloes reached even us humble folk so far from the City. Yet, now you want everyone to believe you'll be content to live at St. Stephen's? But what will happen if in a month or two you decide you are tired of it here and yearn to return to London? How long do you think everyone who was to have benefited from your cattle venture will survive when you abandon us?"

"Abandon you? You don't trust me to see this venture through?"

She couldn't hide her surprise. "Of course I don't trust you. You expect all of us to put our faith in you and the scheme you've concocted when your reputation only warns us to be wary of you. I'm sorry, sir. Too many children rely on the decisions I make for them. Decisions that provide their next meal."

"Then make the right choice. Just consider how this will benefit the children and simplify the running of the orphanage if my cattle venture works."

"In a year perhaps. Isn't that what you just told Lady Clythe-brook's guests?"

"Yes, but in the long run it will secure the welfare of every child in the orphanage."

"I didn't realize the welfare of our children interested you so."

"The welfare of every child interests me."

"Every child? Or just one?"

"Every child, Miss Foley. And one in particular."

"Well, Lord Rainforth. Every child's welfare interests me as well. And I will always do what I consider best for each and every one of them."

"I'm glad to hear that. I'm also sure you realize it would be in everyone's best interest if you'd tell me where I can find my child."

Josie's resolve to keep a smile on her face faltered as her temper soared. "Best for whom? Certainly not the child."

"You don't know that."

"I know if Mrs. Gardner intended for you to assume responsibility for her child, she would have left instructions to that affect. She did not. And why should she? Not once during the time she lived in the dower house on St. Stephen's did you come to even check on the child. I can only assume your lack of interest indicated you didn't care."

"You are assuming a great deal. Did you ever speak to Mrs. Gardner about me or the living arrangements struck between us?"

"You know I did not."

"Then may I ask how you've acquired such extensive knowledge regarding my interest?"

"Because you are no different than any other peer of the realm. A great number of the children at Sacred Heart are a result of the immoral lifestyle in which men such as yourself engage. The children are branded as bastards from birth and come here to live because they have nowhere else to go. They are children no one wants."

Josie took great satisfaction in watching Rainforth's eyebrows arch upward. "Does that surprise you?"

"Surely you can't cast every titled nobleman in such an unfavorable light."

"I can and I do. It is a common practice for the titled to take their pleasures outside the bonds of marriage with little concern as to what might result from such a union. There is, after all, no great risk to the male. It is the woman who suffers the consequences. Producing a child, however, carries with it a great responsibility for both parents. A responsibility the titled of this land think they have no obligation to assume."

"If that's your opinion, then why do you think I'm so determined to find the child now?"

"I don't know. Curiosity, perhaps. To at least be able to boast to your exalted circle of friends that you've made an attempt to care for the child. After all, how would it look if anyone found out you didn't even know your own child's name?"

"His name is Charles, Miss Foley."

Josie reeled back a step in shock. He knew. Somehow he'd discovered little Charlie's name.

For several long, tense moments, the two of them faced each other, muscles taut, backs rigid and straight, gazes locked. It was as if they both needed a moment to evaluate the other's tactics and decide how to proceed. Finally, Josie unfolded the aching hands she didn't realize she had clenched at her side. "How did you find out his name?"

"Obviously not everyone has heard your edict to keep the boy's whereabouts concealed. One of the tenant's wives I visited earlier today thought the boy's name was Charlie. Your reaction just now confirms it."

The Marquess of Rainforth turned to look out onto the garden, then slowly lifted his gaze to the millions of stars in the sky. "He's mine."

His soft, gentle voice slid through the tension and wrapped around her like a warm blanket. "I know."

"I want him."

"He's happy where he is. He has friends."

"He'll be happy with me."

"No." Josie lost her grip on the deep-down anger she thought she had under control. "Why are you doing this? He can never be your legitimate heir. You *can't* want him. No member of the nobility cares about—"

She clamped her hand over her mouth to stop the words.

"Is that what happened to you?"

The air left her lungs. She swallowed hard, trying to recover quickly. Damn the man. That he had the power to expose the scars she thought no one could see infuriated her. "What happened to me is none of your concern. But the events of my life taught me several valuable lessons. And I will use the knowledge I've gained to protect the children under my care. You have no influence here. None."

"But I do, Miss Foley. I have a great deal of influence. And power. And I won't hesitate to use everything at my disposal to get my son."

Josie recognized the determination behind his threat. She stiffened her spine and faced him squarely. "Then you'll have the fight of your life. The children are mine to protect."

"You can't protect the whole world, Miss Foley."

"I don't intend to protect all of it. Just the parts that I can."

"And who will protect you?"

"I can take care of myself. But the children have no one but me."

With a heavy sigh, he reached out to smooth the collar of his jacket beneath her chin. "We continuously seem to be at loggerheads with one another. I want you to give over my son, Charlie, but you refuse. I want you to support my plan to make our estates profitable, but you refuse. I want you to rely on me to help the children at Sacred Heart, but you can't. What will it take before you give in on just one point?"

"A miracle, Lord Rainforth. It will take a miracle."

His expression froze, then a smile slowly lifted the corners of his mouth. As if he couldn't help himself, his lips separated and he smiled fully at her.

"Do you know much about miracles?"

"Enough to know they rarely happen."

"Ah, but they do happen. Especially during the full of the moon."

Josie looked at him, not quite understanding what he meant.

"Miracles. A gypsy once told me that very special miracles happen during the full of the moon."

"And you believed her?"

"I have no reason not to. Shall we test her theory?"

Josie stamped down the strange feeling that he was drawing her into a trap.

"See," he said, pointing up into the sky. "The moon is full."

"And what miracle do you expect to happen?"

"What miracle do you think?"

Josie relived the hours she'd spent with Lady Clythebrook earlier, not giving up until she was certain she'd convinced her not to do anything for at least one month. "Perhaps the moon is fresh out of miracles tonight, sir."

A heavy sigh escaped his lips. "That's a sadly jaded view, Miss Foley." He shifted slightly away and squared his shoulders. "At any rate, we'll soon see. The moon is full and Lady Clythebrook said she'd like to speak to us before she retires. I assume she's ready to tell us what decision she has made."

Josie knew he was probably right. "Then we'd best not keep her waiting. We'll see if you can count on your gypsy's full-moon magic or if we are left with only its jaded side."

"The moon's jaded side?"

"The side we see when there is no hope for a miracle."

He hesitated as if thinking about her words, then bowed politely and offered her his arm. They were on the far side of the patio and the soft lights from the candles glowing through the long, multi-paned windows gave the outdoors an ethereal effect.

"I have a question I'd like to ask you before we find out Lady Clythebrook's decision."

Josie stopped but she didn't look at him. She waited until he spoke.

"Would it be so difficult for you to trust me?"

His question wasn't what she'd expected, yet it didn't shock her. There'd been a connection between them she hadn't understood from the night he'd stopped her in the woods. A connection that turned her hot and cold and left her stomach churning whenever he was near. It was a tumultuous emotion she refused to try to understand. Nothing good would come of it if she did.

She turned toward him and looked into his ruggedly handsome features. He was the epitome of strength and dominance and for a moment she thought how freeing it would be to share her worries and concerns with him. How much lighter the burden would be if he would shoulder some of her responsibilities. But each child's wellbeing was at stake. And the man offering to help her was a peer of the realm. A man whose reputation was no better than the man who'd gotten her mother pregnant then abandoned her and the child he didn't want. A man who could order his fancy clothing packed tonight and be on his way to London tomorrow without a thought as to whether the children went to bed hungry or full.

She looked up to find him waiting for her answer. "No, Lord Rainforth. It would not be so difficult for me to trust you."

She lifted her chin a fraction more. "It would be impossible."

Chapter 10

JOSIE SAT IN ONE OF THE TWO CHAIRS a footman had positioned facing Lady Clythebrook. The marquess sat in the other. The air in the room still held a great deal of the tension she'd created before she'd left him on the patio. Oh, how she wished she hadn't meant those words, but she had.

She'd only briefly glanced at his face when she'd handed back his jacket. The slight lift of his lips told her he considered her words a challenge. The gleam in his eyes as he'd looked down his noble, aristocratic nose at her was clearly a vow that no matter how hard she fought him, he wouldn't be bested by her.

But he had no idea how determined she was. To her mind, this venture was nothing more than a diversion for him as he whiled away the time until reaction to what his father had done died down. Then he'd pack his trunks and head back to the debauched lifestyle that had earned him his reputation in the first place. He'd forget all about the people he'd abandoned here.

She thought of little Charlie and Robbie and Glenda and all the others. Without the smuggling, there was no way to make certain the children had enough food to eat or warm enough clothes to wear. No matter what it took to keep the supplies coming in, she would do it. She didn't intend to watch the children go without.

Josie focused her attention on Lady Clythebrook and saw the

familiar overflowing of warmth and affection she'd known from the first day she'd come to live here. That look gave Josie reason to hope.

Lady Clythebrook smiled reassuringly, then spoke.

"I know you both think that when you leave here tonight one will have won and the other lost. I hasten to assure you that neither of you will come out the loser." She looked from one of them to the other. "Or you both will."

Josie opened her mouth to speak but Lady Clythebrook held up her hand and stopped her words. Josie's heart beat a little faster. There was no way they could both win. She knew that. The marquess knew it too. But from the corner of her eye, she saw him relax back into his chair as if he were enjoying the riddle Lady Clythebrook had given them.

"Lord Rainforth, you have presented an idea you believe will ease the economic problems that plague us. And Josephine, you are just as convinced Lord Rainforth's venture will not provide all he has promised."

Lady Clythebrook held her hand out toward Josie and Josie slid forward in her chair and took it.

"I have always valued your opinion and relied upon you to know what is best for us." She squeezed Josie's fingers with tenderness, then dropped her hand and sat back against the cushions. "I also know how difficult it is for you to take any chances with the children. But perhaps it's time you changed."

The blood rushed through Josie's head, shutting out all sound. Lady Clythebrook was going to agree to Rainforth's plan. But she'd said neither of them would come out the loser. Josie's heart thundered in her chest and thrummed in her throat, nearly choking her.

"Lord Rainforth, I believe you may have the answer to our prayers. The two of you, however, are not the only ones involved in this. I, too, have something to gain. It is a promise I made Lord Clythebrook before he died but thought I would never be able to honor. Until now."

Josie shook her head. She knew what that promise was and wanted no part of it. Lady Clythebrook however was addressing her conversation to Lord Rainforth.

"From the day Lord Clythebrook brought Josephine into our home, she was the child we never thought we'd have. It was always our intent to take her to London. Not to give her a Season, but simply to introduce her.

"No."

Josie jumped to her feet and moved to the sofa next to Lady Clythebrook. "I don't want to go to London. I never have. I'm perfectly content here."

Lady Clythebrook smiled. "But I am not."

She patted Josie's hands, then turned her attention back to Rainforth. "For a long while after Walter died, I didn't want to go to London either. I was perfectly willing to hide away here in the country with my grief and loss. Then, I woke up one day to find that several years had passed and Josephine and I were so entrenched here it was impossible for us to leave.

"As you've probably noticed, my health is not what it once was. But," she said with a twinkle in her eyes, "I'm not so decrepit yet that I cannot survive at least a few months of balls and soirées and musicales. Josephine needs to experience London at least once in her life."

"But I don't want any of it."

"I know you don't, dear. But I'm giving you no choice. For the first time since I've handed over the responsibilities of running the estate as well as the orphanage, I intend to have my way."

Rainforth shifted in his chair. "I'm not sure I understand where I come into this."

"Josephine didn't grow up learning the intricacies of London Society. She fits in perfectly here in the country, but I cannot take her to London without preparing her for what she will encounter. It would be like throwing a lamb to the wolves. And I have been absent for so long I would be of little help to her. I wouldn't even know who to warn her away from, or instruct her on how to avoid the worst of the libertines in Society."

"But, of course, I can."

"Who better, Lord Rainforth, than one of Society's most notorious rakes?"

Rainforth lowered his head, but not before Josie saw the sheepish grin that covered his face.

Lady Clythebrook smiled, then continued. "You have asked for access to the land bordering St. Stephen's. It's yours. With one condition."

Josie sat rigidly still, barely hearing the rest of Lady Clythebrook's words. She had chosen to let him use the land. She had chosen a stranger over the person she claimed to care for as deeply as her own daughter. Lord Rainforth had won and she and the children had lost. She tried to think of what her next move should be but the mention of her name jolted her back to the conversation.

"In return, you will prepare Josephine for what she will need to know when she goes to London."

"No!"

Lady Clythebrook ignored her and continued. "You will instruct her in what liberties to allow men of good breeding and what tricks those same men will use to ruin her good name. You will teach her the latest ballroom steps so she won't be found lacking, and provide her the opportunity to improve her conversational skills. I have no doubt more than a few there will take note of her, especially when they discover the estate that will someday be hers. I want her to be prepared so that no advantage will be taken of her. And Josephine…"

Josephine slowly lifted her shoulders and locked herself in a stance that stated plainly her refusal to go along with Lady Clythebrook's scheme.

"You didn't want me to agree with Lord Rainforth's plan. In fact, you made me promise that I would give you thirty days no matter what decision I made. I therefore agree to your stipulation. If you allow Lord Rainforth to tutor you in the intricacies of

London Society, you will have the thirty days you asked for."

Josie wadded the fabric of her skirt in her fists. "And if I do not?"

"Lord Rainforth may bring his cattle in tonight if he so desires."

Josie felt the room shift around her. This couldn't be happening. "Please—"

Lady Clythebrook held up her hand to stop her. "This is my final word."

Josie knew she'd been defeated. She stared first at the calm, compassionate expression on Lady Clythebrook's face, then the unreadable mask of resolve on Lord Rainforth's.

Lady Clythebrook intended to take her to London to mingle with the cream of Society as if she belonged in their midst. This good woman expected her to parade through the glittering ballrooms in hopes that a desperate second or third son might overlook the fact that she's an illegitimate orphan trying to pass herself off as one of the elite members of Society and condescend to offer for her. And if she refused…

Josie thought of the children. Thirty days. She only needed thirty days and the final shipment of goods would be here. Thirty days and *if* they were very frugal, and *if* Lord Rainforth's scheme actually worked, and *if* the Marquess of Rainforth didn't tire of country life and desert them, then maybe the children would have enough to make it through the rest of the year. Or at least get by until she came up with another way to provide for them.

She turned on the sofa and lifted her chin until she looked directly into Lady Clythebrook's caring face. "Thirty days, my lady. I will allow the Marquess of Rainforth to tutor me against the dangerous pitfalls of London life for the next thirty days. But not one day more. And I will set down the guidelines for our meetings."

She turned her attention to where the marquess sat. "We will always meet here. I will not have the children involved in this."

He nodded. "As you wish."

"We will only meet twice each week. And for no more than

an hour each time."

The marquess's eyebrows shot upward. Josie thought she saw a glimmer of a smile but if there was one, it was gone the second she glared at him.

"I'm sure twice a week is sufficient. One hour, however, is not enough time. It will take far longer than that to share my vast knowledge as a renowned rake and scoundrel. I reserve the right to extend our sessions to two hours, should I require more time."

There was an obvious glint of humor written on his face and she felt an intense desire to scratch out his eyes. "I find nothing humorous in this."

"I'm sure you don't, but that doesn't alter the fact that I will require two hours on occasion. Since you are stating stipulations, I am simply countering with demands of my own."

Josie gave him an even harsher look but he didn't back down from his demand.

"Two hours, Miss Foley."

"Very well. Two hours, should the need arise. And we will meet only on Wednesday and Sunday afternoons. Those are the only days I can spare."

He started shaking his head before she even finished. "I'm afraid that is unacceptable. I will agree to your request of Sunday afternoons. That is an ideal time to meet as it will give us an opportunity to take an afternoon drive, as I'm sure you will do when you go to London. Hyde Park is ideally suited for such outdoor excursions. Isn't that correct, Lady Clythebrook?"

Lady Clythebrook nodded, the faraway look in her eyes telling of remembered carriage rides through the Park on long-ago afternoons.

"But I cannot agree to the time you've set up to meet on Wednesday," Rainforth continued. "Afternoons do not provide the correct atmosphere one finds at balls, musicales and dinners. These will nearly all take place in the evening and there is a certain…ambiance, if you will, that one only feels when the stars are twinkling overhead and the moon is shining brightly. Didn't you find that to be so, Lady Clythebrook?"

"Oh, yes."

"For accuracy's sake, I must therefore insist that one of our weekly tutoring sessions be held in the evening. Perhaps I might come for dinner and stay for a game of whist or a musical selection."

"No."

"That would be delightful," Lady Clythebrook said, the expression on her face not hiding the fact that this evening was turning out better than she had hoped it would. "Do you play, Lord Rainforth?"

"Alas, not well enough to risk damaging either your or Miss Foley's sensitive ears. But I am a good listener."

Josie refused to let him get away with his machinations. "I'm not a fool, Lord Rainforth. Even though you are without question the rake everyone thinks you are, I am not so naïve not to realize what you're doing."

"And what would that be, Miss Foley?"

"Using us, my lord. Using Lady Clythebrook and abusing her trust to gain acceptance from the people who live in Clytheborough. Using every device at your disposal to fool us into thinking that you want Carrie Gardner's child because you intend to do what's best for him. But I know differently. I may have lived my entire life in the country, but I'm not such an innocent that I'll be taken in by your handsome face and your smooth tongue. You are a dangerous threat and I'll never forget it."

"I can assure you I am only complying with Lady Clythebrook's demands. I have no intention of threatening you or the child, or putting either of you in any danger."

"You've been a threat to everything I hold dear from the moment you stepped through the doors of Sacred Heart. Don't tell me what your intention is. I know only too well. Lady Clythebrook may be blind to your faults, but you will find I'm not so easily intimidated."

Josie glared at him again but he wisely held his tongue. The carefree humor was gone from his face and the expression that remained deepened the steel-gray of his eyes until they were nearly black.

"Do your worst, my lord. I'm prepared to battle you."

"You think this is a battle?"

"You don't?"

He shook his head. "Hardly. More a game with friendship as the prize."

"Then, let the game begin. I look forward to our first session. It should prove very interesting. If you will excuse me, Lord Rainforth. Lady Clythebrook. It has been a long day and I'd like to retire."

Lord Rainforth stood. "Allow me to see you to the stairs."

"No. I'm perfectly capable of seeing to myself. In fact, you'll soon discover I'll need your help for very little."

Josie leaned down and kissed Lady Clythebrook on the cheek, then walked from the room.

Yes, let the game begin. Thirty days made four weeks. Eight matches at two hours each equaled a total of sixteen hours. She smiled. She'd put in longer days at the orphanage and survived. Surely she could survive this with no trouble.

Ross leaned against a boulder and watched the waves roll to shore. The moon was full and bright and the water was calm now, the waves lapping against the rocks with a soft, gentle slapping sound that soothed him deep down to his soul. Below him were dozens of caves but from his earlier investigations, only one or two of them were large enough for the smugglers to store shipments of opium. And he was standing directly over their entrances.

He crossed his arms over his chest and thought about his conversation with Lady Clythebrook and Josephine Foley earlier. The evening had gone much better than he'd anticipated. He'd hoped to convince the local landowners his plan would benefit them. Just as he hoped that Lady Clythebrook would see the advantages of joining with him in the venture. But never had he anticipated that having to spend two days a week with Miss Foley would be part of the bargain. Especially when the agreement included that he educate her in how to protect herself against men exactly like himself.

He'd nearly laughed out loud when Lady Clythebrook had first announced what she wanted him to do. At the time it had seemed like a lark. An enjoyable lark, but a lark nonetheless. Now he wasn't so sure. The thought of spending even one hour with Josephine Foley in the moonlight caused his body to react with a fiery heat that reached to the marrow of his bones. He didn't want to think what might happen the first time he pulled her in his arms to practice the waltz. Or the next time he couldn't stop himself from kissing her.

Ross stepped closer to the edge of the cliff and stared out onto the water. Thirty days made four weeks. Eight visits at two hours each equaled a total of sixteen hours. Ross swiped his hand across his jaw in frustration. *Sixteen bloody hours.* His enjoyable lark could turn into a torture unlike anything he'd ever imagined.

He shook his head then turned around to go back. A twig snapped to his right and he stopped short. He wasn't sure how he knew he was in danger, but the warning came through with vivid clarity. He darted in the direction of the boulder, but a sharp burning pain knifed through him before he reached it. He clutched his side and stumbled forward but a second shot took him to his knees. His shoulder burned like someone had stuck a blazing poker through his flesh and he dropped to the ground.

Escape was impossible. His chest heaved with each breath he took. He crawled behind the boulder and pressed his back against the hard rock. A heavy sheen of perspiration dotted his forehead and he swiped at the wetness with the back of his hand. He reached for the pistol he'd tucked into his jacket pocket and raised himself up, then fired two quick shots in the direction he thought the assassin was hiding. His shots weren't returned.

Wave after wave of nauseating pain slashed through him and he sank back against the rock until the earth stopped spinning around him. Another stabbing pain sliced through him and he clutched his fingers around the flesh at his upper left arm. His hand came away sticky and wet.

The full moon was to his advantage, large and bright, lighting up the area all around him. He prayed it held another miracle. The air was turning colder by the second but the pain seemed more tolerable now. He hardly felt any of the sharp stabs that had buckled his legs beneath him.

He put his hand to his side and pressed hard, praying the warm, sticky liquid would stop oozing through his fingers. Then he prayed that whoever had shot him would make a move before he lost consciousness.

Neither happened.

Ross concentrated on the sounds around him. Everything was quiet. Even the birds and animals were burrowed deep in their hiding places or they'd been frightened away by the gunshots. Nothing moved. Nothing made a sound.

Ross closed his eyes. In his hazy, pain-filled darkness, he realized that whoever had shot him had left him to die.

He tried to picture a bright-eyed little boy with dark hair the color of his own, but couldn't. Even the moon which had been so full and bright only moments ago now seemed to show only its dark side. And as darkness consumed him, he thought of Josephine Foley and said a silent prayer that somehow she'd find it in her heart to take care of his son so he wouldn't grow up alone and unloved.

He pictured how she'd looked earlier that night. And he was lost to the darkness.

Chapter 11

DAMN HIM!

Damn him. Damn him. Damn him.

Josie stormed down the back pathway that led away from Clythebrook Manor, then marched past the vegetable garden and through the orchard next to the stables. She looked up at the damnably full, "magical" moon and made her way across an open meadow, calling the Marquess of Rainforth every black and diabolical name she could come up with. This was all his fault. And the worst was yet to come.

Somehow he'd managed to convince Lady Clythebrook that if she went along with his venture, Clythebrook Estate and the children at the orphanage would never go without again. And Josie only had this one last shipment and she and the children would be at his mercy. A nobleman. A man who couldn't be counted on to provide for the children any more than her mother had been able to count on the nobleman who'd fathered her.

Damn him! Why couldn't he have left well enough alone? It wasn't that St. Stephen's Hollow needed this new venture to survive. Why couldn't he have continued to ignore his estate as he'd done his whole life?

Oh, how she wished he'd never have come. How she wished he'd never kissed her. Or held her. Or looked at her with eyes so warmly silver she thought she was drowning when she looked into them. Oh, how she wished he hadn't stirred the traitorous emotions that betrayed her right now. Emotions she knew she could never allow to surface.

She marched through the dewy meadow and approached the cliffs where the marquess intended to graze his cattle. She swore that when she got her hands on him she'd make him suffer for the trouble he'd caused her. If he thought she was going to meekly submit to Lady Clythebrook's plan to educate her in the nefarious schemes of the nobility to ruin innocent ladies, he was sadly mistaken. The next four weeks were going to be the longest weeks of his life. And the most frustrating.

An animal snorted close by and Josie stopped. The sound was out of place. She wasn't anywhere near the few livestock the closest tenants kept. But a horse, still saddled, stood ahead of her, contentedly munching on tender shoots of grass.

She recognized the horse instantly, but its owner was nowhere to be seen. The fact that it was loose this close to the caves only raised her fury.

Damn him! Couldn't the man give her the thirty days she'd been promised? Did he have to come before daybreak on the very night he'd won Lady Clythebrook over to his side? Was he that impatient to make more calculations about how to best utilize the land that he had to traipse the grounds in the pre-dawn dark? What if this were the night the shipment had been scheduled to come in? He'd have seen everything!

Josie stepped to where the horse chomped on the tall grass and grabbed its reins. She'd been given thirty days and that's what she'd demand from him. If he didn't like it, he could forfeit the whole venture.

By the time Josie had convinced the big bay to follow her, her temper was as close to exploding as it had ever been. She marched across the meadow toward the cliffs where she knew he'd be—but stopped short when she saw his crumpled body lying in the tall grass.

She dropped the reins and raced toward him, saying a prayer

she desperately wanted God to hear.

"Lord Rainforth, can you hear me?"

He was deathly pale, or maybe it was just the silver glow of the moon shining on his face, but Josie didn't think so. She knelt beside him, hoping he'd just fallen from his horse and had the air knocked out of him. She knew the minute she pressed her hand against his forehead and felt his cold, clammy flesh he hadn't.

"My lord?"

She put her hand beneath his head and examined his scalp. When she could find no bump, she focused her attention elsewhere. With trembling hands she unbuttoned his jacket and spread the material wide. The light from the moon illuminated the large dark spot that covered the left side of his shirt at his waist.

Josie ripped at her petticoat, tearing huge strips of material and haphazardly folding them into large squares. Next, she gently lifted his shirt away from the wound. The minute she touched him, he moaned and tried to pull away.

"Lie still," she said, pressing one hand against the wound and the other against his shoulder to keep him steady.

He turned his head and looked at her through pain-filled eyes. "Miss…Foley?"

"Don't talk. There's a cottage not far from here. You'll be better once I can see how badly you're hurt."

"Not bad," he moaned, but from the amount of blood soaking the cloth at his side, she wasn't so sure.

"I'm sure you're right, but I won't know until I check. Put your arm around my shoulder and I'll help you up."

"I'm too heavy. Go for…help."

"And leave you here? I hardly think so."

Josie didn't give him a chance to argue further, but eased his arm around her shoulder and helped him sit. Even though she didn't think the bullet was still in him, she had to get the wound cleaned and sewed and the bleeding stopped.

She fought the painful lump that knotted in the pit of her stomach. His skin was already cold and clammy, and there was always the threat of fever. But he was young and healthy. That was to his advantage. If she could stop the bleeding soon enough.

She helped him sit, then raised him up. He was heavy but at least he was conscious and could help her.

"I brought your horse. Can you mount?"

"Do I have a choice?"

"No."

Josie held out the leather stirrup and guided his foot into the strap. With an agonizing moan, he pulled himself up.

His breathing was labored now, every gasp heavy and jagged. The color of his face seemed paler and he dropped his head back to breathe in a heavy sigh while and clutched the saddle with both hands.

"Hold on," she said, leading the horse toward Granny Farland's cottage. "I don't want you to fall off."

"I…won't."

Josie led the horse across the meadow, then the short way into the wood. Twice she had to call out to him when he slipped to the side. With a muffled moan he righted himself. The concentration she saw on his face was heart-wrenching and she pushed the horse to move faster.

"We're almost there," she said, making their way across the meadow. She could see the cottage just ahead and quickened her steps.

"Granny Farland's not here right now because Matilda—her daughter—is expecting her fourth babe and she's gone to help."

"Will she mind…"

"If she does, you can always turn on your charm. That seems to work quite well for you."

"It hasn't seemed to work on you."

She reached up to help him dismount and he placed his hands on her shoulders. "I'm immune. Now, let's get you down before you fall."

He took a deep breath and slid to the ground.

His torso fell against her and she staggered under his weight.

But she stayed steady on her feet.

She wrapped her arms around his waist and held him close. He was weaker that he'd been earlier and a sharp stab of concern raced through her. She placed his arm across her shoulders and helped him through the gate that led to the house.

The door to Granny's cottage was unlatched and she propped him against the wall while she went in to light a lamp. When the room was bright, she brought him into the cottage and sat him on a chair beside the bed.

"Did you see who shot you?"

"No."

She took off his boots and removed his jacket and waistcoat, then lifted his shirt over his head and looked at his wounds. The one at his upper arm wasn't as bad as she'd first thought, only a graze, but the one at his waist was worse.

"Hold this against your side," she ordered, pressing a cloth against his ribs. "This will need to be stitched."

He attempted a smile. "How are you at needlework?"

"Passable." She started a fire and put some water on to boil. "I haven't sewn any pant legs together in more than a week now."

"I'm glad to hear that because—"

His words died when another wave of pain gripped him. Josie rushed to check Granny's cupboards for a bottle of whiskey. When she found one, she filled a glass nearly full and handed it to him. "Drink this," she said, then retrieved a needle and thread from the sewing basket by the hearth. "All of it."

When he drank what was in the glass, she filled it again and handed it back.

"Are you trying to get me drunk?"

"Is it working?"

He drained the glass. "Afraid not. I'm a hardened drinker, you know. All rakes are."

"I should have known that."

She smiled at his slurred words then eased him over to the bed. "The bullet went all the way through. You're lucky whoever shot you wasn't terribly good."

"They were good enough," he whispered, then sucked in a harsh breath when she dabbed at his flesh with a damp cloth.

"What on earth were you doing out there in the middle of the night?"

"I couldn't sleep."

"Next time, try counting sheep. It's safer."

"I'll remember that."

She helped him lie on his side and lifted the whiskey bottle over the wound to cleanse it. "This is going to sting," she said, placing her hand on his shoulder to hold him steady. "Try not to move."

She heard him take a shuddering breath as she poured the whiskey.

He was braver than Josie thought it was possible for anyone to be. He gripped the wood frame of Granny Farland's bed until his knuckles turned white while she poured a generous amount over his wounds. Huge beads of perspiration dotted his forehead, then ran in heavy rivulets onto the pillow. Josie ignored the blue words he uttered beneath his breath. She didn't know what most of them meant, but thought they must be very bad indeed. They sounded even worse than the words Banks used the time he slammed his fingers in the front door.

When she was sure the wound was clean, she picked up the needle and thread and moved to his side. His fingers clamped around her wrist, his grip evidencing a strength she didn't think he had.

"If something happens and I don't—"

"Nothing's going to happen to you."

"I know. But just in case."

The look in his eyes held a desperation she couldn't ignore. "What do you need?"

"There's a trust set up for the boy. It's in Mrs. Gardner's name. See that he gets it."

She nodded.

"Then contact my cousin…Major Samuel Bennett. Take the

boy to him. I don't want Charlie to grow up…thinking no one wanted him."

Josie swallowed hard.

"Promise me."

"I promise."

"Thank you. Now, let's get this…over with. I know how much…you're going to enjoy this."

With a heavy sigh, he dropped his head against the pillow and closed his eyes. Josie blinked back the blurred wetness in her eyes and deftly sewed the gaping flesh at his side.

She was glad when she finished, as much for his sake as her own. This was far from the first time she'd had to stitch someone's flesh together, but never had it been someone whose touch caused her breath to stop. Never before had it been someone whose nearness caused her heart to ache with a longing she didn't understand.

When she looked up, his eyes were closed and his breathing had slowed.

"I didn't enjoy it at all," she whispered, pulling the covers over his shoulders.

She pushed an errant lock of mahogany hair from his forehead and sat in a chair beside the bed to keep watch for a fever she prayed wouldn't come.

Josie sat in the chair where she'd been the last several hours and sipped the last of the tea she'd brewed earlier. He still slept, thankfully more peacefully than he had during the night.

Josie studied the strong features of his face, the high cheekbones and sharp angles of his jaw. They were ruggedly handsome features, as magnificently hewn as if patterned after perfection. But it wasn't only what she saw on the outside that drew her to him. His inner strength also served as a magnet, pulling her constantly toward him. Giving her one small glimpse after another of what it might be like if she would, for just one small second, give in to him. If she would, just one time, give over her worries and responsibilities for him to carry. But of course she would not.

She *could* not.

He was a member of the nobility and could never be trusted. Her mother had made that mistake as had countless other women whose children had been raised in the orphanage. Women who'd given in to a man's handsome features and sweet words had been left with a babe growing in their bellies and a future that promised nothing but heartache and disgrace. Josie's own life had been a living example of how cruelly a man could use a woman. And how easily a man—especially a member of the nobility—could abandon the child he'd created. And yet…

The Marquess of Rainforth's last thought before he succumbed to the pain was for his child. There was a trust fund already in place for him and if the marquess didn't survive, he'd made her promise to take Charlie to his cousin, Major Samuel Bennett. If Rainforth didn't care about his son, why would he have gone to such lengths to provide for him?

Oh, she wished she hadn't seen this side of him. It was so much easier to protect herself from him when she thought he didn't care.

Josie watched him sleep until his slow steady breathing caught and his head moved slightly. She knew the instant he was awake enough to realize where he was and remember what had happened. He released a pain-filled sigh and his breathing turned rapid and shallow.

"Don't move," she said, placing her hand on his shoulder. "Just lie still."

"Miss Foley."

He whispered her name then sank back into the mattress. Josie filled a glass with water and took it to him. "Here, drink this," she said, putting her arm beneath his head and raising him enough to drink. He sank back when he was finished.

"Thank you."

"Are you in a great deal of pain? I can lace some tea with more of Granny's whiskey."

The corners of his mouth lifted slightly. "I think I had enough of Granny's whiskey last night. If I'm not careful, my head's going to hurt as much as the rest of me."

Josie smiled and sat back down on the chair where she could keep a certain distance from him. For some reason she couldn't understand or explain, she wanted to reach out and touch him. She wanted to lift the errant lock of dark mahogany hair from his forehead, then run her fingers across his brow and down the side of his face. She wanted to press her palm against the dark stubble on his cheek and jaw and feel its prickly roughness. A knot formed in the pit of her stomach, leaving her with a sensation she'd never felt before—a warmth that rushed with fiery speed through her chest, then settled down low in her belly. The force of it nearly stole her breath. She clutched her hands in her lap to keep them from reaching out.

"Are you sure you didn't see who shot you?"

"No. I thought perhaps you might have an idea who it could have been."

Josie stared at him in disbelief. "Are you suggesting I had something to do with what happened to you?"

"No. But you know the people around here better than I do. Perhaps you know who might be opposed to bringing in cattle other than you and Baron Lindville."

"Surely you don't suspect Baron Lindville."

"I don't suspect anyone. Although Baron Lindville did make it plain I wasn't welcome here."

"But that doesn't mean he'd try to harm you."

"No, it doesn't."

But Josie knew it was more than possible that Lindville had fired the shots that injured the marquess. Knew it because other than herself, he had the most to lose from putting cattle above the caves.

He turned his head to look at her. "What were you doing out there in the middle of the night?"

"I couldn't sleep either and I was too busy counting all the cattle you intend to bring in to think of sheep."

He smiled, then the look on his face turned serious. "I'm sorry Lady Clythebrook made the demands she did."

His quiet statement pulled her thoughts back from where she'd been. "Then you regret the hours we'll have to spend together, too?"

His eyes were closed but a slow, lazy smile lifted the corners of his mouth. "That wasn't the demand I was talking about." His eyes opened. "I was talking about Lady Clythebrook's plan to take you to London."

"That won't happen."

"You don't think her health will allow her to make the trip?"

"It's a trip I have no intention of making."

"But you agreed—"

"No. I agreed to suffer through thirty days of your tutoring to gain supreme knowledge of all the designing schemes your fellow disreputable rakes might use to destroy my reputation. I agreed to learn from you to avoid being ruined when I go to London."

"Why did you bargain for thirty days? What is so important about that amount of time?"

Josie refused to lower her gaze. That would be a sure sign she had something to hide. "Because that is all the longer it will take."

"Take for what?"

"For you to tire of the country and go back to London where you belong."

"You don't have a very good opinion of the nobility, do you, Miss Foley."

"They've earned my low esteem. Suffice it to say I haven't had many positive experiences with the exalted members of our Society."

"So you lump all of England's nobility into the same reprehensible heap like so much garbage? Even the late Earl of Clythebrook?"

The air caught in her throat. "How dare you."

"I dare because you're letting your jaded impression of the nobility cloud your thinking. How old were you when your mother died?"

His innocent-sounding question stopped her cold. This was a topic she didn't want to discuss. "You've talked enough. Sleep now. You need the rest."

"How old?"

Josie knew he had no intention of giving up. She'd seen examples of his tenacity often in her dealings with him. She breathed a heavy sigh and capitulated. Besides, what did she care if he knew? Her past was no secret.

At least the part she was willing to share.

"My mother died when I was seven. That's when I went to live at the orphanage."

"And your father?"

She raised her chin. "I have no father. Not one who would claim me."

A brief silence separated them before he asked the one question that had the power to pull the breath from her lungs.

"What title does the man who sired you boast? An earl, perhaps? A marquess? Or is he a duke?"

"I don't know."

"Yes, you do."

"His title is hardly worth mentioning," she said, trying to keep the bitterness from her voice.

"Isn't it?"

The look he gave her challenged her and she lifted her head high when she answered him. "He's a marquess. A man living the life of the leisured without a care for anyone but himself."

"Even his daughter?"

"He has daughters, sir. Two of them. As well as two sons. All born legal and within the bonds of his marriage to his marchioness."

"And you resent—"

"I resent nothing! He means nothing to me. I put any thought of him behind me years ago."

"You wouldn't like to meet him? To see him face to face? To talk with him?"

She paused, then answered honestly. "No, I wouldn't. Just as he has no desire to meet me. It's too late. Twenty-seven years too late. He's never been a part of my life. Other than to serve as a valuable lesson. My mother made the mistake of loving a man who took everything she had to give including her heart. Then he abandoned her along with the child she was carrying. It is not so uncommon a story. Especially where the privileged are concerned."

"So you condemn all nobility? Including me?"

"You are worse, my lord. The man who fathered me never pretended to want me. Your son is not so fortunate."

Josie stood and looked down on his pale face. He showed distinct signs of the pain he must be feeling.

"Someone is trying to kill you, Lord Rainforth. Which means the child you claim to care so much for is not safe anywhere near you."

Chapter 12

ROSS SWUNG HIS FEET OVER THE EDGE OF THE BED and stood. He couldn't lie in bed any longer, not with Josephine Foley's words crashing through his mind like an attacking army.

Someone is trying to kill you… Which means the child you claim to care so much for is not safe anywhere near you.

He had to discover who was behind the smuggling operation and put a stop to it. He wasn't safe until he did.

He couldn't be a father to his son until he did.

Ross walked across the room and pushed back the curtains at Granny Farland's window. The wound at his side still ached when he moved but he'd already spent four days abed and during that time the shipment of opium could have been delivered and he wouldn't have known anything about it. He couldn't waste any more time pampering himself when so much was at stake.

Everything was falling into place, and now that Lady Clythebrook had decided to go along with his venture, he needed to make the final arrangements so the work could begin when the thirty days of meeting with Miss Foley were up.

Ross fought the unwelcome heaviness that settled deep inside him every time he thought of her. Just having her tend him for the past four days had been a torture of its own. He wasn't sure how he'd survive the next thirty days, but he would. Nothing this side of heaven would keep him from meeting with her—even the slash in his side that still burned like hell. He wasn't about to give her the slightest opportunity to say he hadn't complied with his part of Lady Clythebrook's demands.

Ross dropped the curtain back into place and sank down on the chair in front of the fire. This was the chair where she'd sat for so many hours during the last four days. He remembered the glow of her skin from the fire as it blazed. He remembered other things too. Things he wished hadn't had such an impact on him, like her soothing voice breaking through the pain during the first few days, or the gentleness of her ministrations while she cleaned his jagged flesh and put fresh bandages on him. Or the light touch of her fingers against his forehead when she thought he was asleep, or the warmth of her hand nestled in his long after she'd fallen asleep and thought he had, too.

He pushed himself to his feet. He would be glad to be gone from here. Granny Farland's cottage held too many memories he was better off forgetting. He turned around to go back to the window and stopped when the door opened. Josephine Foley stood with the sun at her back and a halo of light framing her face. A frown deepened on her forehead and when she spoke her voice contained a tone of concern.

"What are you doing out of bed?"

"Waiting for someone from St. Stephen's to come for me."

She stepped into the room and closed the door behind her. She was beautiful today, more beautiful than even yesterday, if that were possible. Her hair was pulled loosely from her face and several tendrils of golden tresses had escaped their pins. Her face was flushed from walking in the outdoors and her cheeks had a rosy glow that made her look young and carefree. The knot that formed low in his belly every time she came near him was back with a vengeance.

She stepped into the room and pulled at the ribbons from her bonnet, then removed it. "Are you sure you're well enough to travel?"

"Yes, I'm much stronger today. Besides, I have to prepare for Sunday. I have a very important engagement I cannot miss."

She was in the process of setting a small bag down on the table and looked up sharply when she realized what appointment he meant. "You're barely well enough to make it the short distance to St. Stephen's in a carriage. I won't allow you to even think about coming to Clythebrook to take me for a ride."

"And have you accuse me of failing to fulfill my part of the bargain?"

"Lady Clythebrook doesn't expect us to meet after what happened to you."

"But I do." He took a step closer to her. She answered his maneuver by stepping around the table to put a kettle of water over the fire. Her subterfuge amused him. "I refuse to let you say I broke my word."

"I wouldn't say that."

He laughed. "You would. You'd use any excuse you could to avoid having to spend the next four weeks in my company."

Her dainty chin raised an inch in defiance. "I didn't sew you up to have you tear your stitches out bouncing along the rutted roads around here."

"I agree I'm not looking forward to trying to manage a team just yet, but that doesn't mean I intend to let you escape the stipulations Lady Clythebrook insisted upon. You have much to learn about disreputable rakes."

"I already know more than I need to know, thank you very much."

He laughed again. "We'll compromise then. We'll spend the time together as per our agreement, but perhaps a stroll through your garden will be enough for our first afternoon. I'll compare you to the beautiful flowers."

"There aren't any beautiful flowers."

"See how little you know. When a man is in a woman's company, he's not expected to notice the flowers. He's supposed to be blinded by his companion's beauty and tell her that."

She sank down on one of the chairs by the table and looked at him with the most adorable smile on her face.

"And that lie works?"

"Your naiveté is showing. I'll have you know that that particular comment has been known to cause women to swoon at my feet on more than one occasion."

She laughed. "That doesn't say much for the women with whom you associate."

"You wound me," he said, clasping one hand over his heart.

"I doubt you wound so easily. Even you, experienced as you are in the art of deception, cannot be fooled by such a shallow reaction."

"What would you rather I said?"

"The truth. That you see there are no flowers on our walk through the garden, but since we are forced to spend time in each other's company, we will ooh and ah over the bare branches, the lack of blooming colors, and the occasional early green shoot."

The expression on her face was so serious he had to laugh. "Ah, Josephine. Surely a rake of my renown can do better than that?"

In the blink of an eye, the teasing remarks and easy camaraderie they'd shared were gone.

"Please, don't call me that."

"What?"

"Josephine."

"Why? That's your name. Mine is Ross. I'd like you to call me that."

She spun on him. "For what purpose? We can never be on a first name basis. You're a marquess. Is getting rid of your title the initial step in breaking down the barriers that separate us? And who will be the weaker for it?"

"Weaker? Does one of us have to be weaker?"

"In the game you're playing, someone is always weaker. And it's not the pursuer. It is the pursued."

"And why do you assume I am pursuing you…*Miss* Foley?"

"Your son…*Lord* Rainforth. I have something you want."

Her words dropped around his neck like a tightly pulled noose. "Do you think I would use charm to get my son away from you?"

"I think you'll do whatever you think will benefit you." She paused. "But you no longer have to waste your efforts. I've decided not to fight you any longer."

His heart tripped, then raced faster in his chest. "You'll give me the boy?"

"He's your son. I can't keep him from you. I never could."

"But you did."

She shook her head. "I just held onto him as long as I could."

"Why the change?"

"Because I know if you truly love him as you claim, you won't take him."

She stood, then walked over to the window. With her back to him, she pushed aside the curtain to look out. "Someone tried to kill you. And they might try again. Is having Charlie with you worth the danger you'll put him in?"

Ross felt a rock fall to the pit of his stomach. He stared at the cookies she'd placed on a cloth and the cup of tea she'd poured and set in front of him. She was offering him the child he'd wanted since he found out Charlie existed. But only because she knew he wouldn't take him.

Ross sat a second longer then slid his chair back from the table and stood. "Does Lady Clythebrook know how good you are at games, Josephine?"

He saw her shoulders lift at the use of her first name.

"I don't have to resort to games when dealing with Lady Clythebrook."

"That's not true. Your request of thirty days was a game. I know what you told me, but there's something more significant to the time you demanded."

"It will only be significant if I win, and that's yet to be seen."

"And what will you win?"

Josie let the curtain drop with a definite snap and turned around.

"Not nearly enough, sir. Not nearly enough."

"Then we have both gained the same. You're only offering me my child because you know I won't take him." He glared at her. "But that doesn't mean I don't want to at least see him."

He waited for her to give him some indication that she'd allow that concession but all he heard was the sound of an approaching carriage. She held his gaze a moment longer, then, as if still weighing her answer, turned her back on him and began the process of gathering his belongings. When she was finished, she walked to the door and opened it. A servant from St. Stephen's stood outside and when she motioned toward Rainforth's things, the man carried them to the waiting carriage.

She stepped back and stood beside the dying fireplace. Ross couldn't leave her like this, not while this uncomfortable chasm separated them. He closed the door, then walked up behind her and put his hands on her shoulders.

"We're not finished—you and I."

Every muscle beneath his fingers tensed but he didn't release her. Instead, he slowly skimmed his hands downward and clasped her around the upper arms, then turned her to face him. He could tell she wanted to step away from him but forced herself to stay. Perhaps one day he would tell her how much he admired her courage.

"You play the game well, Josephine."

He cupped her cheek in the palm of his hand and rubbed his thumb along her lower lip. She tried to turn her head but he wouldn't let her. He framed her face with his hands and lowered his mouth to kiss her.

He hadn't intended for the kiss to be anything more than a brief touching of their lips, but that wasn't the result. The minute his lips met hers, a searing blaze kindled inside him, unleashing a display that rivaled the Queen's birthday fireworks. He pulled back from her before he was tempted to kiss her again.

The set of her chin matched the lift of her arched brows. "Was this my first lesson?"

He smiled. "Oh, no. An experienced rake would never be so

obvious. So overt. So…blatant."

She stepped back. "Did you think your kiss would break down my resolve to keep Charlie where he was safe?"

His smile faded. "I would *never* risk my son's safety. I only want to see him."

With a heavy heart, he turned and walked to the door.

"Lord Rainforth."

Her voice reached him just before he stepped out into the sunshine. He stopped and turned.

"If the weather holds tomorrow, I promised the children I'd take them on a picnic. You're welcome to join us."

"Will *all* the children be there?"

"Yes."

Ross swallowed past the lump in his throat. "You are full of surprises, Miss Foley. Thank you."

A ray of sunshine streamed through the open door and bathed her in a wash of brightness. A strange tightness settled in his chest and he smiled at her before he walked to his waiting carriage.

He was finally going to see his son.

Josie watched the children play games, and all the while her gaze kept darting to the top of the rise the marquess would come over if he planned to join them. And surely he would. She couldn't imagine him giving up the opportunity to see his child. Not after he'd gone to such lengths to find him.

"Miss Josie! Look what Amanda found!"

Josie looked down as two little girls raced toward her, the one's hand outstretched as if carrying the most precious gift in the world.

"We found it climbing up the side of the tree. Robbie says it lives there."

Josie looked down to find a brown, fuzzy caterpillar crawling determinedly over Amanda's palm and wrist, then further up her arm.

"Isn't it beautiful, Miss Josie?" Amanda said.

Josie watched the four-year-old tentatively reach out, then brush her pudgy little finger lightly over the top of the furry creature. The caterpillar kept moving.

"It tickles," she said on a giggle.

Josie ran her finger along the insect. "That's because of all his tiny little legs scampering at the same time."

"Cissy wants to hold it but it won't go to her and I'm afraid to pick it up."

Josie brushed a smudge of dirt off Cissy's face then took her hand. "Hold out your finger, Cissy."

The three year old held out one short finger and Josie placed it in front of the caterpillar. Amidst peals of giggles and after two aborted attempts, the insect finally crawled from one little girl's arm to the other's hand.

"Have you given it a name?" a deep voice asked from behind her.

Josie jerked up and turned. The Marquess of Rainforth was standing at her side. He wasn't watching the caterpillar, but the two little girls. He smiled a breathtaking smile, and when he transferred that smile to her, Josie felt a jolt that made her cheeks flush hot.

"You can't name a caterpillar," Amanda said, looking first at the marquess, then Josie. "Can you?"

"Everything's got a name, 'manda," Cissy said, her deep blue eyes wide as she tilted her head back to look at the giant of a man standing in front of her.

"Can we name it, Miss Josie?"

"I don't see why not."

"Then I think we should call it Henry," Amanda said, sucking thoughtfully on her lower lip.

Cissy looked down at the insect. "But Henry was our dog's name. And he's dead."

Amanda was silent for a moment, then her eyes filled with

big, wet tears. Josie dropped down so she was eye level with the little girl. "I think Henry's a wonderful name for your caterpillar. Henry would be proud that you named something after him."

"I miss him."

"I know you do."

Amanda pointed to the caterpillar. "He's brown like Henry was."

Josie watched the caterpillar turn around and crawl back down Cissy's arm. "Yes, he is. The very same color as Henry."

"Can I take Henry back with me, Miss Josie? I'll keep him in my room and won't let him out?"

"No, Amanda. This Henry lives near the tree where you found him. He needs to be outside."

Amanda transferred the caterpillar from Cissy's hand back to her own. "Robbie wanted to step on him. He said Henry was just a bug."

Josie lifted her gaze and met Rainforth's smiling gray eyes. She could tell he was having as hard a time as she keeping a straight face.

"But Charlie wouldn't let him."

The mention of Charlie's name was like an explosion rending the silence. The humor went out of his eyes. Even his face seemed a shade paler than before.

Josie stood and turned Amanda back toward the tree where they'd found the caterpillar. "Take Henry back now, Amanda. The other caterpillars he lives with probably miss him."

The two little girls ran off and the marquess' gaze followed them, searching the spot close to the stream where seven or eight little boys played tag.

"Is he down there?"

"Yes. Do you want me to—"

He shook his head and took a step. Then another. He didn't walk fast, but neither did he walk slow. Just steadily down the small dip in the meadow to where Charlie played.

Josie went with him, not because she thought he might need her help to recognize his son. She knew the minute he looked into Charlie's deep-gray eyes it would be like looking into a mirror. And if the eyes weren't enough of a confirmation, or the shape of Charlie's jaw, or the tilt of his nose, the dark mahogany hair that curled slightly at the ends was certain to give him away. And the dimples on either side of his mouth that were identical to the creases that deepened each time the marquess smiled.

The group of boys ran toward the stream, all of them chasing after Eddie Clower who must be the one they had to tag, and after squeals of excitement, they all stopped and formed a circle around something they'd found lying on the ground.

"Miss Josie! Come look!"

One of the little boys broke away from the circle and ran toward them. Before she had time to prepare Rainforth, Charlie was in front of them.

She knew the second the marquess recognized him. Knew what a jolt it was to come face to face with a child you didn't know you had. He took several quick breaths as if he couldn't find enough air to breathe, then stood still as a statue with his gaze fixed on Charlie as the little boy skidded to a halt in front of them.

"Miss Josie! Wait 'til you see what we found."

"What did you find, Charlie?"

"A toad! The biggest toad you ever saw. You gotta look at it."

Charlie reached out his hand and grabbed hers, pulling her along behind him. He was so excited she knew he hadn't even notice the Marquess of Rainforth walking beside her. But the marquess had noticed Charlie. The air sparked with anticipation.

"I think he came from the stream."

Josie stepped through the opening the little boys made for her and looked down to the ground. The toad on the bank was of average size, although large by any four- or five-year-old's standards. But not nearly so gigantic to an adult. Josie, however, made all the appreciative sighs to show she was as impressed with their find as they were. It wasn't until the novelty of watching something that refused to hop wore off that they noticed she wasn't alone.

"That's not just any toad," a male voice said from outside their little circle. Their gazes all lifted to Lord Rainforth at the same time. Richie was the first to recognize him.

"I remember you. You came while Miss Josie was reading to us that other time."

"That's right," Jeremy piped up. "We had to tell you our names and you shook our hands and everything."

"You didn't shake mine," Robbie chimed in, "'cause I wasn't there. Miss Josie sent Charlie and me to the orchard with Jenny. But we heard about you. Didn't we Charlie?"

Charlie nodded in agreement, then lifted his pewter-gray eyes upward. He looked into his father's eyes. And a father saw his son for the very first time.

Josie heard the rush of air come from the Marquess of Rainforth, saw his massive chest expand and hold, as if his body was locked in place and could not move. A look of pain and joy and wonder and amazement was written on his face. For a long time he simply stared at Charlie without speaking. And Charlie stared back.

"Is it a special toad, sir?"

Lord Rainforth cleared his throat and forced a smile. "Why yes, it certainly is. See that yellow stripe on its back?"

They all whirled to look at the toad just as it hopped off the rock and back into the stream.

"That little stripe tells me this particular toad is a natterjack toad."

"Natterjack?" they chorused.

They stared another moment then broke into competing comments revealing what they would do with a natterjack toad if they ever had one of their own.

Josie waited, smiling, but the marquess didn't say more. She stepped closer to him and placed her hand on his arm. His muscles knotted beneath her fingers and a hand squeezed around her heart.

She'd imagined every reaction she thought the marquess might have at finally seeing the child who'd been foisted off onto him by his mistress's untimely death. From curiosity to dislike to the cold insignificance she remembered from the one and only time her father had briefly glanced at her. But none of those expressions were on the Marquess of Rainforth's face as he looked down on little Charlie. Only open astonishment and something even more intense. Something similar to the look on a mother's face after the birth of her child.

"My lord, I don't believe you've met Robbie and Charlie." She separated the two from the yammering group. "Lord Rainforth, this is Robert Jenkins but he likes to be called Robbie."

Rainforth gave a quick nod, then turned to Robbie and extended his hand. "How do you do, Robbie? It's a pleasure to meet you."

After hearing all the glowing accounts of what had been expected of the children when they met the marquess, Robbie followed protocol and held out his hand as if he'd been looking forward to participating in the grown-up gesture."

"A thank-you would be in order, Robbie."

"Oh, yes. Thank you, my lord."

"And this, Lord Rainforth, is Charles Gardner."

The Marquess of Rainforth held his son's gaze for several long, silent moments. Josie waited for him to move. Waited for him to show some reaction to his son, but the two only looked at each other as if quietly studying the other.

There was nothing obvious in the meeting that indicated how earth-shattering these minutes were, but Josie knew. She saw the wide grin of wonder as Charlie stared at the impressive man in front of him. She sensed rather than felt the turmoil churning inside Rainforth. How often was a man forced to come face to face with a part of him that was nothing short of a miracle?

"Lord Rainforth?"

Josie stepped forward to break the spell. She placed her arm around Charlie's shoulder and beckoned the marquess from where he'd been. He blinked once, then held out a trembling hand.

"How do you do, Charlie? It's a pleasure to meet you."

"Thank you, Lord Rainforth," Charlie said, holding out his small hand.

The Marquess of Rainforth took his son's hand as he had taken all the other children's hands. But he didn't release it. He stood with his fingers clasping the child's as if the blending of their flesh was a lifeline that connected them.

"I'm glad you called me Charlie. Everybody does except Miss Josie when I forget to wash my hands. Then she calls me Charles."

"Does that happen often?"

"Not as often as she calls Robbie 'Robert'."

All the boys laughed, then with Charlie's little hand nestled in his, the marquess knelt in front of the boy so they were eye to eye. "How old are you, Charlie?"

"I'm four. I had my birthday the other day. Cook baked me a cake with lots of frosting just like my mama used to make and I didn't have to do any chores all day. Nobody does on their birthday. Miss Josie says so. And I got to pick the story I wanted her to read."

"And which story did you choose?"

"Jack and the Beanstalk."

Lord Rainforth smiled and placed his hand on the boy's shoulder. "I'm afraid I don't remember much of that story."

"If you ask Miss Josie, I bet she'll read it to you. It's real good and there's a beautiful lady in it that plays a harp. She's got golden hair just like my mama had."

"I'll have to ask her to read it to me, then."

"Did you know my mama died?"

Josie saw the Marquess of Rainforth swallow hard.

"Yes, I'd heard that."

"She went to live in heaven. Miss Josie said she's happy there, but I wish she'd come back and live with me."

"I'm sure you do," the marquess said, rising to his feet. "Perhaps some time you can tell me all about her."

Charlie smiled his answer.

Josie tried not to let the tortured look in Rainforth's eyes affect her, but the mention of the boy's mother put the reason Charlie was here into perspective. She fought to keep the tears from building in her eyes and knew any attempt would be impossible if she gave in to the raw emotion Charlie had laid bare. She knew she had to change the subject.

"Are you boys getting hungry?" She stepped up to Charlie and put her arm around his shoulder. There was a chorus of ayes she answered with a smile she didn't feel, then gathered the children around her.

"Charlie, why don't you and the other boys help Mrs. Lambert set out the food. I think she brought blankets for us to sit on. But don't put them under the trees. We want to sit in the sunshine."

"Did Vicar Chadwick remember our gumdrops?" Robbie asked over his shoulder.

Josie held up a little bag filled with the treats the vicar had given her earlier.

"Can I have a red one? They're my favorite."

"I want an orange one," Charlie echoed. And one by one each child put in his order for their special color.

Josie watched them scamper away until they were nearly out of sight.

She was alone now with the Marquess of Rainforth. She didn't turn to face him, but even without looking in his direction, she could feel his hurt and pain. She could feel his loneliness and loss. She could feel his heart breaking because he had a son he couldn't take in his arms and hold.

Then, she lifted her eyes and it was nearly her undoing. He stood with his back to her and one outstretched arm braced against the trunk of a thick oak tree. His head hung in defeat and his broad shoulders rose and fell as he took in one heart-wrenching gasp after another.

This wasn't what she'd expected at all. She hadn't thought to see such pain; such loss. She hadn't expected him to care one way or the other when the boy had celebrated his birthday, or which story was his favorite. And she certainly had not expected to see such regret in his eyes. Regret and pain that made her want to take the grown man in her arms and comfort him like she had his son.

And she knew herself for the biggest kind of fool in the world. A fool no different than her mother had been.

Chapter 13

It was Sunday.

Josie paced from one side of the drawing room to the other. It wouldn't be long and he would be here. She stopped before the wide, multi-paned window that looked out onto the garden and concentrated on nothing in particular. She was ready for him. Ready for any tricks he might try.

If only yesterday hadn't happened.

She allowed herself a moment of self-reservation then tried to erase the heart-wrenching emotion she'd seen on the Marquess of Rainforth's face when he'd seen his son for the first time.

She had to remind herself that the scene from yesterday had nothing to do with today. The man who would be here shortly wasn't the man who'd watched his son walk away from him with tears in his eyes. He wasn't the man who hadn't been able to hide the hurt when his son called him 'my lord' because he didn't know he was his father.

The man coming today was the real Marquess of Rainforth. A man whose reputation as a wastrel and a scoundrel was so widely known no one in their right mind would place an innocent child into his care and keeping. A man who'd tossed aside his mistress the second he'd found out she was carrying his child. A man who hadn't cared enough for the child he'd created to come to see him once in the four years since he'd been born. Yet that was exactly what everyone was proposing she do. Place the wellbeing of not one child, but every child at Sacred Heart into his hands.

From the moment he'd introduced his cattle venture, everything had been a game to him. Convincing everyone to go along with his plan had been his first victory. Finding his son when she'd vowed to keep him hidden had been his second. Agreeing with Lady Clythebrook's preposterous scheme to prepare her to go to London had been his crowning achievement because he was guaranteed the prize no matter the outcome. But so was she if she survived the next thirty days. Which meant the children would be winners too.

Thirty days would buy her one last shipment of supplies and a year to find another way to support the orphanage. Surely she could tolerate being with a man who caused her heart to race every time he came in sight for a few weeks. By then maybe he would have tired of life here in the country and have gone back to London. And she would be alone with the children. And her memories.

Josie steadied her resolve and spun around when she heard voices in the hallway. He was here and she was ready for him. She'd be damned if she'd let him win without a fight. The stakes were too high in this game. Not just the children were in jeopardy. She was in danger too—at least her heart was.

"The Marquess of Rainforth, miss."

"Show him in, Banks," she said. "And please bring tea."

"Yes, miss."

Josie thought she was prepared to see him, but what a fool she'd been. Her breath caught the second he stepped through the doorway. As if that wasn't bad enough, a warmth spread through her that had nothing to do with the heat from the fire in the grate. This heat started in the very center of her and burned with an intensity he had the power to fuel.

Oh, she didn't want him to affect her like he did; as if he alone controlled the air she needed to survive.

He was in black and gray today, colors that made his eyes seem even more vibrant and dangerous. His cravat was tied perfectly and the cut of his clothes emphasized his broad shoulders and muscled thighs. She knew before he spoke his first word that she had much of which to be wary.

"Miss Foley," he said, crossing the room. He took her hand in his and lifted it to his lips, then stepped back with an admiring look on his face. "How lovely you look. Absolutely stunning in that particular shade of green."

Josie smiled. "This happens to be the same gown I was wearing the first time we met, Lord Rainforth. You didn't remark upon my stunning appearance then—"

"An oversight, I'm sure. I had other pressing matters that occupied my mind, if you recall."

"…and I don't expect you to notice now. Complimenting a dress that is nearly seven years old is ludicrous."

"Rule number one. When you get to London, I can promise that what you wear will be noticed and complimented by every male you meet. Men enjoy giving compliments and women enjoy receiving them."

Josie arched her eyebrows. "It doesn't please me when I know the man is offering a compliment he doesn't really mean."

"Then may I suggest you hide the fact that you suspect an admirer of being insincere and graciously accept their well-wishes. London is a far different place than Clythebrook Estate. It is much easier to offend a stranger's sensibilities and much harder to repair the damage done by a careless word."

Any rebuttal she intended to make was cut short by Banks's arrival with the tea tray. Josie had purposely placed two chairs opposite each other with a small table between them. Banks placed the tray on the table and left the room.

"Lord Rainforth," she said after she'd poured the tea and given him a cup. "I think we should settle something between us right now."

"Where is Lady Clythebrook?" he interrupted.

"She was afraid she was coming down with a cold and stayed in her rooms."

"Rule number two. A single woman of gentle breeding *never* entertains a male visitor alone without a chaperone present, preferably another lady of unquestionable character."

"I am hardly a young schoolgirl. My character has never been in question. Now, to get back to my previous point—"

"Your character has never been in question because Lady Clythebrook has always been here to protect it. You are, however, single, and London Society plays by a different set of rules than those adhered to in the country."

Josie set her cup down with a clink. "So what, pray tell, should I have done when you arrived."

"Refused to see me, of course."

"And have it be said that I had broken the terms of our agreement with Lady Clythebrook? I think not!"

"Then you should have insisted that one of the servants remain in the room."

"They have more important things to do than sit in a corner and listen to us argue."

The Marquess of Rainforth sat back in his chair and smiled. "Is that what you think we're doing?"

"What would you call it?"

"I'd say we are having a lively discussion. I am instructing you on the difference between what is acceptable here in the country and why that same action will expose you to scandal in London. Society loves nothing better than to sink their teeth into someone's character. And entertaining single men in private without a proper chaperone is guaranteed to set tongues wagging."

"Spoken by a man who is an expert at creating scandals."

"Touché, Miss Foley. Why else would Lady Clythebrook consider me the ideal candidate to teach you the traps to avoid when you reach London?"

Josie rose to her feet and walked away from him. "Regardless of what Lady Clythebrook has led you to believe, I have no intention of going to London. And if I do go, it won't be to parade around the theaters and attend a number of fashionable balls. Nor will my intent be to attract a husband, but only to accompany Lady Clythebrook. I am tolerating your company for the next thirty days because Lady Clythebrook has left me no choice. If I do not, she will allow you to begin bringing in cattle immediately."

"And you think thirty days will make a difference?"

"I think thirty days will be more than enough time for you to tire of country life and yearn to go back to the City, leaving us with a gaggle of cattle about which we know nothing."

"It's a herd."

"What?"

"A herd, not a gaggle. But never mind. What if I told you there was no chance of my leaving?"

She studied him, her gaze taking in the serious expression on his face. "I wouldn't believe you," she said, but there was something in the way his silver eyes turned a darker gray that told her she shouldn't dismiss his comment so easily. "Why are you so insistent upon bringing cattle here?"

His brows arched. "Don't you think St. Stephen's could use the added income?"

"If half the rumors concerning your wealth are true, the money from the sale of a few hundred head of cattle won't be of any great significance. You could dip into the Rainforth coffers and take any amount that's needed and the money would never be missed."

He slowly set his cup and saucer back on the table, then stood to face her. "I only have St. Stephen's to support me. My cousin has control of everything else, not me."

"You gave away the income from your estates?"

"I gave away what I didn't want. Which leaves me with St. Stephen's."

Josie stared at him in disbelief. What could have possessed him to turn over such a substantial income?

"Why did you keep St. Stephen's?"

"Because I like it here."

"So did your mother. It was hers, wasn't it?"

"It had been in her family for generations. She and I used to come here when I was a child."

"Did your father come with you?"

The corners of his mouth tipped upward. "No. He hated it here. St. Stephen's was much too provincial for his taste."

So St. Stephen's would have been the only place his father had not left his mark.

Could she have been so wrong about him? Could she have been so convinced all the rumors about him were true that she hadn't looked for any good? If that were true, she was in greater danger than she'd even imagined before.

"I would like that walk you promised me," he said, as if he could read her thoughts and wished to escape them. "The flowers may not be in bloom, but the garden beyond the window is well tended. Is that your doing?"

"Banks and mine. We both enjoy digging around in the dirt."

"Then I will imagine what it will look like in a month's time. And we will leave the door open and make sure we stay within view of the windows."

"But there's no one here to watch us."

"But in London there will be."

"Another rule?"

"Yes. That should be number three. Not bad for half an hour's work."

He held out his arm and she placed her hand on it. The flesh beneath her fingers was hard and she remembered how it had looked and felt without the barrier of clothes when she tended his wounds. Her cheeks warmed and she lowered her head before he noticed.

"Do you feel the need for a shawl?"

She shook her head.

"I don't want you to risk getting a chill."

She wanted to laugh. She was more likely to suffer blisters from the heat that warmed her face. "I'm perfectly fine. You were the one who was injured. Are you certain you're up to a walk?"

"Yes. I'd like to ask you some questions about the boy."

"Charlie?"

They'd crossed the patio and were at the three narrow steps that led out into the garden. He stopped before they went down the first step and turned to face her. "Do you doubt Charlie is my son?"

She shook her head. "Some people guessed he was yours when Mrs. Gardner moved into the dower house and Charlie was born not five months after. Now, you only have to look at him to know you are his father."

"There's a picture that looks exactly like him hanging at Rainforth Park. It's a picture of me when I was about his age."

"Why did you never come to see him?"

"I'd like to think I would have, if I'd have known he existed."

She stopped in the middle of the path and darted him a look filled with shock and surprise.

"But, perhaps I wouldn't have," he continued before she had a chance to say anything. He looked down on her and smiled his most seductive smile. "It's hard to say what a rake such as myself would ever do."

Her heart beat faster in her chest. "You didn't know you had a son?"

"Her condition was one detail Carrie failed to mention when she asked me to provide her with a home in the country where she could start again. I didn't even know about her death until a few weeks ago. That was when I came to the orphanage in search of the child."

"But how could you not know? The dower house isn't that far away from the manor house."

"That was part of the bargain Carrie and I struck when she

left. She wanted to put her past behind her and start a different life from the one she'd been living in London. At the time, I thought there was little possibility I'd ever return to St. Stephen's so I gifted her the dower house. She asked that I never make any effort to see her again and I saw no reason not to agree to her request. I assumed if she ever needed me, she knew where to find me."

"Did you love her?"

"No. I didn't love her. Nor did she love me. A wise woman never falls in love with a scoundrel. And Carrie was very, very wise."

Josie felt the weight press heavier against her chest. He was right. That was the mistake her mother had made.

They walked further and he stopped when they reached a small fountain with benches facing it where they could sit. "Would you mind if we rested here a while?"

She sat down on one end of the bench and he sat on the other. They weren't so close they were touching, yet close enough that his nearness caused her body to warm by several degrees.

"What kind of boy is he?"

She listened to the lazy lapping of the fountain and watched the water spray. "He has a gentle disposition and is very bright. He loves books and never wants me to quit reading when I get to the end of a chapter."

"He's a good student?" he asked, clearly interested.

"He's going to be an excellent student. He's only four, Lord Rainforth. He hasn't been taught to read yet, but last week Mrs. Lambert found him in the library practicing his letters on his own."

Josie looked up to see the smile on his face.

"When this is over, I'm going to take him to live with me."

"Why?"

"Because he's my son."

"But he'll never be your son in the legal sense of the word."

"Do you think that's all that matters? It doesn't to me. And I'll make sure it never matters to him either. You more than anyone should understand that."

Josie looked over at the man who was such a conundrum to her. He was a threat to everything she'd always guarded herself against, and if she were smart, the only emotion running through her would be distrust and wariness.

Instead, she found herself in danger of losing her heart.

She stood as if separating herself from him would make everything better. Leaving his side only made her shiver.

"You're cold."

"No, I'm fine," she started to say, but he was already placing his jacket around her shoulders.

A rush building with the force of a tidal wave shot through her, heating the blood in her veins and not easing until it settled with a molten heaviness at that place low in her belly.

If only he'd never come to St. Stephen's.

This was why he was a man to be feared. Even though she'd aligned all her defenses to fight him, she was weakening at every turn. Then, he stepped closer to her and looked down on her.

She knew what he was going to do when he reached out to cup his palms on either side of her face and she knew she should do something to stop him, but she didn't.

"Ah, Josephine," he whispered, then leaned forward and brought his mouth down on hers.

She should have been prepared for the force with which she reacted to him. His voice alone had the power to cause her insides to stir and tumble, and every time she was near him the air separating them sparked as if it had been charged by bolts of lightning. His kiss had the power to tip the earth from its axis.

The pressure of his mouth against hers was not so demanding to frighten or intimidate her, yet not so innocent she missed his intent. With a slight moan, she accepted his kiss and tilted her head as a sign of her willingness.

Josie leaned into him, taking in the passion building between them and suddenly, without understanding where such a need sprang from, she wanted even more.

Her whole life she'd ignored thinking about what it might feel like to be kissed by someone she cared for. She'd shoved her curiosity aside because she knew giving in to any man was forbidden. As if any man would want her if they knew.

But when she kissed the Marquess of Rainforth, she forgot. The passion raging within her made her willing to risk it all and give into him with all the abandon of a starving person after a crust of bread.

He must have realized what she wanted because he deepened his kiss, then opened his mouth atop hers and skimmed his tongue along her lips. The second she parted for him, he entered her mouth, his tongue mating with hers in a ritual that sent her emotions into rampant flight. It wasn't only their closeness that sent fiery sheets of heat spiraling through her, but his arms wrapped tightly around her, pulling her to him.

Josie wound her arms around his neck, holding on to him with a desperation that brought him closer. On legs that were almost too weak to support her, she leaned against him, her body nestled next to him. There they stood, mouth to mouth, chest to chest, and heat to heat. And she couldn't have found the will to move if it meant her very life.

She was lost to what he was doing to her. A molten river swirled low in her stomach to awaken a place that was unfamiliar to her. The woman standing in her shoes was a stranger, wanton and hungry with desire. She tightened her grip around his neck and kissed him back with a desperation that couldn't be assuaged.

She wasn't sure when she realized she'd lost control of the passion that soared through her. Wasn't sure when she didn't care about anything except his hands moving over her, skimming the sensitive skin at the back of her neck then running up and down her spine. Or the feather-like strokes of his fingers as he brushed them against her cheek, then down the column of her throat, and lower yet over the rise of her breast.

Flames seemed to lick at her flesh, flames of desire and passion far hotter than any fire she'd ever known. The chilly air was warm now and every inch of her burned as if she were standing in an inferno, the heat from his kisses sapping her of her strength.

He lifted his mouth from hers and kissed her cheek, then moved downward over her jaw and to the column of her throat. She gasped for air, knowing there was not enough restraint in the whole universe to save her now. For the first time she understood the passion that had destroyed her mother, and Carrie Gardner, and every other woman who'd given herself to a man and been left behind with a babe in her belly and an empty future that offered the woman nothing but a broken heart.

Without willing it to happen, all the nightmares she thought she'd buried surfaced until the man kissing her was not the Marquess of Rainforth but someone else. The hands holding her were not his but someone else's.

She knew the moment he realized she was no longer a willing participant. He lifted his mouth from her and stepped back. The void that separated them seemed cavernous.

Neither of them spoke for several long minutes. She struggled to find her voice but it took more than one false start before she was finally able to utter any sound.

"I don't think Lady Clythebrook intended for you to take your assignment so seriously, Lord Rainforth."

"Don't you? I think this is exactly what she intended."

Josie darted her gaze upward and caught the seductive glint in his eyes.

"Rule number four," he said, his voice thick with emotion. "Passion is a very dangerous game to play. You can never let a situation go beyond your control or no matter how many rules you try to follow, they'll all be for naught."

Josie didn't care a fig about his rules. The only words worth remembering were the ones he'd spoken earlier.

A wise woman never falls in love with a scoundrel.

Chapter 14

JOSIE DIDN'T COME TO THIS SECTION of the orphanage unless she had to. Tonight, she had to.

She lifted her lantern higher while she made her way down the steep stairs that led from a secret door at the back of the old larder in a wing of the orphanage that was no longer used and consigned to storage.

When she reached the cellar, she went down another set of stairs and through a second locked door that opened to a maze of tunnels. She took the path to the right then turned right again and stopped. She stepped behind a false stone wall and moved forward until she reached a thick, oaken door. She took a separate key from her pocket and worked it into the lock then turned it. The hammer clicked and she pushed downward on the heavy latch until the door opened.

She wasn't the only one who knew where this door was— one other person did. But she was the only one who had a key. That had been her first stipulation when she'd agreed to let the smugglers use the secret tunnel beneath the orphanage to move their contraband from the caves to their waiting wagons on the other side of the meadow. Not all the men who delivered the goods were savory characters and she would never let anyone who might be a threat anywhere near the children.

Tonight she didn't have to worry, though. She wasn't here to open the passageway so the men from Captain Levy's ship could bring in their goods. Tonight she'd come because she'd received a message from Baron Lindville that he wanted to meet.

A part of her hoped he was going to tell her that they'd found another way to bring in the goods and they wouldn't need to use the caves any longer. Another part of her hoped it was to tell her things had gotten too dangerous and this would be the last shipment that would come in.

She wanted to laugh. When had she begun to consider an alternative to the smuggling? The most disastrous effect of her meetings with the Marquess of Rainforth was believing that his cattle venture would be able to feed and clothe the children, or that he intended to stay around long enough for it to happen. It was frightening when she thought of how much she'd weakened since she'd met him. Before he'd come she wouldn't even have considered trusting anyone else with providing for the children.

Josie walked down the long passageway until she heard the gentle slapping sounds of the waves coming ashore. The air felt different here. Heavier. Wetter. She didn't mind looking at the waves from up above, but every time she came through the caves, she felt as if she were suffocating. Tonight though, she'd had no choice in the matter. Baron Lindville's message had been most insistent.

Josie walked further into the cave, then stopped when she reached the widest section. She lit the two torches stuck into the wall and looked around. She dreaded meeting with Lindville but told herself that after this last shipment she'd never have to come here again. Even if he didn't realize the smuggling had to stop, she did. Once Rainforth began work above the caves, there'd be no way they could continue without risking that they'd be seen.

"I could have had the torches burning when you came," a voice said from the shadows, "but I wasn't sure you'd be able to come and I hated to take the chance that someone would see the light."

Josie spun around and clamped her hand over her mouth to stifle the scream that wanted to escape.

"Did I frighten you?"

Josie gasped. "You could have at least made some sound to warn me you were here."

"So sorry, my dear. Didn't occur to me."

Josie hung the lantern she'd brought with her on a peg stuck in the wall and walked to where Lindville stood. She wished he'd come out of the shadows. She didn't like talking to him in the dark. He gave her no choice.

"I'm not sure why you wanted to meet here, and at this time of night. Surely you could have come to Clythebrook, or at least to the orphanage."

"I didn't want to chance we might be overheard. Talking about smuggling and illegal contraband is not exactly appropriate parlor conversation."

Josie hated it when Lindville referred to the goods they brought in as illegal contraband. She tried not to think of it that way. There was nothing illegal about what they were bringing in, only cheaper. Because of their remote location, they were unable to buy the items they needed without paying a tremendous freight charge. Captain Levy offered to ship in what they needed for half the cost, but only if they told no one what he was doing. That had seemed simple enough to Josie and she'd never had reason to question what they were doing until now.

"Why did you need to see me?"

"To see if you think there is any chance Rainforth will abandon his plan."

Josie shook her head. "He won't abandon it. The plan's a good one and he's getting too much support from everyone not to go ahead with it. I doubt he'd give up even if he received no support. He's a very determined man."

"That's too bad."

Baron Lindville took a step closer and Josie countered his maneuver by inching back. He followed until they were both out of the shadows.

She could finally see his face and the first thing she noticed was the vacant look in his eyes. She hated when he stared at her as if he were looking through her. There was something frightening about him. "Did you shoot at Rainforth last week?"

"Someone shot at Rainforth?"

There was a genuine look of surprise on Lindville's face and although she should be relieved it hadn't been him, his denial created another question—one even more disturbing. "If not you, then who would try to frighten him away?"

"Oh, there are many people who might have shot at the man, my dear. But I doubt they were simply trying to frighten him away. Too bad they missed."

Josie felt an unmistakable wave of fear. "You don't mean that."

"Don't I?"

Lindville took a flask from inside his jacket and pulled out the stopper. After he'd taken a swallow, he tucked it away and looked up. "So, what do you suggest we do now?"

Josie faced him squarely. "It's getting too dangerous to continue. The next shipment of goods should arrive in approximately two weeks. It'll be the last one we can chance bringing in."

He clicked his tongue while shaking his head. "Not the right answer, Josephine. Not the right answer at all."

She studied his reaction as another niggling of concern sprouted inside her. She moved back another step. "I've convinced Lady Clythebrook to keep the marquess from bringing in the cattle for one month, but after that this whole area will be covered with cattle and the men taking care of them. It'll only be a matter of time before we're discovered."

"Then we'll have to think of something else."

"What?"

"I have the solution. A solution that's perfect."

Baron Lindville uncorked his flask again and drank deeply. Josie wondered how much he'd already had to drink tonight. If the slur of his words and the glassy look in his eyes were any indication, it had been quite a bit. And yet he didn't seem drunk to her. Just…different.

"What solution?" she asked, knowing she wasn't going to like the answer.

"Marriage."

"Whose marriage?"

"Our marriage. Yours and mine. To each other."

Josie wanted to reach out to steady herself against something but there wasn't anything within reach to grab hold of. "What are you saying?"

"We'll marry. We're already partners of a sort. It only seems natural that we extend our arrangement to include personal aspects of our lives, too."

Josie couldn't breathe. "It's preposterous. I can't marry you. I—"

"Don't refuse so quickly. Just think of the benefits. Getting my hands on the inheritance my father left me has always been a problem, but once I'm married, Mother won't have a reason to withhold the money any longer. I'll need a great deal of ready cash to set up my own household as any newly married husband must, and if Mother doesn't part with some of the reserve she's been hoarding, she'll be seen as a miserly tyrant. Which, of course, I'll convince her Society will discover."

Josie took a shaky step away from him. The blood rushed against her ears and she couldn't think. "You can't be serious."

He smiled. "But I am. It's a known fact that one day you'll inherit Clythebrook Estate. As the future owner, I'll forbid Lady Clythebrook to have anything to do with Rainforth's scheme. It'll solve all our problems."

He closed the distance between them and brushed the back of his fingers down her cheek. Josie jerked her head away from him.

"Don't look so horrified, my dear. Our marriage will be especially beneficial for you. Just imagine what you'll gain from marrying me. You'll go from being Miss Josephine Foley to Baroness Lindville."

"I'm not interested in your title."

"Of course you're not. But you *are* interested in providing for the children. Once the smuggling stops, where will the resources come from to feed and clothe the children? Marrying me will ensure that none of your precious charges ever go without." He laughed. "Your generosity will put the meager gifts my mother donates to Sacred Heart to shame."

"Your mother will never allow you to marry me."

Lindville swiped his hand through the air in an angry arc. "My mother has no say in this."

Josie was frantic to come up with reasons to squash Lindville's idea. "This is ludicrous. Your mother will faint dead away when you tell her you intend to take someone of my station as your wife."

He laughed. "One can only hope."

She shook her head and stumbled back. He didn't let her put any distance between them.

"I agree the circumstances surrounding your birth are regrettable, but once Mother realizes the benefits, she'll be forced to welcome you with open arms."

Josie spun away from him. He was daft. Completely insane. "What benefit? I know what the goods bring in. Surely your share of the money we receive isn't worth what you're suggesting?"

He laughed. "You have no idea what our little venture is worth to me. What I gain affords me at least a small amount of independence from my mother and keeps me from toadying to her at every turn."

She stepped back another foot. The torches cast shooting shadows against the stone walls, making the room seem frighteningly confining. "No, I won't—"

He grabbed her by the shoulders. "Is it a show of affection you want? Do you need some proof that we will fit together on the physical side of our marriage?"

Before she could protect herself, he backed her up against the wall and brought his mouth down over hers.

Lindville's abhorrent kiss was nothing like Rainforth's. Lindville's lips were cold and lifeless atop hers—completely without passion. And when he stopped, she was left with nothing but a disgusting emptiness followed by a resurgence of the confining panic.

Josie clamped her hand over her mouth and fought a sensation that bordered on revulsion.

"I'll call on Lady Clythebrook tom—"

"No! I need time. Until the end of the month."

"We don't have until the end of the month!"

"Two weeks, then."

"Procrastination won't save you, Miss Foley. Nothing will. Neither of us has a choice, really. You will marry me to save the children. And I will marry you to save myself."

He brushed the backs of his fingers down her cheek and turned away from her. He took a few steps into the shadows, then stopped. "The smuggling will not cease. Don't think for a minute you have the power to make it stop. And when you speak to Rainforth next, you might explain to him that he was lucky to escape with his life. He might not be so fortunate next time."

Josie stared into the shadows and listened to the soft padding of his footsteps against the packed ground of the cave. She couldn't believe Lindville had just suggested they marry, although his words had been closer to a demand than a proposal. She was sure he hadn't meant them. He'd been drinking. That *had* to explain his ludicrous idea. And even if he had been serious, his mother would never allow it. Not in a million years. An uncomfortable knot settled in the pit of her stomach.

What if he wanted access to the caves so badly he would do anything to get it, even marry someone for whom he didn't care a whit?

She hugged her arms around her middle. Marrying Lindville was a sacrifice she could not imagine making, even for the children's sake. No, she'd chosen her path. The next shipment would be the last one to which she would be a part.

Surely she was reading more into Lindville's demand that

they marry than he intended. When he woke in the morning, he more than likely wouldn't even remember that he'd foisted the idea upon her.

Yet, she couldn't forget the threatening tone in his voice when he'd told her the smuggling would not stop.

Or the threat he'd made against the Marquess of Rainforth.

Ross dismounted from the carriage and strode up the short walkway. He couldn't help but smile when the door opened before he reached it. His visits with Josephine over the past ten days had been well noted by everyone in the area. Even Ross's steward had commented on it this morning.

"Good afternoon, Banks."

"Good afternoon, my lord."

Ross handed the butler his hat and gloves. The weather was splendidly warm today and he hadn't bothered with a coat. "Is Miss Josephine at home?"

Banks smiled. "She's waiting in the drawing room. If you'll follow me."

"I know my way, Banks."

"Very good. Will my services be required later, do you think?"

Ross shook his head. "No. Perhaps Lady Clythebrook needs your assistance in the other part of the house."

"I'm sure she does," Banks answered with a smile he quickly hid.

Maybe he could cajole Josephine into taking a ride with him today. He hadn't been able to talk her into leaving the house on his last visit. Even though she'd assured him nothing was the matter, he knew that wasn't true. Dark circles rimmed her eyes as if she hadn't slept well for nights, and the last two times they'd met she'd been uncommonly subdued.

Ross walked down the hall until he reached the room where

he always met her and looked inside. The door was open and she stood on the other side of the room looking out onto the terrace and beyond.

She was so lovely, small and petite, her golden hair pulled atop her head to expose her long, graceful neck. She wore a pale blue gown today that fastened high at the neck with a ruffle of white lace. Ivory buttons pulled the dress tight around her narrow waist and Ross remembered how perfectly she'd fit against him. He wanted to walk up behind her and put his arms around her and pull her into his embrace. Instead, he cleared his throat and waited until she turned around to face him.

The breath caught in his throat. She had the most stunning blue eyes. Every time she looked at him they sparked with a vibrancy that warned him she was prepared to challenge his attempt to raise the number of rules he'd accused her of breaking. Today, though, it was obvious that something was wrong. The circles he'd noticed days ago were even darker and the smile that lifted the corners of her mouth didn't reach her eyes.

He greeted her with a smile and walked across the room to take her hands in his. They were icy cold.

"Good afternoon, Miss Foley. How lovely you look today."

"Thank you, Lord Rainforth. How kind of you to say so."

Ross laughed at her perfect execution of drawing room manners and gave her fingers a gentle squeeze. "How exquisitely you've mastered rule number two."

She played her part to perfection and smiled. "I believe rule number one concerned the gracious manner in which to accept a compliment. Rule number two was that a single woman of gentle breeding must never entertain a male visitor alone without a chaperone present, preferably a lady of unquestionable character." She pulled her hands out of his grasp. "I'll ring for Lady Clythebrook to join us. She's conveniently occupied herself at another part of the house again this afternoon."

"No," Ross said with a laugh. "Don't bother her. It's the middle of the afternoon and I'm sure we can count on Banks to hover nearby to protect your reputation. I promise to conduct myself with exemplary decorum so there's no need for you to concern yourself."

"Very well. I'll ring for tea."

"Would you mind very much if we walked through the garden? The day is unusually mild and I've been locked indoors all morning working on water estimates and cattle prices. I prefer to feel the sun on my face, if you don't mind."

"Not at all."

Ross couldn't help but notice the look of relief on her face. It was as if she didn't want to be confined to the house any more than he did. Or, perhaps her nerves were so tightly wound she needed to walk off the strain she was under.

Ross opened the door and followed her across the patio, then down the narrow steps. When they reached the bottom, he held out his arm and she placed her hand atop it. Perhaps it was his imagination, but her hand seemed to tremble upon his and the involuntary grip on his arm was much harder than the relaxed touch to which he was accustomed.

"Did Mrs. Lambert tell you I went to the orphanage yesterday?"

"Yes. She said you took the boys fishing. I'm sorry I wasn't there when you returned but I was called away."

She turned her head, making it impossible for Ross to look at her face. Her cheeks, however, seemed flushed. Something was wrong. If he didn't know her better, he'd almost accuse her of lying. He wondered what was so important to take her away from the children, but knew she probably wouldn't tell him.

"Thank you for spending the day with the boys. They're almost always around women and it's good for them to be around a man."

"I'd like to say I did it out of the goodness of my heart, but I have to admit my motives were more selfish than that. I wanted to spend time with my son."

"It doesn't matter why you did it. The boys had a wonderful time. They were still talking about it at dinner."

"Next time I'll have to do something that includes the girls, too. They felt left out, but Vicar Chadwick saved the day by giving them each a gumdrop."

"He keeps a jar of them on his desk for just such occasions." The smile slid from her face and she looked at him. "Are you going to tell Charlie you're his father?"

"Not yet. Not until I know it's safe to take him home with me."

"You're not going to be safe until you give up your plan to bring in cattle."

Ross could hear the water in the fountain just ahead of them and led her to the same bench where they'd sat before. "Are you saying someone might try again to shoot me?"

She pulled her hand from his arm. "Don't make sport of what happened. You could have been killed."

"Do you know who shot me?"

Her face paled but she didn't answer. He wouldn't give up. "Do you, Josie?"

"Rule number seven, Lord Rainforth. A gentleman may not call a lady by her first name until she gives him permission."

"Then may I ask your permission, Miss Foley?"

She shook her head. "That wouldn't be wise."

"Wouldn't it?"

"You know it wouldn't."

"You haven't answered my question. Do you know who shot me?"

"Of course not."

"But you have an idea."

"No, I don't. But I do know whoever shot you wanted you dead."

"And you're concerned for me?"

She came to a halt and glared at him. "Of course I'm concerned. Isn't it enough that your son is going to grow up without a mother? Do you want him to go without a father, too? Give up your cattle venture. If you truly want to be a father to the boy, don't put yourself in danger."

Ross opened his mouth to explain that making St. Stephen's profitable was the only way he could provide for his son. St. Stephen's would someday be Charlie's and the cattle were the assurance that he would be provided for. But none of that mattered if his son wasn't proud of who he was. Discovering who was behind the smuggling was one small step in redeeming the Rainforth name. Not until he saw the smugglers hang would he finally feel like he'd done something good to make up for all the lives his father had destroyed.

"I can't give up. There are reasons the cattle venture must go forward."

"No."

Ross wasn't surprised by Josephine's negative response. There'd always been a combative fierceness to her stand against bringing in the cattle. But for the first time, as she sank onto a nearby bench, he saw an emotion that hinted at desperation. Or perhaps it was fear. He slid onto the bench and clasped her hands in her lap.

"Something's wrong, Josephine. Let me help."

She didn't pull away as he was afraid she would but held on with a grip that sent waves of concern racing through him. The simple holding of hands was a bond that connected them. The clasp it had on his heart was more powerful than the tightening of her fingers or any of the kisses they'd shared.

A squirrel scampered across the lawn and raced up a tree, but he could tell she never saw it. Her eyes were focused on an empty patch of ground, and the way she worried her lower lip said something else occupied her mind.

Ross placed his arm around her shoulder and brought her close to him. She went willingly, then with a heavy sigh, she laid her head against him. He didn't move, was afraid to move for fear he'd break the spell. Finally, she broke the silence.

"Give up the cattle venture."

"I can't."

She stiffened, then pulled away from him. "I have to go to the children," she said, rising to her feet. "I've been gone too much lately."

Ross rose with her and offered her his arm. "I'll take you then. I've got my carriage outside."

She started to walk away. "That's not necessary."

"I know, but I'd like to."

He walked with her across the terrace and back into the house, hoping she'd trust him enough to confide in him. But she kept her silence until they entered the drawing room. Then, a small gasp of surprise echoed through the room and her hands closed over her open mouth.

Two huge bouquets of hothouse flowers sat on tables on either side of the settee, their fragrance filling the room.

"Servants from Lindville Grange brought these, for you, miss." Banks said carrying in a third. "There's a note attached to this one." He brought the flowers over so she could take the note.

She stared at the piece of folded paper nestled between the blooms of the flowers but she didn't take it.

Banks didn't set the third bouquet down but held it in front of her. "Would you like me to have them wait for a reply?"

The fingers clasping his arm had tightened almost painfully and when Ross looked at her, the little color she'd had when he'd arrived was gone, leaving her as pale as the white orchids in the vases.

He put his hand over hers. "Josephine? Would you like to read it?"

"No," she said, clasping his arm even tighter. "Send them back, Banks. Have the servants take them back."

"Are you sure, miss?"

"Yes. Take them back!"

Her fingers still gripped his arm, wadding the material in her fist until it was a mass of wrinkles. Banks left with the first vase of flowers then came back for the second before she moved. The breath left her body in a rush.

She swallowed hard, then looked down at the material clenched in her fist. She released her hold of him. "I'm sorry. That was silly of me."

"Would you like to sit down for a while?"

"No, I'm fine."

"Why would Lindville send you flowers?"

"He didn't."

"Josephine, don't lie to me. Why?"

She jerked her head up, her eyes filled with an expression he was positive he had misinterpreted. "Lord Lindville sent the flowers as a joke. They didn't mean anything."

She watched as Banks returned for the third vase.

"Are you ready?" she asked, her chin high and her shoulders back. "To take me to the orphanage?"

"Of course," he said, and followed her from the room.

He had no idea what the flowers meant, but whatever it was, their arrival had frightened her to death.

Chapter 15

ANOTHER RUMBLE OF THUNDER echoed in the distance, but Josie didn't slow down. If anything, she walked faster. She was desperate to come up with a plan to discourage Lindville. But no matter how fast she walked or how far, the same overwhelming fear suffocated her when she thought of how determined he was to get his hands on Clythebrook Estate. Why else would he consider marrying her?

It was well after midnight. The moon had been out and the sky clear when she'd left the manor house. But that had been hours ago. Since then, clouds had filtered in until there was a heavy covering that concealed the stars. It was black now with nothing but shadows and an occasional clap of thunder to intrude upon her thoughts.

How could he even consider such a preposterous scheme? Surely the land above the caves wasn't worth so much he'd consider marrying her to get it. He knew the circumstances of her birth. Yet the scathing message she'd received after she'd returned the flowers was closer to a threat than a suitor's proposal.

For the first time, Josie sensed the lurking of a danger even more frightening than she'd felt after Rainforth had been shot.

She made her way across the meadow, then down a shallow ravine and up again. She didn't stop until she reached the edge of the cliff overlooking the caves, then pulled her woolen cloak tighter and let the wind whip around her.

She couldn't do it. Even if marrying him were the only way to save the children, she couldn't do it. She'd always known she would never marry. From the day she'd escaped the abuse she'd suffered at Foster's hand, she'd known she would never be a bride. But now, Geoffrey Lindville thought he could force her by threatening Lady Clythebrook and the children.

She hadn't taken him seriously at first. Why should she? The very idea of a baron marrying a bastard was unthinkable. Yet, that was what he was proposing and he was becoming more insistent every day.

Yesterday he'd come to the orphanage to see her and she'd barely escaped him before he could corner her again. But he'd left a note for her. A note that made his threats terrifyingly real.

Josie looked down onto the cove where the boats brought their supplies ashore. She couldn't believe the money was so important to him. The amount wasn't that substantial.

The first raindrop hit her cheek and she wiped it away with her fingertips. Another drop struck her face. She reached up to wipe at it but froze when the grass rustled behind her. She spun around, fearful it would be Lindville. She nearly cried out in relief when the Marquess of Rainforth came toward her.

"Josephine?"

She grabbed her hand to her chest and waited for her heart to stop pounding. "Don't *ever* do that to me again. You scared me half to death."

"Seeing you standing out here in the middle of the night didn't exactly calm my nerves either," he said, coming closer to her. "Step away from there."

She looked out over the edge. "Are you afraid I'm preparing to jump?"

He laughed. "No. Jumping isn't your style. You're more the stand-and-fight type. I just wonder who it is you're getting ready to fight."

"Are you worried it's you?"

"It wouldn't be the first time."

He reached out and pulled her from the edge, then brushed away a drop of rain from her cheek. He didn't step away from her or remove his hand, but cupped his palm against the side of her face. His touch was gentle and emitted a strength she needed badly right now.

She looked him in the eyes, their gazes locked in a heated blaze that sent currents rippling through her chest. Standing this close to him always did this to her—stole her breath and caused a cascading waterfall to plummet to the pit of her stomach.

It was raining harder, not a downpour, but coming steadily enough that her pelisse was showing water spots. She didn't care. Rain always made her feel good—clean. He brushed another drop from the tip of her nose.

"You shouldn't be here," he whispered, then wrapped his fingers around the back of her neck and pulled her toward him. She went willingly.

Raindrops fell, but she didn't notice. He placed a finger beneath her chin and tipped her face upward. He was going to kiss her and she was going to let him.

She closed her eyes and waited.

His mouth came down on hers, his lips firm and warm, his need vibrantly demanding. How could one man's kiss be so different from another's? How could one man's touch be something she craved, while another man's so repugnant to her? She leaned into him until no space separated them.

There were no words that needed to be spoken, no permission to be granted. The understanding between them was mutual. They'd both realized that a force far stronger than either of them could control had brought them to this point. A primal need she'd always been able to stamp down with ingrained mental discipline raged within her and demanded to be satisfied. Just this once, she thought with an ache that burned deep inside her, she didn't want to deny the needs growing within her. She wanted to replace all her nightmares with one night of passion. She wanted his face to be the one she saw when she remembered. She touched his cheek. "We need to find shelter."

He placed his hand atop hers and looked down at her. "You need to go home."

His face was wet now. Drops of rain spiked his lashes and made them seem darker. "Granny's cottage is just ahead. We can go there."

"You won't be safe with me there. You're barely safe with me out here in the rain."

"I don't want to be safe. I want to be loved. Just this once."

Josie didn't know where the words had come from or what person had spoken them. It wasn't the Josephine Foley she'd known all her life. This was a stranger. The Josie she'd been just yesterday was watching from a distance while this outsider found the courage to ask for something she'd been craving her whole life.

"Please."

"You don't know what you're asking."

"Come," she said, taking his hand and guiding him.

He wrapped his arm around her shoulder and walked with her into the woods. Twice he stopped to kiss her. Once she stopped to kiss him. Rain poured down now and they ran the last steps into the same cottage where they'd spent time together while he healed.

He tossed his wet jacket over one of the chairs, then unfastened her pelisse and laid it over the other chair. "Let me light a fire."

"No light. Just the darkness and the rain."

He ground his mouth against hers again, demanding what she'd never dreamed she'd be able to give to any man. His mouth opened and he gently urged hers to do the same. The second her lips parted for him, he entered her mouth.

His tongue searched and found its mate. He moaned a sound she caught and would not release, then he tilted his head and deepened his kiss.

Their clothes were damp and more difficult to remove than if they'd been dry, but he seemed to accomplish the task with little difficulty. His mouth stayed on her—on her mouth, her cheeks, her neck, her shoulders. She didn't simply allow it, she encouraged it. When he moved his kisses upward to recapture her mouth, she threaded her fingers into his hair and pushed him lower, offering herself to him.

She was naked when she climbed beneath the covers and waited with a racing pulse while he undressed. She didn't know if it was normal for a woman to help the man remove his clothes, but she couldn't have done it even if it was. She wasn't that brave.

The mattress sagged when he knelt beside her and she opened her arms to him. Not because he needed the invitation but because she wanted to hold him. He came down over her and touched her, flesh to flesh, warmth to warmth, desire to desire.

She should have been embarrassed. She should have been self-conscious and shy and remote, but she wasn't. The darkness helped but that wasn't the reason she felt no embarrassment. It was him. How could she regret something she'd waited her whole life to experience?

He kissed her again, his kiss deep and hungry and filled with need. And while his mouth drank from hers, his hands moved over her, touching and kneading and caressing. He nestled himself over her and looked into her eyes.

Oh, she loved him. Even though she'd fought the emotions from the day she'd met him, she loved him with every fiber of her being. She cupped her hands on either side of his face and brought his mouth down for a kiss.

"Teach me," she whispered when he lifted his mouth. He kissed her again lightly in answer.

"There will be pain," he said before he took her, but she knew there would not. There was only pain the first time.

He was a gentle lover, careful not to hurt her. He came into her slowly as if anticipating the barrier he knew he should find.

When he met no resistance, he embedded himself fully.

The ritual was as primitive as life itself and she met every thrust with a growing need and passion. The end, when it came, was as powerful and beautiful as she knew it would be. He'd taken her to a place she'd never known existed and when she leaped off that very high ledge into the unknown, he'd been there with her.

Then, with a loud moan, he stiffened atop her and found his release.

She clung to him, holding him tightly as if she'd never have to let him go, but she knew she would. When this night was over, there would be no others. She was taking a huge enough risk making love with him once. She wouldn't risk it again.

She held him close to her, running her fingers over his sweat-dampened flesh. His skin was firm and taut and his muscles rippled beneath her touch. He was perfect and for just these few moments he was hers.

"Are you all right?"

She smiled. "Yes. Perfect."

He rolled off her but took her with him. With a contented sigh, she nestled her head in the crook of his neck and listened to his heart thunder beneath her ear. Her heart matched his rapid beating and she snuggled closer when he wrapped his arm around her shoulder and brought her nearer.

Neither of them spoke for several minutes and she waited, not wanting to be the first to break the silence. He finally ended the reverie.

"Who was he?"

At first Josie didn't comprehend what he'd meant. For several long seconds it didn't register that his tone contained an accusatory note or that the way he held her had changed. The difference was minute and if her senses hadn't been heightened as a result of what they'd just shared, she probably wouldn't have noticed. There was still a tenderness in his touch—a gentleness, but there was also a stiffness that separated him from her, an aloofness that made him a stranger to her.

"Who?" she asked, but knew what he meant.

"The man you gave yourself to first. Or should I be speaking in the present? The man to whom you are still giving yourself?"

Josie felt the air suck out of her lungs and freeze.

"Is it Lindville?"

"No."

"He sent you flowers."

She tried to ease away from him but he wouldn't let her. She tried again but gave up when he made it impossible. "The flowers didn't mean anything."

His chest rumbled beneath her ear. He was laughing.

"The man must have emptied out every hothouse between here and London. Those were orchids you sent back to him. Was it a lover's spat?"

She jerked out of his arms and this time he let her go. She grabbed one of the loose covers from the bed and wrapped it around her. She suddenly felt very self-conscious, even in the darkness.

Her clothes lay on the floor. She snatched them up and quickly slipped into them. From the sounds she heard from the other side of the room, he was dressing too. She was glad the room was dark. She didn't want to see the accusatory expression on his face. Or the revulsion in his eyes.

As she fastened the last of the buttons up the front of her gown, the room glowed from a candle he'd placed in the center of the table. Before long, a fire raged in the hearth.

A welcome warmth sifted through Granny's cottage. But it didn't reach deep inside her to the block of ice lodged in her chest.

She'd been such a fool. She'd hoped he wouldn't notice that he wasn't the first one to have her and if he did that it wouldn't matter. The fact that he thought he had the right to throw her past in her face only made her angry.

Without a by-your-leave, she grabbed her pelisse from the chair and walked to the door. His hand shot out against the door so she couldn't open it.

"It's still pouring out there. You can't leave."

"I've walked through the rain before. It's preferable to being in here."

She tried to open the door again and this time he stood in front of it. Moving him was impossible and rather than fight a losing battle, she turned back. She pushed out the coat tree Granny kept in the corner and hung her wrap over it so the fire would dry it. A shiver raced through her when she heard him step up behind her.

"Why didn't you tell me?"

"Tell you what?"

"That you weren't a virgin."

"Why should I have? Whether you were the first or the one hundred and first is no one's concern but my own."

The look he gave her said that what he felt reached far beyond anger. Revealed in the depths of his steel-gray eyes were other emotions she didn't want to acknowledge, the most obvious of which were disappointment and regret. Josie felt another jolt of her temper and she clenched her hands into tight fists at her side.

"You expected to be the first man to have me and you feel angry and betrayed to discover you weren't." She took another step toward him and leveled him with every defensive instinct battling within her. "You don't have the right to be angry. You don't have the right to be anything."

"Don't I? We just made love. Perhaps that doesn't mean much to you, but it does to me."

Josie felt like she'd been slapped. Before she could recover he fired his next question.

"What is your connection to Geoffrey Lindville?"

"There is no connection between us. We're neighbors. That's the only connection between us."

"When I went to the orphanage yesterday, Mrs. Lambert told me Baron Lindville had been asking for you, too. When I arrived at your house today, Banks said Baron Lindville had been there earlier but you hadn't been home to him. His eagerness to see you on top of all the flowers must mean something. Why would he go to all that trouble if there is no connection?"

"I don't know."

"Then perhaps you know why he is so adamantly opposed to the cattle venture. Every other man at the dinner Lady Clythebrook hosted endorsed my idea—except Lindville. And his land is not even involved in the venture. Why do you think he's pursuing you?"

"I don't know."

"Could it be because you will someday inherit Clythebrook Estate?"

Josie couldn't give him an answer. Instead, she stepped away from him and gripped her fingers around the top rung of one of the chairs tucked against the table.

Rainforth moved to the opposite side of the table. He braced his outstretched arms on the worn wood and stared at her. "And why do you think keeping everyone away from the land above the caves is so important to him?"

"I don't know!"

"Well, I do. It's because the caves are being used by smugglers."

A floating feather could have felled her. *He knew!*

"What do you know about that, Josephine?"

She shook her head, unable to speak.

"Do you know what I think?"

A long silence separated them.

"I think perhaps Baron Lindville is involved with the smuggling and that is why he is so opposed to anyone using the land and discovering what's happening. Maybe the smuggling is so important to him he even shot me to frighten me away."

"Then pay attention to the warning!"

"And let the smuggling continue?"

"Whoever fired at you could have killed you. Stopping them is not worth your life."

He straightened. "It's worth more than my life. It's worth

my honor. It's worth my place in Society. It's the means to redeeming the Rainforth name."

Josie was more shocked than she'd been before. How could stopping them from bringing in a few insignificant goods restore his place in Society? How could it redeem his name?

He turned, and Josie watched him pace the space before the fire. His features were taut with determination, his eyes set with a fierceness she'd seen on his face the first time when he'd come to get his son.

"I assume you know that my father sold military secrets that cost hundreds of men their lives."

Josie nodded.

"I've been given the opportunity to make up for a small part of the suffering he caused."

"Even if it means your life?"

"It's the least I can give after all the lives my father took. The government has asked for my help to discover who is behind the smuggling operation. And I will not fail in doing it."

A cold chill raced through her. "What possible interest could the government have in a harmless band of smugglers this far from London?"

"Harmless? Oh, Josephine. What's happening is far from harmless. These people are murderers and the government will not rest until every one of them is hanged."

Josie reached for the nearest chair and lowered herself to it. How could he accuse them of being murderers? "How could bringing in a few simple items be considered murder?"

"A few simple items? Thank heavens you're so ignorant of what's going on here. If the look on your face weren't filled with such blatant shock and horror, I might suspect you of being involved with the smugglers."

He stepped in front of her and placed his finger beneath her chin. With the gentlest of pressure, he tipped her head back until she looked into his hardened gray eyes. "If you know anything at all, you have to tell me."

"Tell you what?"

"Anything. When the next shipment might come in? Who brings it? Where and when it is unloaded? How they get it from the caves inland? They have to have someone working with them that knows a way to get it from the caves to a place further inland—an underground passageway. Perhaps even through the orphanage. We have to stop them."

She struggled to find her next breath. "Why? What is so threatening about bringing goods in by sea to avoid the high cost of inland freight?"

"Is that what you think they are doing?"

"Of course. What else could they be doing?"

"Opium, innocent child. They're smuggling in opium."

Chapter 16

JOSIE RUSHED THROUGH THE ORPHANAGE and back down the steep stairs that led to the secret door at the back of the larder. It was the middle of the afternoon and using the secret passageway when there was so much activity was more dangerous than coming here during the night, but she couldn't chance waiting until dark. She needed to confront Lindville. Now.

What Rainforth had told her couldn't be true. Captain Levy couldn't be bringing in opium. That meant she'd been part of the smuggling ring from the beginning. And when they were caught, she would hang just as surely as the rest of them.

Her hands trembled as she fumbled with the key to the door that led to the maze of tunnels. When the lock clicked, she lifted her lantern and rushed through the opening.

She went to the right, then right again, and stepped behind the false wall to the thick, oaken door. She opened it, and locked it again when she was inside.

How could she never have suspected what was really happening? How could she have lit the signal to tell Captain Levy that the coast was clear, then unlocked the secret passageway that ran beneath the orphanage for all this time and not once realized they were bringing in something other than the goods that went to Cornelius Sharpe? She called herself every kind of fool imaginable and knew that didn't come close to what she really was.

She paced the room while she waited. He'd be here soon. She'd sent him a note and knew he wouldn't miss the chance to meet with her. He'd tried often enough the last few days.

Her heart pounded in her throat and she fought the waves of anger mixed with rage. He'd used her. He'd used her to bring in opium that he was selling on the black market. She stopped pacing and listened to the footsteps echo in the long tunnel. He'd made her an unwitting accomplice in his crime for the last time. She gritted her teeth and waited for him to step out of the shadows.

"Josephine," he said, coming toward her. He clasped his fingers around her shoulder and kissed her lightly on the cheek in greeting. "I've been to see you several times during the last few days but missed you each time. If I didn't know better, I'd think you were trying to avoid me."

Josie shrugged out of his grasp and stepped back from him. She'd lit three of the torches on the wall and there was more light in the tunnel than there'd been the other night. The brightness made her feel safer and let her see him better. She was glad he was looking at her through clear eyes today. Glad to know he'd understand every scathing word she said to him.

She wanted to laugh. She'd always thought the glassy look and his fragmented sentences were due to the amount of liquor he drank. Now she knew that wasn't it. He was addicted to the drug as deeply as the men he supplied.

"Is it too much to hope that you asked to meet because you've changed your mind and want to marry as soon as possible?"

"Hardly. I asked to meet because I'd like you to answer a few questions."

"Of course. Anything."

She stepped closer. She wanted to stare into his eyes when she asked her questions. Wanted to see the truth or a lie in his answers. "Why are you so opposed to the Marquess of Rainforth's cattle venture?"

"You know the answer to that as well as I. Neither one of us can afford to let him use this land. Have you forgotten what we use the caves for?"

"I haven't forgotten. I'm just confused. I know what you told me, that you need the money to live a certain lifestyle and to provide independence from your mother. I'm not sure I understand how the meager amount from the sale of the goods we bring in provides you that."

His face hardened. "What are you saying, Josephine?"

"That the amount we get from the sale of the goods, although a blessing that goes a long way to provide for the children's needs, is nothing compared to what you need to live a Season in London." She pointed to the expensive clothes he wore even in the country. "The amount it must take to pay your tailor alone is probably more than our shared profit for the year."

"I have a certain standard to maintain. You know that."

"Just what is it Captain Levy brings in that allows you to live such an extravagant lifestyle?"

"You know the answer to that as well as I. French wines, tea, crockery. Goods Cornelius Sharpe sells for a tidy profit."

"What else?"

Lindville clasped his hands behind him and rocked back and forth on his heels. "You are terribly inquisitive all of a sudden. There's a saying about the effect such curiosity has on certain species."

"I'm hardly a feline. What else does Captain Levy bring in other than the goods we sell to Cornelius Sharpe?"

"I don't know what you think is going on, but—"

"I *know* what is going on. I *know* you're smuggling opium."

Lindville blanched, the guilt on his face plain to see. Josie waited for him to speak, half expecting him to deny her accusation. He didn't. He circled her like a wolf closing in on its prey.

"How unfortunate you found out. What do you intend to do with your new-found knowledge?"

"Put a stop to what you're doing."

He laughed. "I don't think so. I'm not about to let you ruin everything."

"What you're doing is illegal! It's immoral!"

"Smuggling of any kind is illegal. Did you think what you did was justified simply because the money went to provide for the children?"

"What I did didn't destroy innocent lives."

"Oh, please. Don't be so melodramatic. The crime is smuggling. Which makes you as guilty as the rest of us."

"Then it's a crime I refuse to be a part of any longer."

"Are you threatening me?"

She stepped up to him. "There will be no more shipments. Not one more item will come ashore on Clythebrook land. Not one more bundle of contraband will pass through the tunnels beneath the orphanage."

He laughed. "Do you honestly think you can stop us? Do you think for one moment anyone cares if you don't approve of what we're doing?"

"You're a fool if you think you can get away with this. Rainforth knows about the smuggling and he's going to stop you."

"Unless someone eliminates him first."

Josie stopped short. "Do you hear what you're saying? You're talking about murder."

"I'm talking about protecting my interests. I don't give a damn about the stupid French wines or the tea or anything else that comes in? I only care about the profits from the opium."

Josie stared at him in disbelief. "You won't get away with this."

"Who's going to stop us? You?" He took a step toward her. "Not if you care what happens to Lady Clythebrook and the children."

"You can't mean that."

"Can't I?"

Josie was suddenly frightened of him. There was a look in his eyes so different than the placid, emotionless glaze she was used to seeing. The unadulterated malice glaring back at her gave her cause to fear.

She took a tentative step backwards but he followed her. With a smile on his face, he clamped his fingers around her upper arms and stopped her.

"Everything's going to remain the same. The goods will arrive as they always have. You'll signal Captain Levy that it's safe to unload and when the boats bring the goods ashore, you'll open the door to the secret passageway beneath the orphanage just like you always have. If you don't…"

He squeezed her arms until she wanted to cry out.

"Well, I'd hate to think that something might happen to someone you cared for."

Josie tried to pull away from him but his fingers dug deeper into her flesh and he pulled her up against him.

"That's no way to act toward the man who intends to make you his wife."

She struggled. "I have no intention of marrying you. I thought I'd made that quite clear."

"You mean when you returned the flowers?" He clucked his tongue and stroked the side of her face with his fine leather-gloved hand. "How ungrateful."

She slapped it away with a crack. "I haven't given you permission to touch me, sir. Nor do I share your sudden ardor. Now, get your hands off me."

He didn't release her. Instead he pulled her tighter against him. She brought both her hands up against his chest and shoved but he didn't release her.

"I don't think you've considered just what I'm saying. I suddenly realize I have no choice but to marry you. How else am I to gain control of the caves so this problem never arises again?"

"You would marry me for a piece of land?"

He slid his hand down her throat and stopped at the slight rise of her breast. "Oh, I'm sure there will be other benefits to our marriage. But yes, the land would be enough."

Josie twisted to the side and slapped at his hand. "Get away from me."

The look in Lindville's eyes changed and a mounting wariness gnawed inside her. Not since she'd been sent to live with the Fosters when she was thirteen had she been as afraid. Then he kissed her.

His kiss was hard. Brutal. The more Josie struggled to free herself from his grip, the deeper his fingers dug into her flesh. She tried to twist her head away from him, but his thumb and fingers clamped like a vice on either side of her jaw and held her tight.

She couldn't move and the harder she resisted, the tighter he gripped her.

He ground his lips against hers, forcing her to open her mouth and take in his tongue. Blood thundered in her ears, rage and fear consuming emotions as she battled to free herself. And then he touched her. His one hand dropped from around her to cover her breast.

She fought him with all her might, finally freeing one hand. She pummeled his chest with her fist but it was as effective as beating a rock with a feather. Then, in a move of desperation, she raised her hand and scraped her fingernails down the side of his face.

"Bloody hell!"

With a yelp he pulled away from her. Josie turned but before she could escape, he brought his hand up and slapped her hard across the face.

Her cheek stung and her eyes watered, but she didn't wait for the ringing in her head to stop before she ran toward the door.

She didn't turn around. She wasn't sure if he followed her, but couldn't hear the thundering of his footsteps in the tunnel behind her. All that concerned her was getting to Clythebrook Manor and figuring out how she could keep the next opium shipment out of Lindville's hands.

Then figuring out a way to keep Rainforth from finding out that she was one of the opium smugglers he'd come to arrest and hang.

"I can't imagine what's keeping Josephine," Lady Clythebrook said, setting down her cup of tepid tea. "There must have been some problem with the children. She can never bring herself to leave if there's some dilemma."

Ross had been conversing with Lady Clythebrook for nearly an hour while waiting for Josephine to return from the orphanage. Today he intended to take her for a ride. They needed to be alone so he could talk to her. The way she'd reacted when he told her about the smuggling was alarming.

He knew she'd be upset to know someone was using Clythebrook land to bring opium into the country, but her reaction indicated something much more serious was wrong. The way she'd had to reach out to steady herself when he'd told her what he'd discovered gave him reason to wonder. Perhaps her feelings for Lindville were stronger than he'd thought and finding out that he might be connected to the smuggling was something she couldn't deal with.

He also needed to apologize for the way he'd reacted after they'd made love. He hadn't meant to say the things he had or sound so condescending, but his unchecked words had come out without his bidding when he'd realized she wasn't a virgin. If he were totally honest with himself—which he was loathe to be—he'd have to admit he'd been angry.

She'd been right. Even though she was seven and twenty years old, he'd expected her to come to him untouched. And when she hadn't…

Why had he been so shocked to realize she'd loved someone before him? How could he have been so foolish to think there'd never been someone special in her life? She was beautiful. She must have had a dozen or more suitors. It's just that she held men at such arm's length he couldn't imagine her taking a lover. And with vivid clarity, he knew she never would.

His heart jolted in his chest. He knew her well enough to know she'd never give herself to any man unless she loved him.

And she'd given herself to him.

He glanced toward the empty doorway. He wished she'd get here. He wanted to make sure she was all right. He wanted to see her again. Hold her.

Just be with her.

Lady Clythebrook sat back against the cushion of the floral print sofa and looked at him with that directness that hinted that there was more wisdom behind that gentle smile than people gave her credit for. He knew she'd realized his thoughts were far away from what they'd just been talking about. And he'd wager a year's profits she knew he'd been thinking about Josephine.

"So, Lord Rainforth. Will London be such a great shock to her?"

Ross returned her smile and lifted one brow. "Other than being a little headstrong and outspoken, Miss Foley was ready to face down London Society long before I came on the scene. Perhaps you'd care to tell me your real reason for putting both of us through this little charade. Other than to stall for the time she seemed so desperate to have."

Lady Clythebrook laughed. "I was right from the start. You're a very bright fellow. Walter would have approved most heartily."

"Approved of what? Surely you haven't attempted to play matchmaker?"

"Oh, no. I would never play matchmaker with two people's lives. At least not people I cared for. What I attempted to do was much more serious. Much more."

The warm, friendly smile on her face faded. What remained was a little glimmer of sadness. "I am ill, Lord Rainforth."

She held her hand up to stop the words of sympathy he started to speak.

"Oh, I'm not dead yet, but God has given me a glimpse of my mortality."

"Does Miss Foley know?"

"No." Lady Clythebrook smiled. "She, of course, believes I will live forever. While I don't intend to die tomorrow, neither am I so confident I will see another spring. God willing, that will give me enough time to take care of one very important detail before I die"

"Would I be wrong to assume that Miss Foley is the one detail you must see to?"

"You are very astute. I am going to tell you something I have never told anyone else. Something I doubt you'll hear from Josephine herself.

"You know Josephine came to live with us when she was quite young. For more than a year after we brought her to live with us she hoarded a portion of every meal she ate. She stuffed her pockets with anything she could manage to steal from the table when she thought we weren't watching and hid it in a small box she kept beneath her bed. We found out later the children often went to bed hungry when the orphanage did not have enough to feed them.

"When she was thirteen, she was released from the orphanage to work for one of the local merchants, a man by the name of Foster. There was nothing unusual about this as nearly all the children were fostered out by that age.

"Although new to the area, the Fosters appeared to be upstanding people and Walter approved of Josie going to live with them. She was to be a companion to Mrs. Foster, who was an invalid, and work in the shop when she wasn't needed at the house. It was exactly the future Walter envisioned for her.

"A few weeks after she was there Walter went to visit Foster with the express purpose of checking up on Josephine. Walter came home disturbed because she didn't seem happy. I laughed off his concern and told him she was probably homesick for the other children at the orphanage and in time she'd be fine.

"Neither Walter nor I gave her another thought and left soon after for London. We were gone several months and when we returned Banks greeted us with news that Josephine had run away from the Fosters and the local tenants had been searching for her."

Lady Clythebrook smoothed the lace handkerchief she'd wadded in her hand and folded it in half. "It took Walter four days to find her. She'd been hiding in the woods for more than a week." She stopped and took a breath before she continued. "Foster had…raped her. She was hurt so badly she nearly died."

Ross tried to speak but no words would come out. Rage exploded inside him. "What happened to Foster?"

"I don't know. Walter went to find him but he and his wife had already left Clytheborough. Walter tried to track him down but the reports were that he'd left England."

A gnawing started in the pit of his stomach and grew until it was a sharp pain. *Bloody hell!* She'd been raped when she was only thirteen.

"Because of her experience with Foster, she's devoted her life to the children at the orphanage, partly to protect them so what happened to her doesn't happen to any of them. But protecting them has allowed her to use them as a shield to hide behind.

"They consume every hour of her time, both day and night. But even more frightening, she's convinced herself the children fill every emotional need and she doesn't need anyone else.

"The children can only give her one kind of love," she said, resolutely lifting her chin. "She needs to be shown what she's missing and I intend to take her to London, not only to prove to the world that she's as much a daughter to me as if I'd given birth to her, but to provide her the opportunity to find another kind of love."

"You are hoping she meets someone and marries?" Ross didn't know why, but the thought that she might made him uncomfortable.

"Perhaps. Perhaps she will gain nothing more from her

experience in London than to feel young and beautiful and free for a little while. I only know if I don't force her to go now, the easiest path will be for her to stay here forever. Then, one day she'll wake up to find herself an old woman and it will be too late."

Ross stood, then walked to the window. Something bothered him but he couldn't quite put a finger on it. He turned around and saw her watching him closely. "Why are you telling me this now?"

"Because I don't want to see Josephine hurt." She lifted her chin and looked at him with grim determination. "You, Lord Rainforth, have the potential to hurt her even more than Foster hurt her."

"You think I am capable of—"

She held up her hand. "She's been able to push what Foster did to her to that secret place each of us have deep within us where we can keep our most unpleasant memories under lock and key. The scars where he whipped her have healed now and are not so noticeable. But you have the power to inflict wounds that will never heal."

The mantel clock slowly ticked away the seconds, seconds that gave Ross more time to evaluate Lady Clythebrook's words.

"You are everything she fears. You're titled. You're a rake with a regrettable reputation. You had a child by your mistress whom you ignored until now. Everything about you is a mirror image of the man who fathered her then abandoned her. And, you've come with a scheme to take the power to provide for the children out of her hands. All she has to do is put her trust in you. Do you see how difficult this is for her? Everyone she has ever trusted has nearly destroyed her. Even Walter and I failed her."

Lady Clythebrook picked up her cup and saucer again and ran one thin finger around the rim. She stopped and lifted her gaze. "I will not allow her to be hurt."

"If you're so certain keeping company with me will cause her some harm, why did you stipulate that we spend two days a week together."

"For Josephine's sake, I had to. I see how she looks at you. I see how you look at her. The air nearly ignites when the two of you are together. Whether or not you're aware of the effect you have on each other is irrelevant. Josephine recognizes it. You've given her a glimpse of something she's pretended all these years not to want or need. She's restless with feelings she can't explain and desperate to replace what Foster did to her with memories she can cherish. I had hoped that putting the two of you together would help her decide what course of action she must take.

Ross felt the blood drain from his face. He knew what Josephine's decision had been. He tried to remember the words she'd used. *I don't want to be safe. I want to be loved. Just this once.* Her goal had been to replace what Foster had done to her. And he'd given her another nightmare to lay alongside the one she'd lived with since she was thirteen years old.

Ross braced his hand against the window frame and remembered every one of his accusations. Why had he let his anger and disappointment show? Why had he thrown her past in her face as if it were a dirty piece of laundry?

He looked out the window again. He wanted her here. He wanted to hold her like he should have done last night, and comforted her. And given her something she could remember without regret. Instead, they'd parted with angry words and bitter accusations.

He looked up. She'd have to come across the meadow if she came from the orphanage. Ross swore, when she arrived, he'd take her someplace where they could be alone. Then, he'd apologize for his angry words and his harsh accusations. She deserved better.

He squeezed his eyes shut for a moment and when he opened them he saw her.

"Here she is." He watched her race through the tall grass, the blood rushing through his head as his heart thundered in his chest. He needed to make up for the way he'd treated her and tell her—

The euphoric emotions running through him faded when

she came near enough to see her face. Something was wrong. The way she ran was not the carefree movement of a woman enjoying the freedom of the outdoors. There was a sense of urgency in her gait. As if she were running from something. In fear. Every muscle in his body stiffened in warning.

"If you will excuse me, Lady Clythebrook, I think I'll go out to meet Miss Foley."

He didn't wait to hear Lady Clythebrook's reply. Josephine was close enough now that he could see her more clearly. See the terror on her face and the torn sleeve of her gown.

Ross raced from the room, covering the space down the hallway in long, panic-filled strides. He reached the foyer just as she threw open the door and rushed inside. Eyes filled with terror lifted and she saw him. She stopped. Even though she held her hand over her mouth, a small cry escaped from deep inside her that tore at Ross's insides.

Her hair was disheveled and her chest heaved as her breaths came in huge, ragged gasps she could hardly control. She blinked twice, then swiped at her tear-stained cheeks and bit down on her lower lip as if to keep it from trembling. It only made her efforts worse. Her wide eyes stared at him, the look of fear still evident in her gaze.

He slowly took a step toward her lest he frighten her more, then another. He didn't stop until he was close enough to touch her.

He looked at her, determining what his action should be; whether to reach out to comfort her or give her time and space to be on her own.

He chose the former.

He placed one finger beneath her chin and lifted, taking in the red welt still raw on her cheek. "Are you all right?

She nodded.

There was no way to put the relief he felt into words. "Who did this to you?" he asked, quick boiling anger resurfacing inside him.

She shook her head.

"Who?"

"I…fell."

The panicked look on her face stopped him from questioning her further. Now was not the time. He knew she'd run away from him if he continued his interrogation. So, in a slow, careful movement, he pushed the outer door closed with one hand and brought her up against him with the other. He wrapped his arms around her narrow shoulders and cradled her close. Her cheek lay against his chest, the top of her head nestled beneath his chin. Without prodding, she wrapped her arms around his waist and held onto him as if he were her safe harbor in a storm.

Her gown was torn at the shoulder and the mark across her cheek looked like it had been made by a hand. But otherwise she didn't appear harmed. At least, not in any way that was visible.

They stood in each other's embrace several long, silent moments, until her trembling calmed and her breathing slowed. When he was assured she had recovered, he placed his hands on her shoulders and held her in front of him far enough so he could look into her eyes. "Is this all he did to you?"

Her gaze hit the floor and she nodded.

"You're sure?

She took a fortifying breath that shuddered when she released it. "Yes."

He held her for a little while longer before she stepped away from him. His arms felt strangely empty with her gone. "Go upstairs and put some cold water on your face. You'll feel better after you wash and change."

He saw her worried glance move to the morning room where Lady Clythebrook waited for them. "I'll tell Lady Clythebrook you tore your dress and need to change. I'll wait for you here."

"I can't—"

"You're sadly mistaken if you think I intend to overlook what just happened to you."

"Nothing happened."

"Enough happened. Now, go upstairs and change. I'll tell Lady Clythebrook we're going for a ride. Then I'll wait for you.

"It was noth—"

"Go," he ordered and watched her turn away from him and climb the stairs. He didn't know who was responsible for the welt across her cheek and terror in her eyes. But when he found out, he vowed they'd pay dearly for what they'd done to her.

Chapter 17

JOSIE PACED HER ROOM, dreading having to go back downstairs to face him. She'd already sent a note asking him to leave. He'd sent an answer back in a heavy, bold script that reminded her of the expression on his face. He gave her fifteen minutes or he was coming up to get her. She had less than five minutes before her time was up.

She'd known facing him would be difficult enough after the night they'd spent together, but what happened today only made it worse. If she told him Baron Lindville was responsible for her reddened cheek, he'd want to know why. How could she tell him she'd refused to be a part of the smuggling ring any longer and Lindville wouldn't take no for an answer?

And he'd never believe that she didn't know they were smuggling in opium. What sane person would believe she'd been a major player in the smuggling operation all this time and didn't know what was being brought in? No, he could never find out she'd been involved. Did she honestly think he'd save her from being hanged just because they'd been lovers?

Did she think he wouldn't accuse her of sleeping with him to protect herself in case he found out?

Josie clasped her hands to her cheeks and felt the burning heat seep into her palms. Oh, why had she taken him to Granny's cottage and given herself to him? She'd told herself it had been because she'd wanted him to erase the memories of the night she'd been raped. But that wasn't the reason. She'd slept with him because she'd fallen in love with him.

She wanted to laugh. How had this happened? She'd been so sure she'd never fall in love. But without knowing when or why, it had. She'd fallen into the trap that had destroyed her mother.

Her heart ached inside her chest. Oh, if she'd had to fall in love, why, oh, why, did it have to be him? He was everything she could never trust.

A knot formed in the pit of her stomach. She was such a fool. She thought that giving herself to him once would be enough to last her a lifetime? But it wouldn't. Loving him once only made her want him again. Even today, she'd never been so glad to see anyone in her whole life as she'd been to see him when she raced through the front door. When he took that first step toward her and opened his arms, she couldn't rush into his embrace fast enough. And when he wrapped his arms around her, she suddenly felt safe. As if this was where she belonged.

Josie took the bonnet she'd laid out on the corner of her bed and walked to the mirror on her dressing table. The red mark was nearly gone now. She was glad. At least it wouldn't be there to infuriate him further. She reached for a pair of gloves that matched the light blue gown she'd changed into and left her room.

The gown was one of her better dresses and Lady Clythebrook had always told her the color brought out the blue of her eyes. Josie hoped she was right. She would need every advantage today.

She took three steps down the long staircase and stopped. He was waiting for her at the bottom, his thick brows drawn close in the center. His lips, which usually bore a resemblance to a smile in the process of widening, were clamped tight. Even from the middle of the staircase, she noticed the knotted muscle at the base of his jaw that worked in frustration. He was angry. His eyes told her he was. His rigid demeanor re-emphasized it. And his wide stance and the knotted fists at his side left no room for doubt.

Josie lifted her chin and readied herself to face him. "Lord Rainforth." She took the final steps with a graceful ease she far from felt. "I must insist we postpone our meeting today. My regrettable behavior earlier was an overreaction to a minor incident. It was nothing you need to concern yourself—"

Josie's sentence went unfinished when Rainforth snatched her cloak out of Banks's hands and draped it around her shoulders. Without a by-your-leave, he placed a firm hand beneath her elbow and led her to the door.

"I must insist—"

"Save your breath, Josephine. It won't do you any good."

He ushered her out the door and to his waiting carriage. There was no groomsman to open the door or assist her inside, so he helped her himself.

He jumped in beside her and with an angry snap of the reins, the horses lurched forward. The feel of his taut, muscular frame jostling against her burned through each layer of her skirts to her flesh beneath, and she realized this would be one of the longest rides she'd ever taken.

She kept her eyes focused on the passing scenery, but concentrated her gaze more to the right where she didn't have to look at him. Not that he was looking at her. He was too angry. His eyes remained fixed on the road ahead of him.

The horses moved at a faster pace than she was used to traveling on these roads. The steady clopping would turn into an all-out gallop if he snapped the reins once more and gave the two bays their heads. She knew he was itching to do just that—release his frustration by racing through the countryside with the wind slapping him in the face. But he didn't. He kept the horses under the same tight rein as he kept any effort at conversation.

His silence unnerved her. She gripped her fingers around the edge of the soft leather seat, vowing to allow him thirty more seconds of brooding silence before forcing the issue.

Her resolve didn't last that long.

"You might as well begin your interrogation," she said, noticing that they'd neared the meadow close to Granny's cottage. "That's the reason for this ride and we both know it."

"Do you intend to answer my questions if I ask them?"

"No."

"Then, pray tell, woman, why on earth should I ask them?"

"Because if you don't, you're going to erupt."

He pulled the horses to a stop so sudden that it threw her forward. His arm shot out to protect her and she grabbed onto him.

"Who struck you?"

She loosened her grip and pulled back. "I fell."

"Don't do this, Josie. Was it Lindville?"

"Lindville? Why would you think—" She tried to force a smile. "Oh, the flowers. You think we had another lover's quarrel and—"

"He's not your lover. You don't have a lover. That's what you used me for."

The air left her body. For a long moment, no words would come. "I didn't use you. That isn't what…"

She couldn't let him think that. She couldn't let him cheapen what they'd shared by thinking she'd used him to make love to her.

"Then why?"

They were just two small words, but he'd said them in such a way he'd made their meaning monumental. She started to answer, then closed her mouth. A gentle breeze whipped the ribbons of her bonnet around her face but she didn't move to hold them down. Nor did she make an attempt to answer his question.

"Why me? I know I wasn't the first man to have you, but I would wager St. Stephen's and the land where I intend to put the cattle that I was the second."

She looked down at his hands gripped tightly around the reins. Those were the hands that had held her and touched her and made all the ugly, painful abuses she'd suffered from another man's hands vanish.

She slowly lifted her gaze to his face. She wanted to reach out and erase the deep furrows across his forehead. She wanted to whisper gentle shushing sounds to ease his anger and ask him, *who else but you?* There would never be anyone else.

"Would you at least tell me why?"

She swallowed hard, then lifted her chin and took the biggest chance of her life. She offered him an explanation that exposed every weakness she possessed. "Because I knew I could trust you. I knew you would never hurt me."

He sucked in a breath so harsh it was as if she'd struck him.

She knew she owed him an explanation but it was so hard to say the words. She'd never said them to anyone. Not even to Lady Clythebrook.

"You're right. You weren't the first. The man who took my virginity, took it by force." She paused. "I never thought I'd ever want to give myself to anyone again. Then you came."

Josie dropped back against the cushion and clasped her hands in her lap. "If only Lady Clythebrook hadn't stipulated the time we had to spend together. If only I could have battled you on even terms."

"What terms would those have been?"

"The children. The orphanage." She turned toward him. "Charlie. It was easy to keep you at arm's length as long as I felt I needed to protect Charlie from you. If only you would have remained the villain."

But I fell in love with you and everything changed.

Josie lifted her gaze and followed a small wren that flew past her and darted to a small copse of trees where it sat on one of the branches. "Everyone knew Carrie Gardner had been your mistress. When Charlie was born a few months after she'd arrived, we knew he was yours. Which made you exactly like the man who'd gotten my mother with child then abandoned her." She pulled at a string on her worn cloak. "Until I discovered you never knew about Charlie. And that you wanted to be a father to him."

She followed the wren as it flew from the trees to the roof of

Granny's cottage, then she turned and looked into his eyes. A hooded expression masked whatever he might be thinking.

"And still you tried to keep Charlie from me."

She nodded. "You were everything I feared. Even your reputation warned me against you."

"But he was my son."

She paused as she looked deeper into his eyes. "I couldn't let that matter. I'm all they have. If I fail them, they have no one else. Can you understand that?"

He took a deep breath and nodded his head as if he understood something that had been a mystery before. "Yes, I can. When did you change your mind about me?"

"I don't know. Perhaps the first time I saw you with Charlie. Perhaps even before that. When I introduced you to the children and realized you didn't treat them like I expected you to. Perhaps at Lady Clythebrook's dinner when you looked into Squire Pearson's eyes and told him how sorry you were his nephew had died in the war. And you meant it."

"That's what made you decide that I would be the one you gave yourself to?"

Josie turned her head away from his penetrating gaze. "No. That just happened."

"Was there any emotion involved in what you did?"

She turned back. "Emotion? Such as what? Affection? Of course."

She forced herself not to lower her gaze. "But don't expect me to say I love you. I learned very little at my mother's knee, but I did learn one very important lesson. Loving a member of the nobility leads to nothing but disaster and heartache."

"I see," he said, sitting taller in the seat. "Never love."

She saw the stunned expression on his face and knew admitting that she cared for him would be the biggest mistake of her life. "Don't tell me that's what you expected from me? Have all the women you've met been so enamored of you that they fall at your feet in blind adoration?"

"No, not all. Not even some of those who shared my bed professed to love me. But I always thought I knew the difference."

Josie watched him lean toward her. Her heart thundered in her ears. She knew he intended to kiss her. He cupped his hand to her cheek and brought his mouth down on hers.

Josie knew it would do no good to deny him. This was a test to which he needed an answer. He wanted to prove to her that what they'd shared had meant more than she would admit. He wanted to prove that what they'd shared had been far more than affection. But she already knew it had.

She just couldn't allow him to know it.

She remained limp beneath his grasp, her hands lifeless in her lap and her lips unmoving beneath his. Surely he would give up soon and release her? Surely if she didn't participate she would convince him his kisses meant nothing to her? But he didn't give up.

His fingers loosened the ribbons that tied her bonnet, then pulled it from her head and dropped it to the carriage floor. When his hand was empty, he skimmed his palm up her arm and over her shoulder, then wrapped his long, capable fingers around her nape and pulled her closer. For a few long, agonizing seconds she held her resolve, even when he held her head so close to him she shared her breaths with him. Her head spun, her heart thundered in her breast. Then it was too late.

He deepened his kiss as if he were starving for the taste of her. His lips moved over hers while his hands caressed her with unbelievable tenderness. And she was lost to him. When his mouth opened atop hers, she followed his lead and accepted his intrusion.

His tongue met hers, touching, then mating in a ritual that sent rational thought spiraling into the wind. Common sense no longer existed within her, only a need that was desperate to be assuaged. Only the pulsing, aching desires he'd awakened the night she'd given herself to him.

His hand covered her breast and she arched into him. He

was dangerously close to her and every promise she'd made to remain immune to his touch was suddenly null and void. His other hand held her closer still while he assaulted her with one mind-altering kiss after another.

If making love with him had been the biggest mistake of her life, then giving him her heart had been far worse. But it was too late to change the course she'd taken. She wrapped her arms around his neck and pulled him closer. When she skimmed her fingers over his shoulders, the muscles across his back rippled beneath her fingers and with a moan that matched hers he deepened his kisses.

"I need you," he said, burying his head in the crook of her neck.

She tried to pretend she didn't understand what he meant but she did. She knew only too well. Granny's cottage was only a short distance away and before she could utter a word of protest, the reins were in his hands and the horses were trotting across the meadow.

He stopped the pair in front of the door and jumped to the ground. His hands trembled slightly when he reached out for her. If she were going to stop him, now was the time. All she had to do was stay in the carriage and refuse to go inside. Instead, she stepped into his arms and walked through Granny's door with him.

The curtains were drawn together and the cottage was shrouded in shadows but he didn't light a candle. He closed the door behind them and pulled her into his arms. A voice inside her head echoed that she still had time to run from him but the warnings were forgotten the second his mouth came down on hers.

Between kisses they undressed each other, then lay down on the bed. He kissed her cheeks and her neck, then moved lower to her breasts. His hands caressed her flesh with loving tenderness, burning her skin as he blazed a hundred paths across every inch of her. When he came over her she opened her arms and welcomed him into her body.

They both rode the wild waves of passion and desire and made unfathomable discoveries. With her arms clasped tight around him and her body arched, she shattered into a million pieces. She told herself the tears streaming down her cheeks weren't tears of sorrow, but tears of joy. Except she knew she'd lost a piece of her heart and she would never be whole again.

"Josie," he said, rolling off her and bracing himself on one elbow. He stared down at her and brushed one finger over her damp cheek where the tear had made a path.

She turned away from him but he brought her head back with a finger against her jaw.

"Look at me."

Josie lifted her gaze.

"No regrets. Not ever. Not with what is happening between us."

More tears swam in her eyes, his face a watery outline that had no form.

"You were right the first time you gave yourself to me. You can always trust me not to hurt you. Just as you can trust me to protect you."

She wanted to look at him but couldn't. She focused on a spot beyond his shoulder instead.

"Did Lindville strike you?"

She made a move to slide away from him but he wouldn't let her.

"Look at me."

She didn't want to meet his gaze but the tone of his voice gave her little choice. Even through the softness there was a low rumble that resembled an angry growl.

"What possible reason could he have had to strike you?"

His eyes were intense as they looked at her, then blackened with fury as if a thought just occurred to him.

"Did it have something to do with the land? Did he threaten you to stop me from going forward with the plan to bring in cattle?"

She knew the moment he realized that's what had happened. The shocked expression on his face was openly hostile. She wasn't going to say anything but couldn't keep from voicing her accusation. "Did you just realize that someone other than yourself could be affected by what you intended to do?"

His scowl darkened. "Stay away from him, Josie. He's connected with the smuggling. I can't prove it yet, but when I can, he'll pay for his crime at the end of a rope. And so will everyone else who's involved."

She couldn't breathe. She had to make sure the man lying next to her never found out she'd been one of the band of smugglers.

She took several slow breaths, having already decided what she had to do. She knew with unerring certainty that there would never be another shipment of smuggled goods. Just as she knew this would be the last time she gave herself to him.

She turned her head and met his gaze squarely. "What happened to me is not important. Even what we just shared is of little consequence in the grand scheme of things."

"How can you say that?"

"Easily. You are still the Marquess of Rainforth and I am my mother's daughter. Nothing will ever change that."

"And if who you are doesn't matter to me?"

"Then you are lying to yourself."

Neither of them said anything for quite a while, she, because any other words would only prove how much she wanted such an admission to be wrong. He, because her answer had closed the door with such finality there was no room to maneuver closer.

He would always be the Marquess of Rainforth.

The bastard had hit her.

In all the scenarios Ross had let play out in his mind, not once had he thought anyone else might be in danger because of his plan to bring in cattle. The mark on Josephine Foley's face told him how wrong he'd been.

Was this why she'd been so opposed to his plan from the

start? Had she been threatened from the beginning, and if she had, what leverage had been used? Lady Clythebrook's safety? The children's?

The stark look on her face when he took her home flashed through his mind. The afternoon still had an hour or more before dusk came, but when he walked her to the door and watched her go inside, the darkness that consumed his soul made him feel as if the sun had already faded from the sky.

"Don't expect me to say I love you…You are still the Marquess of Rainforth and I am my mother's daughter."

Her words pressed against him with the aching finality of a death knell.

Ross pushed the team toward home. What difference did it make if he were a marquess and she her mother's daughter? He'd learned long ago that members of Society were the only ones to whom it mattered. He'd also found out how quickly and easily one could fall from their good graces and how difficult it was to make amends. If it were not for his son, he wouldn't be making the effort now to redeem the Bennett name, and the Rainforth legacy. For himself he didn't care. Whether or not Society approved of the woman he loved mattered even less.

Ross pulled the team to a halt in front of his home and jumped from the carriage more determined than ever of the need to convince Josie that her fears were unfounded. He handed the reins to a groomsman and covered the distance to the door in long anxious strides. The door opened before he reached for the knob and Benedict stood in the entryway, ready to take Ross's hat and gloves.

"There's a gentleman to see you, sir. He says it's important. I showed him to the library."

"Thank you, Benedict."

Ross went down the hall to the library and opened the door. The man had been seated in a chair and stood when Ross entered.

"Lord Rainforth?"

Ross nodded.

"Lieutenant Joshua Honeywell, sir. Major Bennett sent me. I'm to give you this."

The man held out an envelope and Ross took it. "Are you to wait for a reply?"

"No, sir. I'll be returning to London right away."

"You'll eat something first," Ross said, calling for Benedict to show the man to the kitchen.

When he was alone, Ross sat down at his desk and broke the seal. The letter was from Sam and identified by the crest he always used.

Ross tore open the envelope and scanned the writing. It was in the code Sam had created when they were young. The same code his father had used to sell military secrets to the Russians. Ross ignored the chill that shivered through him and took out a pen and paper to decipher the message. A few minutes later he put his pen down on the desk and read the message again. An unidentified source had informed them that a shipment of opium was due in London in three days' time, which meant it would arrive here any day. Sam and McCormick would leave as soon as they could make the necessary arrangements and should be here sometime tomorrow, which was Wednesday. In the meantime, they wanted Ross to keep a close watch on the cove and report anything that seemed suspicious.

Ross locked the message away in a drawer in his desk and sat down before the blazing fire.

The time had finally come—his chance to make up for all his father had done. His chance to redeem his name so he and his son could walk amongst the nobility of London with their heads high.

And nothing would stop him.

Chapter 18

JOSIE STARED AT THE MESSAGE in her hands. It arrived as they all did—by special messenger. It was written on the same paper as usual—rough, inexpensive parchment, and penned in Captain Levy's familiar hand—bold and difficult to decipher. The arrival of the letter had always filled her with a new sense of anticipation. An excitement at knowing that for a while longer the children would not go without.

This time reading the instructions made her stomach turn. This time she knew there wouldn't just be supplies for the people of Clytheborough, but a shipment of opium that would leave here and go to London where the deadly drug would destroy more innocent lives. Her blood ran cold.

She'd thought of little else since Rainforth had told her someone was smuggling opium. The decision of *what* to do had been easy. *How* to accomplish it was another matter. She finally had the answer.

She read the message again. She'd been expecting the shipment, so the instructions weren't a surprise. Only this time there'd been a change of plans. The shipment wouldn't be arriving on a Thursday night as it usually did, but tomorrow night—Wednesday. The change would actually work to her advantage.

She sat down behind the desk and pulled out a clean sheet of paper. She needed to put her plan in motion. There was a certain amount of risk involved, but if everything went the way it should, this would be the last shipment to come in and no one would be the wiser.

She'd only met Captain Levy once, but she'd gathered from that first meeting that he wasn't the kind of person to take unnecessary chances. Nor would he willingly risk his ship and his crew if he thought there was the possibility they would all be arrested and hanged. She was counting on that. If she was wrong, she would fail and she'd have to face a short future at the end of a rope.

Josie read the message from Captain Levy once more to make certain of the Wednesday delivery, then dipped her pen into the ink well and wrote a note she would send to Lindville in the morning. The message contained only two words, but he would know what they meant.

THURSDAY – MIDNIGHT

She folded Lindville's message and tucked it into her skirt pocket, then threw the original message in the grate and watched it burn. She didn't want there to be any evidence left behind to prove what she'd done. She stopped short at the knock on the door and stepped away from the tell-tale ashes. The door opened and Jenny peeked her head around the corner.

"Lord Rainforth is here. He says he'd like to see you."

A slight hitch caught in her chest and she looked out the window. It was nearly dark outside. "Send him in, Jenny."

"Will you want anything else, Miss Josie?"

"No. I'm almost ready to leave. I doubt Lord Rainforth will be here long."

"Very well, miss."

Jenny left and Josie stared at the door unable to move. She hadn't expected to see him any more today. Not after this afternoon.

The door opened and he stepped into the room. He seemed to take up all the air and dominate the space that suddenly seemed much smaller. This was the man to whom she'd given herself.

The man whose kisses scattered her resolve to the four winds, whose touch made her flesh burn with desire. Whose lovemaking had caused her to cry out for release. Her cheeks turned hot remembering what had passed between them. He closed the door and looked at her.

"I wanted to make sure you were all right."

"I'm fine."

He walked across the room and stopped when he reached her desk.

"Would you mind if I sat down?"

"Of course not."

He waited until she sat then lowered himself to one of the chairs in front of the desk.

He'd changed since she'd seen him earlier. His face was smooth as if he'd shaved before coming and she was caught again by how handsome he was.

"I went to Clythebrook Manor first but was told you'd left before dinner."

"I ate here with the children."

"Lady Clythebrook said she didn't know when to expect you. When I hinted that I might go to the orphanage, she said I should tell you she was retiring for the night and wouldn't be up when you came in. Do you do this often?"

"When there's an emergency I need to handle. Sometimes late in the evening is the only time it's quiet enough to get anything done."

"Who makes sure you get home?"

She wanted to laugh. "No one, Lord Rainforth. I'm perfectly capable of—"

"My name is Ross. Don't you think enough has passed between us for you to call me by my given name?"

She swallowed hard. "You know I can't."

"Can't? Or won't?"

When she didn't answer, he leaned back in his chair. "You won't let yourself forget who I am, will you?"

"You can never be anything but what you are, my lord. How can I forget it?"

Whatever strange emotion connected the two of them, it seemed stronger tonight than it ever had. Maybe because they'd spent more than an hour in each other's arms earlier in the day. Maybe because willingly giving your body to someone forms a closeness that cannot be explained. Maybe because realizing you've fallen in love forces you to see everything so much differently.

Josie pushed back against her chair because it was suddenly important to keep as much distance from him as possible.

"You shouldn't be here. Please, go home."

He rested the ankle of one foot atop his other knee as if settling in for the duration. "Not until you're ready. I have my carriage outside."

"That's not necessary."

"It isn't? You may have forgotten the mark on your cheek from this afternoon but I haven't."

"I already explained—"

"No, you didn't. And I'd wager you have no intention of explaining."

He stood and the room shrank around her. Even though the desk separated them, she felt as though she needed a wall. A very high, thick wall.

"I've told you who I think was responsible, but you—"

Whatever else he was going to say went unfinished. There was a soft rapping sound and the door opened. Vicar Chadwick walked into the room.

"Miss Foley. They told me I'd still find you here. I was wondering if—"The vicar stopped. "Lord Rainforth. What a surprise."

The marquess turned. "Vicar Chadwick. Good evening. I came to escort Miss Foley home."

"How thoughtful. Yes, quite the thing."

"Did you just return from London?" Josie asked, trying to focus the attention away from her.

"Only moments ago. I left some papers unfinished before I left last week and thought I'd pick them up on my way to the vicarage."

"Would you like some tea? I'm sure Cook still has some of the tarts left from supper."

"No. I'm fine. I would like a glass of sherry, though. Would you care to join me, Lord Rainforth?"

The marquess nodded. "Thank you."

"Miss Foley?"

"Just a small glass."

Vicar Chadwick went to a small cupboard against the wall and took a bottle out of a drawer, then filled three glasses. When he brought them back, he gave each one a glass and they sat before the fire that still glowed.

"You just returned from London?" Rainforth asked.

Josie watched for some hint of longing that he might be anxious for any news from the City but she didn't see it in his expression. Neither did she hear it in his voice.

"Yes. What an exciting place. But I have to admit I long for the peacefulness of the country after a few days. Do you find that too, my lord?"

"I quite enjoy it here," Rainforth said, taking a sip of his sherry. "London can be suffocating at times."

"I know what you mean. There's always something stirring. Right now it's all the talk of the illegal drugs that are coming in."

Josie felt a cold chill sweep over her.

"I even heard some news that will be of special interest to you, Rainforth. Quite exciting. The Queen has set up a new force to combat the rising drug problem and has appointed Major Samuel Bennett to head the program. He's your cousin, isn't he?"

"Yes. The major and I grew up together."

"An impressive fellow. I was fortunate enough to hear him speak before an assembly. The populace is quite concerned over the illegal trafficking of opium and he assured everyone that the government is doing everything in its power to see that anyone involved is brought to justice. I walked away from the meeting feeling much safer knowing someone so capable is combating such a monumental problem. Has the major confided in you at all? Do they have any clues at all as to who is behind the smuggling?"

"I'm sure I wouldn't know. I've been away from London for months now."

"Of course. Of course. At any rate, with Major Bennett in charge, I am confident the problem will cease shortly."

Vicar Chadwick set his empty sherry glass down on the table and reached into his pocket. He pulled out a red gumdrop and popped it into his mouth. "Well, it's been a long day and I'm more than ready to retire."

Rainforth walked the vicar to the door, and Josie stared at the dying embers in the fireplace. Major Samuel Bennett wasn't someone to be taken lightly. She'd forgotten he and Rainforth were cousins. If Rainforth was in the major's confidence, perhaps it wasn't a coincidence that he'd been watching the cove for anything suspicious.

Josie's blood ran cold. Tomorrow night couldn't come fast enough. She needed to stop the smuggling before opium took one more life. She needed to stop the shipments before the man with whom she'd fallen in love discovered that she was involved in the smuggling.

"Is something wrong?"

Josie snapped up her head to find him standing in front of the desk. She didn't know how long he'd been watching her or how much he'd said that she hadn't heard. "No, everything's fine." She fumbled to put the papers she'd been working on in a drawer then stood. "Are you ready to go?"

She grabbed her cloak from the hook against the wall and stepped toward him. He took it from her and placed it around her shoulders. His hands didn't leave her.

"You're shaking."

"Just a shiver. I'm fine."

"It'll be over soon," he said, wrapping his arms around her and pulling her back against him. "Don't worry, I won't let anything happen to you."

Josie's heart turned in her chest. What she wouldn't give to stay in his arms like this forever. But she couldn't. And letting herself think she could was only asking for trouble.

"It's getting late. We should be going."

He released her and banked the fire while she extinguished the lanterns and they left the room.

"Would you take me up to see him?"

She stopped and looked at him. "The children are in bed. He's probably asleep."

"I know. I'd just like to see him before we leave."

Josie felt a knot press against her heart. She remembered the only time the man who'd fathered her had come. Her mother had dressed her in her finest dress, telling her as she curled her hair and put bright blue ribbons in it that when her papa saw how pretty she was, he'd come back to them. But when the man came, he refused to even look at her. He fired some harsh, angry words at her mother, then threw a thick envelope on the table and left. She'd always imagined Rainforth would be the same, but that was before she'd met him. Before she'd given herself to him. And her heart weighed heavier in her breast. The real Marquess of Rainforth wasn't at all like she'd painted him.

Josie led the way up the stairs and stopped in front of the room where Charlie slept. There were three beds in the room and thankfully only two to a bed right now. When it was very crowded, the smaller children would sleep three and even more in a bed. She took one of the small lanterns from the hallway and stepped inside.

Charlie was in the bed nearest the window and Josie led the marquess over to where he slept. When she reached him she set down the lamp on the bedside table where it cast a soft glow on the sleeping child and stood beside the marquess.

"He looks so fragile."

She smiled. "He isn't. Believe me. He's always in the thick of any sport the children play. Quite accomplished at catching the ball. He's usually one of the first to be chosen when the children select teams."

"I've missed so much," he whispered and Josie heard the longing in his voice.

"His best friend is little Robbie," she said, motioning toward the other little body sharing his bed. And he's Glenda's champion. Glenda's small and walks with a limp from an accident when she was very tiny. He always makes sure she's on his team and helps her run when she gets tired. He has a fondness for animals and his favorite dessert is peach cobbler," she whispered.

"I will see to it that he has a puppy and that peach trees are abundant in the orchards at St. Stephen's."

Josie smiled then stood in silence while the marquess studied his son.

For a long time he didn't move, then, he knelt down beside the sleeping child and, with a trembling hand, brushed a strand of hair from his forehead. He placed his fingers gently against Charlie's cheek and stroked it as if his flesh were made of silk, then picked up Charlie's small hand and placed it in his own. The contrast in size gave the perfect comparison of how much the young boy still needed his father's strength and protection.

"He looks…so perfect."

"He is. The world hasn't had time to spoil him yet."

The marquess lovingly brushed his hand across Charlie's forehead once more then rose. There was a soft look on his face as he watched his son sleep and the lump in her throat grew larger. The wall she'd erected to keep the hurt away crumbled and she felt herself weakening. A voice from deep inside her issued a warning to keep her distance from him but she ignored it. Instead, she did the worst thing imaginable. She reached out and took his hand in hers.

Huge tears filled his eyes, then spilled over his lashes and ran down his face, but he didn't brush them away. He squeezed her fingers tighter while the tears ran unabashedly down his face.

Josie's heart ached until she thought it might break. The barrier she'd erected to protect herself crumbled even more when he wrapped his arm around her shoulder and held her close to him. If she hadn't been sure before, she knew in that moment it was far too late to stop herself from loving a man who had the power to destroy her.

Ross paced to the window and looked down the lane, waiting for any sign that Sam and McCormick were here. Sam had written to expect them Wednesday and it was nearing four o'clock in the afternoon. He expected them any moment. They wouldn't want to miss the shipment if it came tonight.

His blood raced in his veins and his heart pounded in his chest. The time had finally come when he could accomplish what he'd set out to do; when he could erase at least some of the black marks against his name. Knowing that he'd helped to save one life from the deadly drugs the smugglers were bringing into the country was the first step in redeeming the Rainforth name.

One was not such a monumental number, but it was the first step to make up for the many his father had taken. Only when the smugglers were stopped could his son grow up proud to be a Bennett. And proud to have the Marquess of Rainforth as his father.

Watching his son as he slept had made him realize how desperately he wanted Charlie to be proud of him. Standing with Josephine Foley's hand nestled solidly in his made him realize how much he wanted to spend the rest of his life with her.

He nearly laughed out loud. He didn't know when he knew he wanted her as his wife. Perhaps when she'd stood up to him the first time he'd come to the orphanage to find his son and wouldn't back down. Perhaps when she hid his son from him to protect the boy. If not then, then certainly it had been at the dinner party when Lady Lindville had openly tried to discredit him and she'd come to his aid.

But if not then, it had been the night they'd made love and she'd trusted him with not only her body, but her heart. From that moment on, he'd known he couldn't live another day without her.

Ross paced across the room and back, then looked out the window to the drive leading from the lane. Two men rode toward the house.

Ross turned toward the door and waited until Sam and McCormick entered the room.

"What have you found out?" Sam asked before he'd barely tasted the whiskey Ross had offered them.

Ross fought the rush of excitement. "I know where and I'm sure I know who. The when is a guess, but my suggestion would be that the two of you get something to eat then rest awhile. I can almost promise you it's going to be a bloody long night.

Chapter 19

Ross crouched behind the boulder near the cliffs and watched the three small boats come ashore. He was struck again by how absolutely perfect this spot was. Someone had scouted the area and chosen this particular site with smuggling in mind.

If the ship carrying the contraband anchored far enough out to sea—as this one had—the sharp rise of the cliffs hid a narrow strip of water where smaller boats could come ashore without being detected. Only one spot provided an unobstructed view of what was going on below—the spot where Ross sat right now.

Unfortunately, there was no way for anyone to reach the smugglers from this high up, which was why Sam and McCormick and the dozen or so men they'd brought with them were posted down below on either side of the area. This put them at the disadvantage of not being able to see what was going on, but close enough so when Ross gave the signal, they could converge on the smugglers and arrest them before they could escape.

Ross looked down at the flares at his feet and bent to pick one up. He'd waited more than a month for this night to happen. He couldn't believe he'd been given the chance to do something good to make up for all the evil his father had done. Not that he would have cared two months ago if his name were connected with the capture and prosecution of the smugglers. But he had a son to consider now. He needed to give Charlie a name he could be proud of.

He looked up to the sky. It was a perfect night. The moon was full and the area shone so bright he could almost see the expressions on the sailors' faces as they rowed the boats ashore.

Ross remembered his conversation with Josie about a full, 'magical' moon. Tonight would be a night of magic and miracles. A night when he would start a new life with Josie at his side. Together they would provide a stable, loving home for Charlie, and perhaps even a baby brother or sister in a year's time.

Ross thought of the two times he'd lain with her and felt a rush of something he never thought he'd feel. Perhaps a babe already grew inside her. Perhaps they'd have a daughter who'd have Josie's bright eyes and golden beauty. Or, if not a daughter, then another son blessed with Josie's winning smile and sharp intelligence.

Lady Clythebrook had wanted to take her to London to experience a part of life she would never know if she stayed here in Clytheborough. Well, he intended to take her to London too, but not just to see the sights. He would take her as his wife.

He'd introduce her to the cream of Society and escort her to the theater and the opera and ball after ball. He'd dress her in the finest clothes money could buy and shower her with so much love and affection it would shock everyone who'd known him before. He'd prove to all the skeptics who didn't think it was possible for him to be faithful to one woman how wrong they'd been.

And if she wanted, he'd stand at her side when she met her father. For no other reason than that the man would know how much he'd given up when he'd abandoned her.

Ross looked over the cliff to watch the progress. His heart raced faster in anticipation. Two sailors manned each boat and were close enough that Ross could see their cargo. From what Sam had discovered, the opium would come in small bundles about a foot square. The raw opium was wrapped in poppy leaves and cotton to keep it dry and was relatively light weight and easy to transport. Only one of the boats looked like its cargo fit that description. Ross watched that boat with particular interest.

When the boats reached the sandy beach, six men jumped out. The captain said something to the men then walked toward the mouth of the cave in front of him. Ross leaned forward, hoping whoever the captain was talking to would step far enough out in the open to be recognized, but he didn't.

Ross suspected it was Lindville. Every detail he'd learned about the smuggling operation made Lindville the prime candidate, from his adamant objection to Ross using the land, to the red mark he was sure Lindville had put on Josie's face. Even if redeeming his name wasn't reason enough to put a stop to the smuggling, keeping Josie safe from Lindville's threats was.

Ross rolled the long, heavy flare between his fingers, but didn't light the wick. Sam had been very explicit in his instructions not to send the signal too soon. Ross was to wait until the men were busy unloading the opium bundles so there would be little chance any of them could escape. It was important that they catch *everyone* involved, from the captain who brought the opium ashore, to the person at the head of the smuggling ring. Oh, yes. Especially the person who was the mastermind behind the smuggling operation—the person standing below him right now.

The captain came out of the shadows and walked to the men guarding the shipment. Ross pulled the matches from his pocket and took one from the box. It was almost time. He stayed where he could see every movement from below and held the match steady, ready to light. The minute the men unloaded the last of the opium, he'd set off the flare so Sam and McCormick could converge on the smugglers and make the arrest. It was a well-planned operation, guaranteed to put everyone involved swinging from the end of a rope.

Ross stayed ready. He swiped his damp palms against his pant legs. It was happening. The moment he'd been waiting for was unfolding before his eyes.

The captain turned back and said something to the person standing in the shadows, then motioned to his men. There was a scurrying from below. One of the men picked up the first bundle of opium and carried it ashore.

Ross stuck the flare into the ground and waited. His heart thundered in his chest as he watched the boat containing the opium empty. It was nearly time. He'd been given a second chance to redeem his name and nothing would stop him. Charlie's future depended on it.

When one of the sailors lifted the last bundle out of the boat, Ross struck the match and turned to light the flare.

A movement from below drew his attention and he glanced down just as the person hiding in the shadows stepped into the moonlight. Recognition hit him with a force so painful it nearly took him to his knees.

He closed his eyes, praying that when he opened them Josie wouldn't be standing below with the full, 'magical' moon illumining her features and the last bundle of opium passing before her. He froze, unable to breathe; unable to move.

Light the flare! a voice inside him ordered. But he couldn't.

Blood roared through his head, pounding against his ears like great clashes of thunder that stole the air form his lungs. Every part of his body was numb with shock and disbelief.

Light the flare!

He'd imagined so many different outcomes to tonight, the best being the smugglers would be captured and all would end well. The worst, that a gun battle would break out and someone would be injured, perhaps even killed. But not once had he thought he'd have to choose between his family's honor and the woman he loved.

Light the flare!

Ross looked down onto the sandy beach. Josie stood like a sentinel while the men around her unloaded the rest of the smuggled contraband. They were nearly finished. If he was going to send the signal he had to do it now.

He turned his gaze back to the flare at his feet. Then stopped.

How could he light the flare, then live with himself when the woman he loved was hanged for her part in the smuggling?

Ross didn't feel the match burn his fingers. He dropped the charred stick to the ground where it flickered and died—along with any hope he had to redeem his name.

A painful grip tightened in his chest. He pulled air into his lungs and pushed it back out even though his body didn't want to function any more. Every instinct he possessed warned him to turn away from what was happening but he couldn't lift his gaze.

The small boats were unloaded now. There was still time to light the flare but he had to do it now.

Now.

Instead, he was unable to move as if he were a marble statue.

The men pushed the small boats away from shore and still he didn't move. He watched as their outlines became smaller and smaller and smaller, and finally disappeared.

At last he tore his gaze away from the ship sailing out of the cove and looked back to where Josie had been. She was nowhere in sight. She'd undoubtedly gone back into the cave where the smuggled goods were stored.

He tried to imagine what she was doing. Perhaps counting the goods that had arrived and estimating the profits she'd made from tonight's delivery. Perhaps offering thanks to her magical moon that had brought her perverse, jaded miracle. Perhaps thinking of what she could buy for herself and for—

That thought stopped him short. Something wasn't right, but his mind was too numb to figure out what it might be.

Bloody hell! She was an opium smuggler. She'd destroyed as many lives as her father. And he loved her!

He tried to put the pieces together but they wouldn't fit. How could she be involved in something so horrific? This was the woman who'd made one sacrifice after another for the children. Who'd tried to keep his son from him because of his reputation. Who kept the children at the orphanage long after they were considered old enough to leave because she wanted to protect them. Had she resorted to smuggling to provide for the children?

She had. He knew she had. This was why she'd been so opposed to his cattle venture. This was why she'd warned him to stay away from this part of the estate. This was why she'd bargained with Lady Clythebrook for one more month. Because of the shipment she knew was coming in tonight.

His mind whirled in confusion as he argued her case. For some reason a part of him still didn't want her to be guilty. Even after seeing her standing there while they unloaded the opium, he still wanted her to be innocent.

But she wasn't.

Ross stood on the cliff overlooking the cove, as still as if he'd been chiseled from granite. The ship was nearly out of sight now. The reality of what he'd done cut deep into him with the deadly aim of a rapier. He'd sacrificed his honor to save her. He'd thrown away his chance to redeem the Rainforth name rather than hand her over to the authorities. He'd lost everything he'd hoped to achieve.

"Rainforth!"

The sound of heavy footsteps pounding against the hard ground behind him was all the warning he had. The fury he heard in McCormick's voice should have set his heart thundering in his chest. But he was too numb to have much reaction at all.

"What the hell have you done?"

He set his shoulders and watched the empty spot where the ship had been. Somehow he'd get through this like he'd gotten through the days and weeks after he'd discovered what his father had done.

"That was the ship!" McCormick bellowed. "You let them get away!"

Ross stepped back from the edge of the cliff and turned to face his accusers. The blatant fury on McCormick's face was plain to see. The vicious rage was an emotion Ross could deal with. He understood it. It was even an emotion he knew he would feel as soon as the numbness wore off and what he'd done set in.

What he couldn't deal with was the harsh disappointment

he saw on Sam's face; the restrained anger Sam didn't put into words; the coldness in his eyes and the open confusion that said no matter how hard he tried, he couldn't come up with one reason why Ross had done what he had.

McCormick stepped in front of him and bellowed in his face.

"You're ruined, Rainforth. If you think your name was worthless before, the disgrace you suffered was nothing compared to the mud people will sling at it as soon as what you did tonight is common knowledge. And don't think it won't be. The twelve men with me can't wait to get back to London to spread how you're the second generation of Rainforths to betray his country."

"That's enough, McCormick," Sam said. "Why don't you see if the men have found anything."

"You know they won't find anything," McCormick fired back, his voice brimming with anger. "Rainforth made sure the smugglers got away. What I want to know is why? How much is your cut from the smuggling?"

Ross felt the barb and fought the urge to throw his fist in McCormick's face. Sam handled the comment much better.

"Check on the men, McCormick. Let me know if they've found anything."

Ross heard McCormick stomp off and he was left alone with Sam. "Do you want to tell me what's going on here, Ross?"

Another cloud covered the moon's brightness. It cast them in semi-darkness that erased everything except the gentle slapping sound of the waves rolling ashore.

"Answer me, dammit! What the hell happened?"

Ross opened his mouth to say something. Anything. But no words would come. At least none that could justify the magnitude of what he'd just done. He closed his mouth and didn't try.

He saw a flash of anger, then concern in Sam's eyes. He turned away.

"I don't know what game you're playing, Ross, but be careful. These are dangerous men and you can't fight them alone."

Ross arched his brows. "What makes you think I intend to

fight anyone? You heard McCormick. I'm the second generation of Rainforths to betray my country."

Ross ignored Sam's harsh expletive and stared at the spot where he'd last seen the ship. He knew Sam didn't intend to let his statement go unanswered, but McCormick coming toward them stopped him.

"The opium's not there, Major. Only some wine and tea and bolts of cloth."

Sam released a heavy sigh. "Well, we can't do anything more tonight. Take the men back to camp and get a few hours' sleep. We'll make a thorough check of the area in the morning when it's light. Perhaps we'll find something more then."

Ross knew Sam wanted to question him further but he didn't. Instead, he followed McCormick back to where their men were waiting.

Ross listened to him go and nearly sank to his knees under the weight of what he'd done. The moon shone bright and full again, the air washed over him with a gentle breeze, but nothing could erase the deathly pall that shrouded him.

He'd lost it all. Given it up. Because he didn't want to lose her.

But because of what she'd done, he knew he already had.

Ross wasn't sure how long he'd stood on the cliff overlooking the caves, but long enough for his life to come full circle. Long enough for every mistake he'd ever made to rise before him with overwhelming clarity. Sometime before dawn he made his way back to St. Stephen's, where only a few hours earlier he'd looked forward to a future more perfect than any he'd thought he would ever have.

Until his world had fallen apart.

He walked into his study and sat in one of the two chairs flanking the fireplace, but didn't light a fire. The darkness suited him well enough.

As the hours slowly ticked by, the depth and breadth of his emotions ran the gamut from numbness to despair to disbelief to rage, and now, to a subtle anger that slowly grew inside him. Anger because she'd betrayed him. And, just as quickly, a determination to make her suffer for what she'd done to him.

Ross looked at the cold, lifeless ashes in the fireplace. He could still see the long stretch of sandy beach where he'd seen her a few hours ago. He still battled the disbelief that engulfed him when she stepped out of the shadows. He recalled the exact moment he realized what her presence meant.

He closed his eyes and wondered if it were possible to hate someone you loved.

When he opened his eyes, the sun was peeking above the horizon, lighting the room in a dusky gray. It was time. Time to confront her. Time to let her know he knew about the smuggling and her role in it. Time she knew he saw her for the lying manipulator she was.

Ross remembered what she'd told him when he'd asked her why she'd given herself to him. *Because I knew I could trust you. I knew you would never hurt me.*

A hard knot formed in the pit of his stomach. She'd used him. She'd used her body as insurance in case he discovered her role in the smuggling. She'd slept with him to protect herself. She'd made him fall in love with her to keep from hanging from the end of a rope.

Well, that may have been what she'd thought was going to happen, but she'd play by his rules now. And she'd pay dearly for what she'd done.

Ross bolted from his chair and walked to the window. With a violent swing, he threw back the drapes and stared at the rising sun. By the time he washed and changed, she'd be at the orphanage. He'd confront her there.

When he was finished with her, she'd know what it felt like to lose everything she held dear. And still have to go on living.

Chapter 20

JOSIE WALKED ALONG THE NARROW PATH that led away from the orphanage. If she stayed to her right, she'd end up near the stream where she'd taken the children not that many weeks ago when Ross had seen his son for the first time. She remembered the look on his face and how her heart had ached for the years he hadn't known he had a son. She would never be able to look at the bubbling stream again without being reminded that even though she'd done everything in her power to stop it from happening, she'd fallen in love with the Marquess of Rainforth.

She swiped her hand across her eyes. She didn't need to relive the memories from that day and took the less-traveled path that veered to the left.

She wanted time to herself. Someplace quiet where she could hide for just a little while until her hands stopped shaking and her legs quit trembling. Someplace where she could come to terms with the fact that she'd just emptied twelve chests of opium cakes wrapped in poppy leaves and cotton cloths into the ocean and watched the tide wash them out to sea. Time to adjust to the knowledge that she'd been involved in something much more deadly than the innocent smuggling of goods to provide for the children. And time to adjust to the fact that

Geoffrey Lindville wasn't her greatest threat.

Blood pounded in her head when she thought of what would happen when the real head of the smuggling ring discovered what she'd done.

On legs that trembled with each step, she walked until she reached the small orchard where she'd sent Charlie to hide that first day Ross had come to search for him. She leaned against the sturdy trunk of an apple tree, then dropped her head to her hands and rubbed her fingers against her temples. Her head throbbed from lack of sleep as well as the stress from last night.

Convincing Captain Levy that this would be the last shipment they would receive had been easier than she'd anticipated. The captain had heard about the agency the government had formed to combat the rising opium addiction problem. He and his men were only too happy to unload the contraband and leave as fast as they could.

What he did question, though, was why she'd come instead of the usual contact.

For a minute, she thought the captain was going to refuse to leave the contraband. Finally, with a shrug and a smile that only lifted one side of his mouth, he gave orders for his men to unload the boats.

As each crate and box passed before her, she pretended to show significant interest in the delivery, while inside her, she thought she would be ill.

For nearly two years, she'd not only allowed, but looked forward to the arrival of the goods Captain Levy brought each quarter. For nearly two years she'd been so thankful for the money Cornelius Sharpe gave her from the sale of the goods, she hadn't once thought to question what else was coming in with the cases of wine and bags of tea the captain could purchase. Instead, she'd turned a blind eye, while the tunnels beneath the orphanage were being used to smuggle in a drug that had destroyed hundreds of lives.

Josie clasped her arms around her middle and took one deep

breath after another. What she'd been a part of made her ill. But the worst was yet to come. Knowing how Ross would despise her when he found out turned her blood to ice. Even the fact that she'd spent the last several hours breaking open each chest and dumping the cakes of opium into the ocean wouldn't make him hate her any less.

She pushed herself away from the tree and swiped at a stray tear that ran down her cheek. She didn't think she had any more inside her that hadn't been shed last night, but somehow one more drop filled her eyes and escaped.

Such moments of weakness made her angry. Crying was useless. She had no one to blame but herself and would have to face what she'd done and suffer the consequences. But she was so frightened. Perhaps, the best she could hope for was that Ross would go with her when she went to the authorities. Not that she expected his title or his appearance to influence anyone, but only so she wouldn't have to go alone.

She swiped her hands down her skirt to dry her sweating palms and turned to go back to the orphanage. She took two steps before she lifted her head, and stopped short. Her gaze locked with Ross's and held.

He stood before her, more terrifyingly handsome than ever. Her heart lurched, then thrummed faster in her breast. Oh, how she wanted to rush into his arms. How she wanted to spill out her story in one long breath and rely on him to tell her what to do. Or just to admit to him what a fool she'd been and have him tell her everything would be all right. But of course she couldn't.

Even if confiding in him would have been possible, something about his stern countenance and the icy coldness of his gaze warned her to be wary.

"You surprised me," she said, gathering her self-control. "I didn't expect you so early."

"I might say the same of you, Miss Foley. I thought perhaps you wouldn't be here yet, but Mrs. Lambert said that you were in your office even before she awoke."

Miss Foley.

He hadn't called her Miss Foley except in public since he'd made love to her that first time. A wave of warning washed over her.

"I couldn't sleep and there was much to be done."

He took two menacing steps toward her and stopped. "Just what did you need to do that had to be done before dawn? Or didn't you go home at all last night?"

Josie braced herself as the invisible wall she'd often found necessary to erect around herself went quickly into place. There was no softness in his voice, none of the warmth she'd looked forward to hearing. Another alarming jolt slammed into her.

"I needed to take an inventory of all the spring clothes to be repaired or replaced. And Cook left a list of items that are running dangerously low. I thought to go over the list and see what can be done to—"

"How ambitious. You have your hands in a number of ventures. Don't you?"

Josie felt the grip of warning tighten and squared her shoulders. "I'm not sure I understand what ventures you're talking about."

"Don't you?"

Blood rushed through her veins, crashing inside her head. She didn't answer him, but waited. He took another step toward her and for the first time, she felt threatened by him. Not in danger, but threatened. His next question gave her cause.

"Where were you last night? It's obvious you haven't slept. Where have you been?"

"I was…"

She couldn't finish. She couldn't lie, yet she wasn't ready to admit the truth. Something about the accusatory tone in his voice and the way he watched her with the wariness of a predator anticipating the kill held her back. This was a side of him she hadn't seen since the first time she'd met him. She felt the need to escape.

"Where I was is none of your business. Now, if you will excuse me."

She took her first step away from him but stopped when he spoke.

"I saw you."

She shook her head, at first unable to comprehend his meaning. Then, the magnitude of his words and the assumption he'd drawn from seeing her last night hit her full force.

"Where did you see me?"

"Beneath the cliff. Standing in front of the cave while the men unloaded their supply of smuggled goods. Did everything meet with your approval?"

"I…It's not what it seemed. I—"

"Isn't it?"

She opened her mouth to continue, then stopped when she realized how lame her words would sound. He would never believe she hadn't known they were smuggling in opium. Not after he'd seen her with his own eyes.

He took another step toward her and she noticed his drawn features. The dark circles that shadowed his eyes seemed even blacker and she realized he hadn't slept any more than she had.

"I finally understand why you bargained for a month when Lady Clythebrook issued her demands. I thought the reason was that you had so little faith in me you thought I'd soon grow tired of the country and head back to London." He laughed. "I couldn't wait to prove you wrong." He took another step toward her. "How long have you been involved in the smuggling?"

She opened her mouth but no words came out.

His second demand was more forceful. "How long?"

"Two years. The children—"

"No!" He swiped his hand angrily between them. "Do *not* use the children."

Josie's first instinct was to stop and let him think what he wanted but something made her go on. Perhaps just the belief that this would be the only chance she had to explain why she'd involved herself in the smuggling.

"Two years ago the children's needs were greater than we could supply. Lady Lindville had always offered assistance in the past but was unable to help as much as we needed."

"So you resorted to smuggling."

She heard the disdain in his voice and fought to stomp down her rising temper. "The children were going without food!"

"Smuggling was your only answer?"

Josie turned her gaze away from him. How could she explain that it had been? There'd been no other way to provide for the children.

"How is Lindville involved?"

"He contacted Captain Levy each quarter to make the arrangements."

"Why did he involve you? Why not someone else? Surely there were others he could have—"

"He needed me. I was the only one who…"

Josie hesitated. This was the most damning of all. The part that would incriminate her and leave no room for escape. "You know how steep the incline is from the cove. It's nearly impossible for anyone to make the climb either up or down without being observed. But, there's a network of tunnels beneath the orphanage that smugglers used more than a hundred years ago. Very few people know they exist."

"But you knew?"

"Yes. Evidently, so did Baron Lindville. He came with a proposition to bring in goods that we could then sell to Cornelius Sharpe. The goods we brought in weren't illegal, just items Baron Lindville managed to purchase for far less than Cornelius could get them. The orphanage received half the profits and Lindville kept the other half."

"How convenient. Except you've failed to explain how your contraband changed to opium."

Josie looked into his eyes, hoping she'd see some hint of softness there, but all she saw was a steely-gray hardness that didn't conceal his intense anger. Her heart felt like a leaden weight anchored in her chest.

"Would it be expecting too much to ask you to believe I didn't know about the opium?"

His hollow laugh stopped her. "Far too much," he said with more bitterness than she thought he was capable of.

He turned his back as if he couldn't stand the sight of her. His words proved it. "I have to give you credit, though. You played the game with amazing ingenuity. Giving yourself to me was a very calculated move." He spun back to face her. "Did you think it would be your insurance? Was sleeping with me part of the plan to assure that if your role in the smuggling was discovered, you could use what we'd done to your advantage?"

"No! What we did had nothing to do with this. I slept with you because—"

The pain inside her chest hurt too much. She couldn't go on.

"I'm waiting. Please, enlighten me. Why did you sleep with me?"

She reminded herself this might be the last chance she ever had to speak with him. She did not want this final time filled with lies. "Because I realized that I lo—"

He slashed his hand through the air in a violent arc. "No! Use any excuse but that! Tell me you wanted to be able to brag that you'd been bedded by a notorious rake. Or that you wanted to be intimate with the Rainforth heir whose father had betrayed his country. Or, try the truth, Miss Foley. You slept with me because you thought it would benefit you. Any excuse, but don't speak to me of love."

Josie felt as though she'd been slapped. She lifted her chin and glared at him. "Very well. You want the truth? Then you shall have it. I slept with you because I was a fool."

His eyes opened wide, as if her words had surprised him.

"If anyone was a fool, it was I. I know prostitutes who are more honest! At least they're up front about the reason they sell themselves."

The lump lodged in Josie's throat threatened to choke her. Before last night, she'd only cried once before in her life and that was when Lord Clythebrook had died. She would not let it happen again. Not now. Not in front of him.

She needed to get away before she embarrassed herself. She

jerked her skirts to the side and started to walk past him. He held out his arm and stopped her.

"I was given one chance to redeem the name my father destroyed. Not just for myself, but for Charlie. So Charlie could claim the Bennett name with pride. Your greed and deceit took that opportunity away from him. I hope you can live with yourself."

The vice clamped around her heart tightened until she could barely breathe. But he didn't intend to give her a respite.

"Major Bennett and Agent McCormick are here. They knew about the shipment and were waiting for the signal so they could arrest the opium smugglers—a signal *I* was supposed to light."

Josie's mind was a muddle of confusion. That was how he knew. She lifted her gaze and saw the blatant fury in his eyes. "You were to signal them?"

He smiled but it wasn't a smile she ever wanted to have directed at her again. "Yes. They trusted me and again a Rainforth turned traitor."

He stepped away from her as if her nearness was too much to bear. "I have to meet Sam and McCormick at the caves later this morning. They're going to investigate where the opium came ashore to see if some evidence might still be there to identify the smugglers. I hope you didn't leave anything incriminating behind or you may not be in the clear yet. And this time I won't do anything to prevent them from arresting you. Or from watching you hang."

He turned to step away from her then stopped and faced her again. "Where did you hide the opium?"

She glared at him. "Where no one will ever find it."

The look he gave her was more murderous than before and it took all her willpower not to shrink from him.

"When I am finished with Sam and McCormick, I intend to come back for Charlie. See that his things are together. You might want to take a few moments to gather your own belongings, too, Miss Foley. I cannot in good conscience allow an opium smuggler to have anything to do with the children."

The ground shifted beneath her. She wanted to grab hold of something to steady herself but Rainforth was the only solid object within reach and she couldn't bring herself to touch him. "You can't mean that."

"Oh, but I do. If I find you anywhere near the children after today I'll do everything in my power to see that Sacred Heart is closed and the children moved to another orphanage."

"But the children—"

"The children need to be protected from you! If you care for them at all you will leave."

Josie stared at him, every inch of her body numb. "Do you hate me that much?"

She watched the change in his features and felt as if the glaring blackness in his countenance pulled her deeper into a pit of despair.

"I don't hate you, Miss Foley. What I feel doesn't come close to hatred."

Each word was like a pointed dagger being thrust through her heart. Keeping her back rigidly straight, she walked past him and made her way back to the orphanage.

She didn't run. Even though she wanted to, she slowly placed one foot in front of the other and walked away from the only man she would ever love.

She made her way to the little room that had always been her sanctuary and closed the door. Then, for the first time in her life, she bolted it, keeping out those who were most dear to her. When she was alone, she walked to the tiny closet where she kept a spare dress in case she ever had to stay the night with one of the children, and folded it into a worn valise.

It wouldn't take her long to gather what was hers. She'd never had much. The children had always needed so much more than she did.

The children. How could she survive if she had to leave the children behind? But she would. What choice did she have?

When she was finished, she set her valise by the front door, then asked Mrs. Lambert to assemble the children outside. She wanted to gather them around her one last time and read them one of their favorite stories. She wasn't sure which one yet. Perhaps she'd let one of the children decide.

Perhaps Charlie.

Josie waited in the garden, knowing this would probably be the last time she'd be welcome here. The door to the orphanage opened and she watched as the children filed down the path. She greeted them all, hugging the ones who hadn't outgrown the need to be hugged, just touching the ones who had. When they were all seated beneath a sturdy beech tree, she read to them from one of their favorite books while they munched on a cookie she'd talked Cook into giving them. All this she accomplished without a tear. As if she were watching every painful event from somewhere outside her body.

She was nearly to the end of her story when a cold chill raced down her spine. She finished quickly, then closed the book, afraid she'd dallied too long and Rainforth had returned already to take Charlie with him. Oh, she didn't want to face him again and had hoped to be gone before he came back.

The prickly warning grew stronger and she forced herself to look down the path that led to the orphanage. Her heart thudded in her breast, then slammed against her ribs. It wasn't Rainforth but Baron Lindville, and even from a distance she could see the fury on his face.

He covered the ground in long, angry strides, with hands clenched into tight fists at his sides. Josie remembered the last time she'd angered him. A fresh wave of fear raced through her and she jumped to her feet.

The children.

"Take the children inside," she said to Mrs. Lambert, who'd recognized that something was not as it should be and had rushed to her side. "And don't let them come back outside."

Mrs. Lambert looked at Baron Lindville then turned back to Josie. She started gathering the children. "Something's wrong.

What is it?"

"Nothing. Take the children inside. Hurry."

Mrs. Lambert looked back toward Baron Lindville. "You can't stay out here. Not alone."

"Go! Now!"

Mrs. Lambert ushered the children toward the orphanage and Josie moved in the opposite direction. She knew why he'd come. She knew the reason for his furious expression. And she was afraid.

"What the hell have you done?" he bellowed before he reached her. "What the bloody hell have you done?"

Josie glanced over her shoulder toward the orphanage. Mrs. Lambert nearly had the last of the children safely behind the doors. The minute they were all inside, she stopped moving. She knew trying to get away from him would do no good. He was intent on punishing her and the more she tried to escape his wrath the more furious he would become. She didn't know what she would do, but she had to get him away from here. Away from the children. Someplace where she stood a better chance of protecting herself.

Josie took a deep breath and turned around to face him. "I stopped you from using the orphanage to smuggle in the opium that was destroying hundreds of young men and women."

"You fool!" he said and drew back his hand. He slapped her hard across the face.

Josie staggered. "Hitting me won't change anything. I told you I wouldn't let you use the children for something so vile. Besides, the authorities have come. They know about the smuggling. They know about the opium."

"I don't give a damn what they know. They can't prove anything. There are ways to get around anyone the government sends."

"No, you can't. They're going to—"

Before Josie could finish her sentence, his hand reached out and struck her again. This time harder than before and she fell to her knees. He grabbed her arm and jerked her to her feet.

"Where did you hide it? Captain Levy said you were there

when they unloaded the chests and you told him there wouldn't be any more deliveries. I went to the caves this morning and there's nothing there. Nothing except the boxes and barrels that will go to Cornelius Sharpe. What did you do with the opium? I want it now or I'll—"

"Miss Josie. I need to tell you something."

Josie spun her head in the direction of the orphanage and took in a huge, painful gasp. Little Charlie was running toward her as fast as his short, pudgy legs would carry him.

"No, Charlie! Go back!"

"But I need to tell you something. Guess what?" he said, coming to a halt in front of her. "Lord Rainforth wants me to come to—"

Josie reached for Charlie but she wasn't fast enough. Before she could push him behind her, Lindville had the boy by the back of the neck and was squeezing so hard tears swelled in Charlie's eyes.

"Let him go! No! Don't hurt him."

"Then tell me where you've hidden the opium."

"All right. Just let him go."

Lindville hesitated a moment then pushed Charlie to the ground. He fell hard but didn't seem hurt. Josie squatted down in front of him and pulled him up to her. "Go inside, Charlie. And stay there."

"But—"

"Tell Mrs. Lambert to put a cool cloth on your knee, then see if Cook has any cookies left."

Charlie gave her a weak smile and limped toward the house, taking a wide path past Lord Lindville. Josie didn't breathe again until Charlie was safe behind the doors.

"Now, where is it?" Lindville demanded.

"It's where you'll never find it."

"Show me!"

Lindville grabbed her elbow and led her to the front where his horse was tied to the brass post. He pushed her up into the saddle and mounted behind her.

"Where to?"

Josie remembered Ross's words, *I have to meet Sam and McCormick at the caves later this morning.*

"The cliffs," she said, knowing leading him there would protect the children from him.

Knowing the cliffs was the place she could least protect herself.

Chapter 21

DO YOU HATE ME THAT MUCH?

Josie's question echoed over and over with each step Ross took as he followed Sam and Agent McCormick down the steep incline to the caves below the cliffs. Did he hate her that much?

He clenched his hands until his fingers ached. No, he didn't hate her that much. He loved her so much that what she'd done had nearly killed him.

A boulder blocked the path and he stepped around it. They were almost to the bottom now, to the place where he'd seen her standing last night inspecting every item the smugglers brought ashore. How could she involve herself in something so vile? How could she love and care for the children to the point she was willing to go without herself, while at the same time, smuggle in a deadly drug she knew destroyed countless innocent lives?

If someone would have asked him that question yesterday, he'd have said it wasn't possible. But he'd seen her with his own eyes. He'd seen her stand right here while the smugglers carried ashore one crate of opium after another.

And yet, as he sorted everything out in his mind, so many things didn't make sense. The sale of opium on the black market was extremely profitable. Profitable enough that Josie and Lady Clythebrook should be living in grand style. And the children should never want for a thing. Instead, from everything he'd seen, no one was living in opulence, and neither Josie nor Lady Clythebrook had worn a new dress in years. The only thing in abundance at the orphanage was love. That had been obvious the first time he'd stepped through Sacred Heart's doors.

If she'd been involved in smuggling for nearly two years, what had she done with the money?

Nothing made sense to him. If only he hadn't fallen in love with her. But how could he have stopped himself? She'd made her way into his heart as if that was where she belonged. As if there'd always been a special place for her and she'd finally come to claim it.

How could she have given herself to him—not once but twice—and not known that what they shared was special? How could she have cheapened what they'd shared because she thought it might benefit her later? Ross stopped at a place near the bottom of the steep decline as an answer to his question slammed into him.

She couldn't have. The Josephine Foley he knew couldn't have. And yet she had.

"Where did they unload the opium, Ross?"

He jerked his gaze to where Sam stood and walked over to the place where the boats had pulled ashore.

"Here. There were three boats and six men. They unloaded several crates and barrels and carried them through there," he said, pointing to the mouth of a cave. Both Sam and McCormick lit the lanterns they'd brought with them and entered the cave.

Ross stayed outside, not wanting to see what they discovered. He knew when they saw the shipment they'd have other questions, like: What else had he seen? Did he recognize any of the smugglers? How long had it taken them to unload the goods? Did he see who had contacted them? The moon was full—that damnably full, magical moon. Surely he'd recognized whoever had come to meet the smugglers and could identify them.

Ross fought the waves of self-loathing. He was as much a

traitor as his father. How could he answer their questions without condemning Josie? Or live with himself after he did?

"Ross, get in here."

Sam's voice crashed in on his thoughts, pulling him back to the present. Ross walked into the cave and toward the light. Sam and McCormick stood in the large opening, the lids of barrels lying on the ground, tops of crates hanging by their hinges.

"Is this all of it?"

Ross looked around. He could see without counting that not all the boxes and crates that had been unloaded last night were here. The opium wasn't there. "There were more."

He grabbed the lantern from Sam's hand and walked to the back of the cave. Sam and McCormick followed. They found nothing until they reached the thick wooden door he'd discovered before.

"Where does this lead?" McCormick asked, trying the door to make sure it couldn't be opened.

"There are tunnels beneath the orphanage that were used for smuggling more than a hundred years ago."

"They must have already taken the opium out this way," Sam said, hunkering down to check the sandy floor of the cave. "But if they did, they were damn careful. There's only one set of footprints and from the size of the imprints, they weren't made by a man."

McCormick bent down to study the evidence then rose and started for the mouth of the cave. "We'll go to the orphanage. Someone there knows what the hell is going on and I want to know who it is."

A heavy weight sank to the pit of his stomach. Part of him hoped Josie was already gone so they couldn't talk to her. Another part knew it wouldn't make any difference. It was only a matter of time until they discovered she knew more about what went on at the orphanage than even Vicar Chadwick did.

A terrible premonition chilled the blood running through his veins. He may have saved her last night but he knew there was nothing he could do to help her today.

"What's going on, Ross?" Sam said when McCormick was far enough ahead of them so they couldn't be overheard.

Ross stared at McCormick's retreating back and shook his head.

"Dammit, Ross. Don't shut me out. Maybe I can help."

Ross wanted to laugh. This was no different than the night he'd realized what his father had done. "It's too late for that."

"Who is she?"

Ross jerked his head to the side. There was a look on Sam's face that Ross had seen often in the past. The intelligent gleam in his eyes that enabled him to look at something and see beneath the outer coating to reveal what was hidden. Ross was certain it was this ability that had made him such a valuable asset to the government.

"What makes you think there's a woman?"

"I know you. I know how badly you wanted to do this. You wouldn't have let the ship leave without signaling us if you hadn't seen something that stopped you. I just hope she was worth it."

"Bennett!"

Sam gave Ross one more second to confide in him, then walked toward the entrance of the cave and stepped out into the sunshine. Ross followed him to where McCormick stood close to the water's edge. His gaze was fixed downward. Sam and Ross both looked out to see what had drawn his attention.

"Bloody hell," Sam whispered, stepping into the water. He picked up some of the debris lapping up to the shore with the waves and held it in his palm.

"I don't understand," Ross said, looking from the water-soaked cakes in Sam's hand to the frown on his face.

"Someone destroyed the shipment of opium."

"Why?"

"My guess would be to make sure none of it reached London. You wouldn't know who that might be, would you Ross?"

Ross's heart slammed against his ribs. Oh, yes. He knew who it had been. He remembered Josie's answer when he asked her where she'd put the opium.

Where no one will ever find it.

Then he remembered the question she'd asked him before that.

Would it be expecting too much to ask you to believe I didn't know about the opium?

What if that had been the truth? What if Josie hadn't known about the opium until he'd told her and she'd come here last night with the express purpose of destroying it before it reached London?

Blood thundered in Ross's head. Did she have any idea what she'd done? Didn't she know what Lindville would do when he found out?

"We have to get to the orphanage."

Ross raced up the steep incline, leaving Sam and McCormick far behind him. He scrambled to the top, but stopped short when he looked up.

Geoffrey Lindville stood at the top of the cliff with Josie in front of him. One arm was wrapped around her chest in a death-grip. The other hand held a gun. She struggled to free herself when she saw Ross, but Lindville pressed the gun harder against her temple. Josie stood still.

"I wouldn't come any closer, Rainforth. It wouldn't be safe for Miss Foley if you did."

Ross jerked to a halt and raised his hands in surrender. He hoped Sam and McCormick saw him and knew to stop. He didn't look behind him to find out.

"Let her go, Lindville."

He took one small step toward them and Josie tried to take advantage of his movement to twist out of Lindville's arms. Ross stopped when Lindville twisted Josie's arm behind her back and she cried out in pain. He took a small step back and Lindville relaxed his grip just enough so Josie's breathing returned to normal.

Her eyes were wide and her face was pale. All except for the deep red mark on the left side of her face that was turning purple. Ross was filled with a deep-down rage that boiled inside him.

"Are you all right?" he asked, knowing she wasn't, but needing to say the words to feel a connection to her. His question forced her to look at him. She nodded.

He held her gaze and tried to put a look of confidence on his face. Her grim expression told him she wasn't any surer of him than she was of Lindville. And he didn't blame her.

"Let her go," he repeated.

"Miss Foley and I have some unfinished business to settle. I don't suppose you'd consider forgetting what you saw here and leave?"

Ross stepped to the side, hoping he could position Lindville with his back to the water to keep him from seeing Sam come over the steep incline. "I said, let her go."

Lindville smiled, then shrugged. "I guess not. That's unfortunate. I really hadn't intended on killing you, too, but…well, you can understand the predicament I'm in."

"You don't have to kill anyone. Your smuggling venture is finished. Just cut your losses and run while you can."

"Cut my losses. Bloody hell, Rainforth, you're a damn fool if you think I intend to walk away from this. You don't even know what's going on here."

"Oh, but I do. You've been using Miss Foley and the orphanage to smuggle in opium that you sell in London. The authorities have been investigating you for months and are waiting to arrest you."

"If they arrest me, they'll have to arrest Miss Foley too. She was as much a part of it as I was."

"No!" Josie argued. "I didn't know you were smuggling opium. I only thought you were bringing in items Cornelius Sharpe could sell."

"You were such a fool. For nearly two years you carried the messages back and forth, then religiously unlocked the doors to the passageways each time before you left and sealed everything back up in the morning after the goods were gone. And not once did you suspect a thing."

"I didn't think I needed to suspect anything! I didn't imagine you would involve yourself with smuggling opium. Or involve the children and me."

Lindville pressed the gun beneath her chin and lifted until she was forced to look at him. "How did you finally discover what we were doing? Not that I care, mind you. I'm just curious."

Ross tried to take a step closer. They were still too far away from him. "I told her. You were right when you put a connection between my cousin and me. The authorities are on to you."

"That's too bad. But they won't be able to prove anything. Not with you dead."

"Don't add murder to your crimes. It's not worth it."

Josie struggled again and Lindville tightened the hand he had wrapped around her.

"Oh, it won't be murder. It will seem like a tragic accident. Miss Foley slipped and fell to her death. In your grief and despair, you rushed down the steep slope to get to her. Unfortunately, you stumbled and fell. Your deaths won't even be suspect because I'll be a witness to the tragedy. I'll tell the authorities how devastated I was to have witnessed the whole event without being able to reach you in time to help."

"Is that what you told the authorities when you reported Carrie Gardner's death?"

Ross saw Lindville's reaction to his accusation and knew what he'd suspected for weeks was true. The sadistic grin on Lindville's face confirmed it.

"You think you have it all figured out, don't you Rainforth?"

Ross moved another step to the side. "Why did you kill her?"

"I didn't kill her. She had a tragic accident."

"You killed her the same as you intend to kill Miss Foley and me. Why?"

He tightened his jaw and spoke through clenched teeth. "Because she was blackmailing me."

Geoffrey Lindville was as a poor an excuse for a human being as

Ross had ever seen and just looking at him made Ross ill. "Carrie Gardner wasn't blackmailing you. She didn't need money."

"She wasn't blackmailing me for money. You provided her with more than enough to live a comfortable life at St. Stephen's."

"Then why would she blackmail you?"

"She objected to the attention I was showing her and threatened to tell my mother about certain…habits I'd acquired if I didn't leave her alone. Everyone knew she'd been your mistress and you'd sent her to live in this Godforsaken part of England when her belly swelled with your bastard. I just wanted her to provide me the same services she'd provided you."

"So you killed her when she refused?"

"It was an accident. We struggled and she fell."

"And you told everyone she had a carriage accident."

"I'm tired of talking about something that happened another lifetime ago. I'm more concerned with what is happening right now. Where is the cargo Captain Levy brought last night, Miss Foley?"

Lindville pressed the gun harder to her head and repeated his question. "Where is it?"

Ross watched Josie brace her shoulders and lift her chin. He'd never seen anyone braver than she was. He'd never loved anyone more. But he couldn't let her tell Lindville what she'd done. He'd kill her as soon as he found out.

"Don't tell him, Josie."

"Shut up! Where'd you hide it?"

When Josie didn't answer right away, Lindville clamped his fingers around her arm and twisted it behind her back. "Where!"

She screamed in pain and Ross took a step toward her but Lindville waved his gun and Ross stopped.

"Where is it?"

"There!" she said on a gasp and pointed toward the ocean.

"Where?"

Lindville looked out over the inlet but didn't understand what she meant.

"Gone."

Comprehension slowly dawned and the features of his face reddened with violent fury.

"No!" he bellowed and brought his hand up. Before Ross could move, Lindville slammed his fist into Josie's face. Her head flew back and blood spilled from her mouth.

Ross lunged toward him. If only he'd managed to get closer. If only he could cover the distance separating them before Lindville had time to fire his gun. But he knew he couldn't. At least Sam and McCormick had heard enough to convict Lindville of smuggling and murder. No matter what, Lindville would hang.

Lindville dropped his hands from around Josie, then lifted the gun and aimed it at Ross's chest. As if the world shifted into slow motion, he saw Lindville's finger pull back on the trigger and he fired the gun. At the same time something moved to his right and before he could reach out, Josie was in front of him.

Her gaze locked with his and her look of confusion turned to surprise, then pain. Her breath caught and she staggered a shaky step toward him before her knees buckled. Ross caught her and brought her up against him.

"Josie, no!"

He took her to the ground and shielded her with his body. A second shot echoed from behind him and Ross turned. Sam stood near the edge of the cliff with his arm outstretched. Smoke streamed from the gun in his hand.

Lindville's eyes opened wide in shocked disbelief before he fell to the ground. McCormick rushed to where he lay and even though it was obvious Lindville was past the point of using it, grabbed the gun from his hand.

It took Ross a second to shift Josie in his arms and when he lifted his hand from around her, his fingers came away sticky and wet.

"Don't move," he said when she tried to lift her head.

"I'm sorry," she whispered. "…all my fault."

"Shh. You can talk later."

Ross pulled his neckcloth from around his neck and pressed it to her back. She winced when he touched her, but she didn't cry out.

"How badly is she hurt?" Sam asked, kneeling down beside them.

"We need to get her home."

"McCormick's getting the horses. It won't be long."

Josie's fingers clamped around Ross's forearm. "Ross. I was… wrong. It wasn't him."

He placed a finger over her lips to quiet her. "Don't talk, Josie."

She squeezed his arm tighter. "The vicar. Get…the vicar."

A lump formed in his throat. "Don't worry," he whispered, then brushed a strand of golden hair from her face. "I'll get him."

She seemed to relax when he promised to get Vicar Chadwick and that frightened him more than the blood he couldn't get to stop.

"Why did you do it? Dammit, Josie. Why?"

She slowly lifted her hand and cupped his cheek. Her fingers were ice cold and her hand trembled, but the feel of her touching him with such tenderness brought tears to his eyes.

"…couldn't…lose you."

Ross leaned down and kissed her lightly on the lips then picked her up when McCormick came with the horses.

Ross mounted first and Sam gently lifted Josie into his arms. Somewhere between the cliffs and Clythebrook Manor she lost consciousness. The bullet was still in her shoulder and Ross prayed she didn't wake up until they had it out.

It wasn't until he carried her into her room that he remembered his promise to her. But now he wasn't sure he could do it. Admitting she needed Vicar Chadwick was admitting that she might die. And he couldn't do that.

Chapter 22

ROSS PACED THE FLOOR at the end of the bed where Josie lay. Doctor Hallam had taken the bullet out and applied salve to the bruises on her face and she'd finally fallen asleep.

He stopped to watch her. Any doubt he had that he loved her was long gone. He only wished he'd have told her when he had the chance. He wished he'd have let her tell him she loved him when she'd started to.

"Why did you sleep with me?"

"Because I lo—"

But he'd stopped her.

He sat down on the edge of her bed and brushed his fingers across her forehead. Doctor Hallam said they needed to watch for fever. The next twenty-four hours were crucial.

He picked up her small hand and held it in his. Why hadn't she come to him when she'd realized what Lindville was doing? Hadn't she trusted him enough to know he'd have done anything to help her? Instead, she'd met the smugglers alone, destroyed the opium alone, faced Lindville alone. And stepped in front of the bullet that would have killed him—alone.

"I love you, Josie Foley," he whispered then leaned over and kissed her on the forehead.

She stirred but didn't wake, and Ross watched as rays of sunshine streamed through the window and bathed her in a soft glow. Behind him, the door opened then softly closed.

"How is she?" Sam asked, walking across the room.

"She doesn't have a fever. Hallam said that could be more dangerous than the bullet wound."

"It is. But she's strong.

"I should have listened to her, Sam. She tried to tell me she didn't have anything to do with the smuggling but I wouldn't even give her a chance to explain. I was so angry and all I could think was that she'd taken away my only chance to redeem my name."

Sam didn't say anything, but Ross didn't expect him to. Sam didn't know the real reason it was so important for Ross to restore his name. "I have a son. His name is Charles."

Ross lifted his head and looked at the surprised expression on Sam's face.

"Carrie Gardner was pregnant when she left London and had the babe after she arrived here. I never knew. When she died, Josie took my son to live with her, then placed him in the orphanage. When I found out he was there, I went to get him." He looked down at Josie and smiled. "She wouldn't give him to me because she said someone with my reputation didn't deserve to raise a child. I should have known then that she wouldn't have anything to do with smuggling opium."

"If she wasn't involved, how did she find out about it?"

Ross laughed. "I told her. I even asked for her help. I told her I was watching the cove and asked her to give me any information she might hear. Then I told her that when the government found the smugglers, they'd be arrested and hanged. She asked me why the government was so interested in something so insignificant. I told her there was nothing insignificant about smuggling in opium."

Ross raked his fingers through his hair. "You should have seen the shocked expression on her face."

"Then, it was Josie you saw below the cliffs."

"I was watching when the shipment came ashore. I had the match in my hand ready to light the flare when she stepped into the moonlight. I thought I couldn't be seeing right yet there she was, checking each crate and barrel as they unloaded them."

"So you didn't light the signal."

"I couldn't."

Sam paced the room as if sorting through the details to make sure they made sense. "All the time she thought they were bringing in goods the merchant Cornelius Sharpe sold in his shops in Clytheborough, Lindville was bringing in opium he transported to London and sold on the black market. So it was Lindville who was behind the smuggling?"

When Ross didn't answer right away, Sam stopped pacing and looked at him. "Why that look on your face?"

"I don't know. A gut feeling there's something I'm not seeing."

"Explain yourself."

Ross placed Josie's hand atop the covers and turned to face Sam. "Right after she was shot, she grabbed my arm and said, 'I was wrong. It wasn't him.'"

"Who wasn't him?"

"I don't know. Maybe she meant Lindville. Maybe she was trying to tell us that someone else was involved."

Ross started to put his thoughts into words but a knock on the door stopped him. Vicar Chadwick stepped into the room and walked over to where Josie lay.

"I just heard what happened. How is she?"

"She's sleeping and Doctor Hallam says that's the best thing for her right now. Vicar Chadwick," Ross said, rising to introduce the vicar to Sam. "I don't think you've met my cousin, Major Samuel Bennett."

Sam and the vicar shook hands. "No. I haven't had the pleasure. I met Agent McCormick downstairs. He asked me to tell you he was taking the men back to your camp but he'd return before they left for London. Will you be going back with them, Major?"

"No. I'm going to stay on until I tie everything up. There are a few details I need answers to first."

"Such as?"

"What can you tell me about Baron Lindville, Vicar?"

The vicar shook his head. "I just came from Lady Lindville. She's taking her son's death very hard."

"She had no idea he was involved in smuggling opium?"

"Oh, I'm sure she didn't. No one here did."

"Was there anyone here to whom Baron Lindville was especially close?"

"I'm not sure I understand."

"Someone who might have been involved with him in the smuggling? A partner perhaps?"

The vicar looked shocked. "You don't think Lindville was acting alone?"

"We're not sure."

The vicar looked to where Josie lay on the bed, then back to Major Bennett. "Do you think Miss Foley knows the smuggler's identity?"

"It's possible. Was Lindville particularly close to anyone here?"

"Not that I know of. He didn't spend a lot of time here. He found country living quite boring so he spent most of his time in London. From the stories that came back, he led quite a wild life, but then most idle young men do, I'm told."

The vicar didn't look in Ross's direction, but Ross felt the implication in his words nonetheless.

"He had a penchant for spending money. I'm afraid that might be what led him to get involved in such an activity."

"Were you aware of the smuggling?"

A sheepish grin covered his face and Vicar Chadwick quickly lowered his gaze. "I'm afraid I was. Or at least suspected it. So did most of us who live in the vicinity. But the children needed the money so desperately that…well, everyone just looked the other way. No one dreamed Lindville was smuggling in opium."

"Did you know about the caves that ran beneath the orphanage?"

"Yes, I'd heard rumors they existed, although I'd never seen them. Miss Foley was the only one who knew their exact location or had a key to get to them."

"Do you know where she kept this key?"

"I'm not sure. There's a small tin box in the bottom drawer of her desk that she keeps locked."

"Can you open it?"

"No, but the key may be one that she keeps on a ring she has hidden in the lining of her cloak. I saw her take it out one day when she didn't think anyone was around."

Ross rushed over to the cloak they'd removed from Josie and turned it inside out. He pulled the ring from a deep pocket and showed it to Sam.

"We need to check out the caves again," Ross said, then turned to the vicar. "Would you stay with Miss Foley until we return? It shouldn't take long."

"Of course," the vicar offered. "I'm sure she won't wake up for a while yet and Lady Clythebrook is just down the hall if I need anything."

Ross looked at Josie. He wouldn't be gone long and if she did wake up, the vicar would be here.

"Thank you," Ross said, and followed Sam to the door. He walked down the hall at a fast clip, certain he and Sam would be able to answer the niggling questions that wouldn't go away.

"What are you thinking?" Sam asked as he tried the key they'd found in the small tin box in the bottom drawer of her desk. Sam turned the key and opened the thick, oak door in the cave. Ross handed Sam one of the two lanterns he had with him and they walked into the tunnel.

"I keep thinking of what Josie said. 'I was wrong. It wasn't him.'"

"What do you think she meant?"

"I don't know. It wasn't who? Lindville? But it was. He as much as admitted it."

They both walked on, following the tracks the smugglers had left behind. "Maybe she meant he wasn't the only one. Maybe someone worked for him?"

"More than likely he worked for someone else."

Sam stopped and knelt down, shining his lantern closer to something he found on the ground. "Why do you say that?"

"I didn't know Lindville well, but I can't believe he could have masterminded such a well-organized smuggling operation. Nor can I believe he had the contacts necessary to bring in the quantity of opium that was coming into London."

Sam rose to his feet and slipped what he'd found into his pocket. "Who do you know in this area who would fit the profile?"

"No one. It would have to be someone with close ties to the orphanage and who knew about the tunnels. Perhaps even someone who works here. Or at least spends a lot of time here. And it would have to be someone who visits London frequently. Someone who goes there enough to make the necessary arrangements both for buying and selling."

Ross lifted his lantern and walked further into the tunnels. "That points us back to Lindville." He stopped at the opening on the other side of the orphanage. "What do you know about this Captain Levy?"

"We've been watching him for some time now. We think he meets a Chinese trader in the Bangka Strait, east of Sumatra, and trades tea from Batavia for opium he brings to England. The Chinese have been major opium suppliers since the early days of the East India Company." Sam stopped to shine his lantern on a piece of colored glass peeking out of the ground. "Once you have a connection with someone local it's simple to make the necessary arrangements."

Sam bent to pick up the colored object, then turned it over in his fingers. "What the hell? This is the second one I've found.

Do you know what this is?"

He handed it to Ross and Ross looked down at a piece of smashed red gumdrop. A gumdrop like Vicar Chadwick always carried in his pocket. But Chadwick said he'd never been here.

Chadwick's lie hit Ross square in the gut along with the danger Josie was in by being alone with him.

"Bloody hell. No!"

Ross clutched the gumdrop in his fist and ran to the opening of the tunnel. It was him. This is what she meant. Lindville wasn't behind the smuggling ring. It was Chadwick. Somehow she'd found out.

And Chadwick couldn't let her live to expose him.

Josie awoke in a foggy haze. Pain shot through her shoulder and down her arm. She tried to go back to the dark place where it didn't hurt so much but she'd lost her way and was trapped somewhere between where she'd been and where she was going.

She tried to open her eyes but couldn't. It was as if heavy fingers held her eyelids closed and she couldn't lift them. She knew something had happened, something that still terrified her enough to make her heart beat faster but she couldn't remember what it was. Only that it had frightened her.

With her eyes shut and her mind racing from one place to another, she let her ears try to decipher what was going on. There were voices. One was Lady Clythebrook's and Josie heard the worry. She wanted to reassure her she was all right and tried harder to open her eyes, but the black hole she had fallen into was so deep. She tried to speak but no words would come so she gave up and sank back to listen again.

The other voice was a man's. She hoped it belonged to Ross. She desperately needed him to be with her. She would be safe then. But when the voice spoke again she knew it wasn't his.

Stabs of warning raced through her. This voice belonged to someone she needed to fear. Josie tried to open her eyes again and this time she saw shadows on the other side of the room.

One of the shadows was Lady Clythebrook and Josie felt safe, but Lady Clythebrook left the room and Josie knew she'd been left alone with the man who wanted to kill her. She forced herself to breathe through the pain, then opened her eyes.

"Well, well, Miss Foley. Welcome back."

"Where is Lady Clythebrook?"

"You just missed her. She's been quite concerned about you but I assured her you were in good hands and convinced her to leave for a while."

"Please, ask her to—"

The sardonic grin on his face stopped her words and Josie looked up at him with new-found fear.

"I'm sorry, but I prefer she didn't return just yet. Not until I'm finished."

Vicar Chadwick reached for one of the pillows on her bed and held it in his hands.

"You realize I have to kill you, don't you." He took a step closer.

"Captain Levy came to me right away. He assumed you knew I was involved, but realized too late that you didn't."

He clutched the pillow tighter. "I was hoping Lindville would take care of you for me but he didn't." He shrugged his shoulders. "Too bad."

She shook her head and tried to speak but no words would come. She tried again. "No one knows. I promise, I won't tell anyone."

He laughed. "Oh, please, Miss Foley. What kind of fool do you think I am? I know you and Rainforth are lovers. He's been determined from the first to stop the drugs."

"If you leave now—"

"Oh, I'm going to leave. Just as soon as I gather what I need. But first I have to make sure you're not around to tell anyone what you know."

Josie's heart thundered in her breast. She doubted she could scream loud enough for anyone to hear her. But surely, in time, someone would come to check on her.

"Why did you do it?"

"Smuggle in drugs?" His eyebrows arched high. "The money, of course." He ran a hand over his worn black frock. "You know the life of poverty we lowly vicars are supposed to be content to live. Well, I don't have the stomach for it. I've gone without my whole life while fools like Lindville have been handed life's riches on a silver platter. I refuse to live out my days watching everyone else enjoy what I should have."

"But why did you involve Lindville?"

"To keep from having to expose myself. He was my insurance. The person I could count on to take the blame if anything went wrong. And he did. Look how perfectly it turned out? Except…"

He frowned and placed a finger against her cheek. "Look what he did to you. You're going to go to your Maker with some terrible bruises on your face. I'm glad he's dead. He got what he deserved."

Josie felt a sickening dread and moved her head to keep him from touching her. "How did you find out about the tunnels?"

The vicar grinned. "My grandfather was a smuggler of some renown years ago. The caves were a part of the stories we all listened to as children."

"If you knew, then why involve me?"

"You were the most reliable person to make sure the passageway was open, then locked again when the goods were removed. You were also the perfect contact person for Cornelius Sharpe. You gave our little smuggling operation an air of credibility. Everyone knew about it, yet because you were involved, the whole countryside turned a blind eye to what was going on.

"You were so focused on the few pounds that were coming in for the children that not once did you consider something else might be going on. You were the ideal choice. So organized. So responsible. The perfect liaison between Captain Levy and the men who would come to remove the goods from the cave when it arrived. Baron Lindville certainly couldn't be trusted.

His dependency on the drug made him more useless every day. But you…As long as you received a small portion of the profits for the orphanage, we could count on you to do what had to be done and keep your mouth shut. The children were your Achilles' heel. You'd do anything for them. And you never suspected a thing. Quite foolish of you, actually."

"But why didn't you—"

"Enough questions. Do you think I don't know what you're doing? Stalling for time won't do you any good. I have to be gone before Rainforth and Major Bennett return from the caves. Not that they'll find anything. Everything has been removed."

He stepped back a fraction and looked at her. "What did you do with it? I looked all over and there was no sign of the opium anywhere. Where did you hide it?"

She glared at him and tried to turn away from him but he clamped his thumb and forefinger on either side of her jaw and turned her face back to him.

"How did you get rid of it?"

"I dumped it in the ocean."

He laughed. "How brilliant. Even in the end you did me a favor. You destroyed any proof that might be used to incriminate me. I owe you a huge favor. Unfortunately, you'll never be able to collect."

Josie watched as he raised the pillow over her head then brought it down. She struggled to free herself but firebrands of burning pain shot through her. She scratched at him with her uninjured hand and felt her nails sink into his flesh. He muttered a vile oath, but he didn't release her. He only held the pillow tighter against her nose and mouth.

She couldn't breathe. Bright lights exploded behind her eyes and her lungs burned as if they were on fire. A thousand voices screamed inside her head but she wasn't sure any of them reached beyond what she alone could hear.

She was going to die. She wasn't strong enough to fight him any longer.

Ross's face shone before her the way he'd looked when he'd seen his son for the first time. The way he'd looked when he'd made love to her. The way he'd looked when he'd smiled at her.

She held onto that image as everything around her went black.

Chapter 23

ROSS DIDN'T WAIT FOR BANKS to open the front door but burst into the entryway at Clythebrook Manor and took the steps that led to Josie's bedroom three at a time. Sam wasn't far behind him but that didn't matter. If they were right about Chadwick, Josie could already be dead.

All the way to her bedroom he tried not to think what might have already happened. But suddenly, the possibility that he might be too late to save her couldn't be ignored and he realized he wasn't sure he could survive without her.

Why had it taken so long to realize Chadwick had been involved? The clues had been there all along yet he hadn't seen them. He threw open the door and stopped.

Josie lay beneath the covers as still as if she were sleeping—or dead. Chadwick loomed above her, the pillow that should have been beneath her head was over her face. The vicar jerked up when the door slammed open but the imprints of his hands still indented the downy feathers.

An eruption of fury raged within Ross and he lunged across the room, pulling both the vicar and the pillow off her. The vicar slammed against the wall and Ross threw himself at him.

Ross was filled with an uncontrollable rage unlike anything he'd ever felt before. He swung out his fist, pummeling at

Chadwick's face with every ounce of strength he possessed. Even after the vicar sank downwards, Ross didn't stop. He pulled back his arm and smashed his fist into the vicar's face again. Then again. And again.

Not caring that blood was streaming from Chadwick's nose and mouth. Not caring that the vicar could hardly stand on his feet. Not caring the groans and grunts after every punch were weaker and weaker.

"Ross! Enough! You're going to kill him."

Strong hands held him; kept him from striking out at Chadwick again like he wanted to.

"Let him go!"

He heard the words but it took several seconds for them to register. When they did, Ross shoved Chadwick's body away from him and watched him drop to the floor.

Josie!

Ross rushed to the bed where she lay. He was almost afraid to touch her, afraid that if the bastard had killed her, even Sam couldn't stop him from murdering him. He took a deep breath and leaned down to her.

"Josie," he whispered, touching her cheek. Her face was pale, her lips tinged with blue, and her eyes rimmed with dark circles. But her flesh was warm.

"Josie."

"Is she breathing?" Sam asked, pressing his fingers to the side of her neck.

"I don't know."

Ross lifted her head and gently cradled her against him. The minute he moved her she moaned.

"Take a big breath, Josie," he whispered, keeping her in his arms.

"Breathe, dammit! Breathe."

After what seemed an eternity, she opened her mouth and filled her lungs with air.

"Again, Josie. Take another breath."

She took another. Then, as if her body told her she'd gone without air too long, she sucked in one gasp after another.

Ross coaxed her to breathe, then calmed her when the nightmare she'd just lived through came back to haunt her. He murmured in her ear, assuring her that everything would be all right now, and telling her she had to recover because the children needed her.

Ross knew the room was a hive of activity but paid little attention. He was more concerned with Josie's struggle to break free of the haze that clouded her mind. That was more important than the commotion in the room.

Sam sent a footman after Agent McCormick who arrested Chadwick and took him away. Lady Clythebrook hovered close by for the next several hours, leaving only after Ross and Doctor Hallam assured her Josie would be fine and needed to rest.

A servant came in with fresh tea and plates of sandwiches and cakes several times, but Ross wasn't hungry and Josie wasn't alert enough to eat. Sam came back just before dark then left with his promise to come back in the morning.

Finally, the sun went down and the house grew quiet. And Ross was alone with Josie.

He sat at her bedside and held her hand in his. For long minutes her sleep would be deep and peaceful, then she'd toss restlessly and he'd gather her up against him and croon her back to sleep. It was hard for him to look at the bruises on her face that evidenced what she'd gone through. It was hard for him to imagine any hurt she'd endured and know he hadn't been there to protect her. He loved her so much he vowed he would never let anything happen to her again.

"You're still here?"

Ross lowered his gaze and saw Josie watching him, her eyes open as if she'd been studying him.

"Where else would I be?"

She shut her eyes briefly and sighed. "Perhaps with Major Bennett…standing guard outside my door…waiting to arrest me."

He held her gaze and fought the inner turmoil that wouldn't let go. "Why didn't you tell me?"

"I thought I could stop them myself. I thought when I told Captain Levy…that Baron Lindville said it was getting too risky…the smuggling would stop."

"But when you mentioned Baron Lindville, Captain Levy knew you were lying because Baron Lindville wouldn't have made that decision. Vicar Chadwick would have."

"I had no idea he was involved." She winced, then closed her eyes.

Ross moved to sit beside her on the bed. "Why did you step in front of me?"

"Because I—"

She stopped, then continued with measured words.

"Because Charlie's lost enough. I didn't want him to lose his father, too."

"You could have been killed."

"So could you."

"I know. It's over now. We'll talk later. You just need to rest."

He lifted her uninjured arm and pressed his lips to the tender flesh of her palm. Pure molten heat shot deep in his belly and he kept her hand nestled in his own. He wanted to tell her he loved her; he needed her to know. But not now. Not until he could prove he meant every word he said.

Ross watched her for a moment then leaned down and kissed her lightly. "Sleep now, and don't worry. I'll see to it that you're always safe." He brushed his fingers down the side of her face. "It won't be long and the cattle will bring in enough so the children will never have to go without again."

Ross heard her breathe a contented sigh as she twined her fingers in his. This was where she belonged. Where he wanted to keep her forever.

He stared into the dying fire and thought of everything he wished he'd told her but hadn't.

"I love you," he whispered. "I nearly lost you once but I won't chance losing you again."

Ross relaxed into the chair, his hand still holding hers, content for the first time since his father had made the Rainforth name synonymous with traitor.

Josie sat propped up against her pillows and watched Ross doze in the chair beside her. Except to meet with Major Bennett and Agent McCormick for a few hours yesterday, he hadn't left her side since she'd been shot three days earlier.

She knew why. He felt he owed her. She'd saved his life, after all. But he couldn't ignore St. Stephen's much longer or the cattle venture he was determined to set in motion. And the business with the smugglers still wasn't settled. She'd overheard Major Bennett tell him he'd have to go to London to verify everything. No, it wouldn't be long now before he'd be too busy to stay with her. Before he'd leave to go back to the life he'd left behind.

She had no idea falling in love was anything like this. She'd never realized it would hurt so much when it was over. Or that watching him leave her would be so hard. But he didn't belong here. He needed to return to London and take his place in Society. It's what he'd wanted from the very beginning.

He didn't talk of London much, only when she asked him a direct question. But when he did, she could hear the excitement in his voice. She could picture him in his formal blacks, going out for an evening, either to a ball or the opera or to one of his clubs.

Even though he didn't admit it, she knew he missed being a part of that life. As soon as word reached the drawing rooms that he'd been instrumental in shutting down one of the largest opium suppliers in England, there wouldn't be a hostess in all of London who wouldn't proclaim him her guest of honor, or a proud papa who wouldn't try to snare the infamous marquess for his daughter. And that was how it should be.

Josie pressed her hand over the heavy weight crushing against her chest. It hurt every time she thought of how this would end. She'd been so foolish, so very, very foolish. She'd fallen in love with the Marquess of Rainforth. *A marquess.* Exactly like her mother had done. Only she would not hold onto the delusions her mother had refused to abandon—that someday her marquess would give up everything to marry his mistress. That had been her mother's fatal error. Josie wouldn't make the same mistake. She wouldn't live her life dreaming of something that could not happen. Or believing in miracles. Even if the moon were full and filled with magic.

She watched him sleep a little longer. He was the most magnificently handsome man she'd ever met. It wouldn't take long at all before some beauty snatched him for her husband. For as much as it hurt to imagine him in someone else's arms and someone else's bed, she wished him well. And she would always have the memories of him in her arms and inside her body to remember. To cherish. She would make those memories last a lifetime.

Josie swiped at a tear that escaped from her eye and looked up at the soft knock on the door.

Major Samuel Bennett took a step into the room then stopped when his gaze rested on where Ross slept in the chair. "I told him country life was making him soft."

"I'm afraid it's my fault. I've been very demanding of his time. He's under the misguided assumption that my injury is his fault and that he must devote endless hours to be at my beck and call."

Ross moved. "The injury *is* my fault and I'd be lying in that bed instead of you if you hadn't foolishly stepped in front of me. I am not," Ross opened his eyes and sat up in his chair to finish his sentence, "devoting endless hours at your side because of some misguided guilt. I am devoting endless hours at your side because I cannot bear to think of being separated from you. You've captivated me, Miss Foley."

Josie made a very unladylike snort and rolled her eyes in an effort to hide the redness she knew was growing on her heated cheeks.

Ross stood. "Are you leaving, Sam?"

"I need to get back to London. McCormick's set up a meeting with the Queen in a week's time. Be ready to join me. As soon as the Queen hears the role you played in capturing the smugglers, she'll no doubt want to reward you for your service. It's no more than you deserve. Her recognition will make it impossible for Society to ignore you."

"Perhaps."

"More than perhaps, Ross."

Sam leaned over Josie and kissed her gently on the cheek. "Thank you for what you did. I'd like to explain the part you played in stopping the smuggling ring and saving Rainforth's life, but it's best if the authorities don't find out you were connected with the smuggling."

Josie knew exactly what the major was implying. "Thank you, Major."

"My pleasure. Take care of yourself and recover quickly."

"I will. Have a safe journey to London."

He nodded and turned to the door. Ross followed him. "I'll see you out," he said and left after promising to be back shortly.

Josie stared at the empty door until he returned. She smiled when he walked back into the room and kissed him back when he kissed her like he was used to doing for no reason at all. That was another memory she would cherish.

"Will you go to London?"

He nodded. "I'll have to. I'll accept all the pomp and accolades even though I cringe at the thought of such exposure. I don't have a choice though. Being accepted back into Society isn't just for me, but for Charlie. I've sent word for my solicitor to draw up the papers that will make him a Bennett, and someday inherit St. Stephen's. I want the Bennett name to be one he can wear with pride. And I want him to be able to walk into any home in London with his head high and the scandal my father placed on our shoulders a distant memory. Can you understand that?"

She nodded. She understood that and more.

She understood that this was the end. She understood that once he left she could never let him come back.

She put a smile on her face and looked up at him. She wouldn't let herself regret what she'd done. The passion they'd shared was the one perfect, magical memory she could hold onto.

Chapter 24

JOSIE SAT ON A BENCH in the garden beneath a shade tree and looked out at the flowers that were just beginning to bloom. Ross had been gone more than a month and she thought that by now the emptiness wouldn't hurt so much. But for some reason she couldn't explain, she hurt more.

On the outside she was healing every day. It wouldn't be long and she'd be well enough to go to the orphanage for at least a few hours. She wasn't sure how much longer it would take to heal on the inside. Or if she ever would.

She tried not to think of the promise she'd stopped him from making the day he left—that it would not be long before he came back to her—because she knew it was a promise he couldn't keep. He was the Marquess of Rainforth. She was the illegitimate daughter of one of nobility's mistresses. She could hardly play a role in his life. Not if he wanted his children to be accepted by Society. So she let him go.

The letter she'd written him had been the hardest words she'd ever composed. She'd had to tell him in terms he couldn't misunderstand that she didn't want him to come back to Clythebrook Manor. That what they'd shared was over and if he ever returned, she wouldn't receive him. She'd given him no reason for not wanting to see him again—what reason could she give him that he wouldn't try to refute. Except that in time, he'd realize she didn't belong in his life. And he must already because he hadn't written her in return, not even to tell her he'd received her message and agreed with her decision.

Josie felt another tear fill her eyes. She seemed to do that a lot lately for no expected reason. But then, she'd heard that was common for what she suspected might be wrong with her. She swiped the tear away and when she looked up she saw Lady Clythebrook coming down the path. Josie put a smile on her face and made room on the bench for Lady Clythebrook to sit beside her.

"Are you enjoying the sunshine, Josephine?"

"Yes, it's a beautiful spring day. Come, sit with me. The flowers are starting to make an appearance."

Lady Clythebrook sat. "I just received a letter by post from my friend, Lady Sheffield. You remember her. I'm certain I've spoken of her before. She's the Countess of Sheffield and she and I have been friends since we had our come-out together. She'd set her eye on the Earl of Sheffield—who wasn't an earl yet, but only a viscount—the minute she'd seen him. I, of course, had already decided I wanted Walter. I'm afraid we both behaved scandalously. But that's another story."

Josie knew all this, but let Lady Clythebrook relive what to her was a special memory.

"Anyway, she says she penned this letter the minute she returned from the Duchess of Dunsmore's ball. You'll never guess who the guest of honor was."

"Who?" Josie asked, even though she knew.

"The Marquess of Rainforth. She says that everyone in London is vying for his attendance at their balls. She says— well, listen to what she says—

> *'You can't imagine the stir young Rainforth is making,*
> *especially after the lavish ceremony Queen Victoria hosted*
> *in his honor. The queen has made it impossible for anyone*
> *to turn their backs on him and numerous affairs are being*

hastily planned with Rainforth as their guest of honor. He has taken the ton by storm. He is such a dashing young man and so very handsome—No, Constance. I'm not so old that I cannot take note of a handsome young man. And he makes sure to find time to attend them all, even making an appearance at two or three events in an evening. He's doing his best to set his foot firmly back into Society and from all signs, even the haughtiest are welcoming him with open arms. Especially anyone with a daughter of marriageable age.

'You should see the young fillies lined up to demand his attention. It's scandalous, Constance. Girls are much more brazen than we were in our day. Why, young Miss Hawkins, that's Baron Hawkins's second daughter from over by Leicester way, had the temerity to feign a swoon while Rainforth was escorting her in to dinner. Everyone knew she'd done it so he'd be forced to catch her. And, of course, her gown just happened to slide down exceedingly low to expose a great deal of her generous bosoms.

'Well, this only increased the efforts the other females are being forced to make to attract his attention. A short while later, the Duke of Perringot's eldest daughter, Lady Margaret, tried to trap Rainforth in a compromising situation in the garden. Luckily for him, his friend Major Bennett and his wife, who was the former Countess of Huntingdon—well, she wasn't really, but that's another story—came upon them to act as chaperone before Lady Margaret had time to put her plan into motion.

'Needless to say, the unmarried lasses are getting more desperate in their attempts to trap him and it won't be long before he finds himself leg-shackled.'

Lady Clythebrook folded her letter and placed it in her lap. "He's making quite a sensation in London. Has he written when he plans to return?"

Josie shook her head. "I don't imagine it will be for quite some time. He needs to be there. I'm sure there are several details to take care of, and it's important for him to regain his place. Not only for his own sake, but for Charlie's and the other children he is bound to have once he marries."

"If you're up to traveling, we could leave tomorrow and, if we proceed with caution, we can be there within the week. Then you could—"

"I know what you're trying to do," Josie said, patting Lady Clythebrook's hand, "but I have no intention of going to London. I think, though, that tomorrow I will go to the orphanage for a couple of hours. The children have all written their good wishes and I miss them terribly."

"I know you do. I also know you miss *him* terribly. I only wish there were something I could do."

"There isn't," Josie said, squeezing Lady Clythebrook's fingers. "We both knew this was how it would be. Lord Rainforth doesn't belong here. He never did."

"I think you're wrong, Josephine. This is exactly where he belongs. We'll just have to see whether or not he realizes it."

Lady Clythebrook gave Josie a smile then stood. "Are you ready to go inside?"

"No. I think I'll stay here a while longer."

"Very well. Don't take a chill."

"I won't."

Josie watched Lady Clythebrook make her way back to the house, leaning on the cane she always had with her. When she was out of sight, Josie lifted her face and let the sun bathe her a little while longer, then stood to go back. She'd spent enough time for one day reflecting on things she couldn't change. She took two steps toward the house and lifted her head. And stopped.

Rainforth was coming toward her, as unbelievably handsome as ever. Her heart began a steady pounding in her chest and she cursed herself for reacting to him.

He didn't call out a greeting, nor was there a smile on his face as he closed the distance between them. The expression he wore was more serious than she was used to seeing, his steel-gray eyes a deep silver. He had something on his mind, and if his stern countenance was an indication, it was of grave importance. Josie braced herself.

He stopped when he reached her, not a respectable distance away from her, but close enough that she could lift her hand and easily touch his face. Close enough that she could step into his embrace and rest her forehead against his chest. Close enough that she could smell leather and outdoors and the clean smell of the soap he'd washed with. She wadded the material of her skirt in her hands to keep from reaching out to him.

Neither of them spoke, but only studied each other as if something might have changed in the time since he'd left. Then, Josie realized she couldn't allow herself to go down this path. "I told Banks I wasn't receiving guests."

"He told me. I ignored him."

"I wrote you a letter, Lord Rainforth."

"I threw it in the fire."

"Don't make this more difficult that it is. Please."

"I wondered," he said breathing in a deep breath that expanded his chest and flared his nostrils, "if I had exaggerated in my mind how I would feel when I saw you again."

She swallowed. "Don't. Please."

"I hadn't come close," he continued as if she hadn't spoken. "I thought my heart would simply pound inside my chest as if it were running a race while the blood thundered inside my head."

"Don't," she whispered while her heart shattered inside her breast.

"And that happened," he continued. "I just hadn't counted on the weakness in my knees when I saw you or the trembling of my hands. Or the ache in my chest because I'd missed you so desperately."

Josie tried to keep the tears from welling in her eyes. How could she keep from giving in to him when he laid his feelings out before her with such an open admission?

"I've missed you, Josie," he said as he pulled her into his arms and brought his mouth down on hers.

He kissed her long and deep, giving her a taste of the emotion that overpowered them whenever they were close. She tried not to react, but lost the battle when he brought her closer to him. She'd dreamed of this. Dreamed of him holding her in his arms, of his lips pressed to hers, of his body surrounding hers. But she thought she'd only have her memories as comfort. Her heart gave a painful lurch. It would have been so much easier if he hadn't returned.

She turned her face to the side and stepped out of his embrace. It was the hardest thing she'd ever done.

"I'm surprised to see you here," she said taking another step away from him. "Lady Clythebrook received a letter just this morning exalting your praises and relating stories of the affect you were having on London Society. I'm glad you were so overwhelmingly accepted. Was it as grand as you thought it would be?"

"Taking my place in Society was necessary for Charlie as well as any other children I might have. Nothing more."

Josie felt a pang of something that resembled pain.

"Though I don't understand why you're surprised to see me back. Surely you knew I was coming."

There was a frown on his face that Josie couldn't bring herself to look at for long. "I knew you'd return eventually, but not so soon. Not until everything was settled in London."

"Other than the business with Sam and McCormick, what other business did you think I had to settle?"

She searched for the right words. "Personal matters. You need to marry. Surely you realize that now more than ever. You need to provide an heir to secure the Rainforth properties, just like you intend for Charlie to inherit St. Stephen's."

He nodded but the look of skepticism did not leave his face. "I'm glad you understand how important it is for me to marry. I was afraid it would be difficult for you to give in on this."

This was it, then. This was where he explained that even though he loved her, it was important that he take a bride from the "right" family. This was where he explained how important it was to marry a woman who already fit in with Society. She braced her shoulders and took a deep breath.

"You could have explained all this in a letter. There was no need to come to see me personally."

His eyebrows shot up. "Something this important deserved to be said in person."

She nodded. "And have you decided upon who it is you will marry? In a letter Lady Clythebrook received from Lady Sheffield, she says there is no small number of females ready to become the future Lady Rainforth."

"Yes. I have the future Lady Rainforth in mind."

Her heart twisted in her breast. She thought perhaps it had broken, but she would not allow herself to know for sure until she was away from him.

"You would approve of her, Josie."

"I'm sure I will."

"She will be the perfect mother for Charlie and the other children I intend to have."

"I'm glad."

"Are you?"

"Yes, of course. You deserve the best."

Oh, she wanted to leave him. She couldn't bear to hear him speak about children he would have with another woman. She couldn't bear to think of him planting his seed inside someone else and having a child by someone else and raising a child with someone else when…

"I have decided I would like a large family. *If* my wife has no objections. I was raised alone and was always so envious of my friends with brothers and sisters. Does that sound selfish of me?"

She clenched her fist and pressed it to her breast. Yes, her heart was breaking. If she stayed here much longer she would disgrace herself by bursting into tears.

"No. That doesn't sound selfish. Now, if you will excuse me, I've been out longer than I'd intended."

She turned away from him and took two shaky steps toward the house.

"How soon will you marry me?"

His question stopped her. Josie slowly turned.

"I know the proper way is to go down on one knee before the woman you love and ask her to marry you. It is no more than you deserve and I'll willingly do it that way if you want me to, but asking you *if* you will marry me demands a yes or no answer. I refuse to take the chance you might choose the wrong answer so I will ask you instead how *soon* you will marry me. That is not nearly so risky."

He took a step toward her. "How soon will you marry me? Tomorrow? Or will you make me wait a day longer?"

The tears that filled Josie's eyes spilled over her lashes and ran down her cheeks. "Oh, Ross. I…We…"

"Don't tell me we can't marry because I am a marquess. I can't help that. I am a marquess by accident of birth. Our firstborn male will suffer the same fate and inherit a title he probably won't want either. But he'll have no choice."

Josie swiped at her wet cheek. "I wasn't talking about you. It's me."

"Surely you aren't going to bring up the irrelevant fact that your father didn't marry your mother?"

"Irrelevant? Do you think Society will let either one of us forget it?"

"And do what? Snub the wife of the man the Queen of England just declared a hero? Risk the ire of Her Highness over something as insignificant as a bloodline? Especially when the woman in question is the daughter of the Marquess of Brookfield."

Josie's heart skipped a beat. "How did you…?"

"Lady Clythebrook told me." He closed the gap between them and clasped his hands around her upper arms. "But whether she had or not makes no difference."

His hold on her made her feel safe. His nearness made her heart race in her breast. The love she saw in his eyes filled her heart with unbounded ecstasy.

"I don't care what Society thinks of you or of me. I only know I can't spend the rest of my life without you. Or worse yet, spend it with some weak-brained, spoiled, debutante, whose pedigree is perfect. Hell, I barely survived the weeks I was away from you."

Josie smiled through her tears.

He leaned down and rested his forehead against hers. "Don't ask me to spend the rest of my life without you. I couldn't do it."

His voice had been low and the words raspy with emotion. A pressure tightened around her heart. "You don't know what you're asking. I'm not even sure who I really am. Foley is just the name my mother went by."

He smiled. "You're Josephine Foley. Foley was your mother's maiden name." He pulled a paper from his pocket. It was a special license. "I didn't want to chance putting the wrong name on our marriage license so I went to your father. He offered to give you away if you would like. The choice is yours though."

Josie looked at him in wide-eyed disbelief.

"You don't have to decide right away," he said, pulling her into his arms. "You have ten days."

She jerked away. "Ten days?"

"Sam and Claire are making the arrangements right now. We will be married in London a week from this Saturday. All of Society will be there because I want them to know how proud I am to have you as my wife, and how happy we are together. When we return to St. Stephen's, we'll throw a party the magnitude of which the people of Clytheborough have never seen. It'll be a celebration no one will forget."

Tears ran freely now and she wiped them away with the handkerchief Ross handed her.

"I love you, Josie. More than I thought it was possible to ever love anyone."

"And I love you. More than you can imagine."

He took her in his arms and gently touched his lips to hers. "Do you know when I first knew I'd fallen in love with you?"

She shook her head.

"It wasn't the first time I kissed you. I only suspected it then." She smiled.

"It was the second time I kissed you. That night beneath the stars and that damned jaded moon."

"Well then, sir, your memory is founded upon a myth."

"What? Impossible. I remember very clearly you called it a jaded moon."

"Not true, my love, not true at all. I called it magical. It was *you* who called *me* jaded. And perhaps I was…just a bit. But you saved me. And that magical moon brought my miracle."

She hugged him fiercely.

The Marquess of Rainforth tipped his head until their noses touched, and let out a long trembling breath. "As long as it's shining down on you, it will only be magical. And it will be the only place I will ever want to be. Forever."

He drew her into a kiss, and Josie knew she would have a whole lifetime of full moons and magic—right here in his arms.

About Laura

Laura Landon enjoyed ten years as a high school teacher and nine years making sundaes and malts in her very own ice cream shop, but once she penned her first novel, she closed up shop to spend every free minute writing. Now she enjoys creating her very own heroes and heroines, and making sure they find their happily ever after.

A vital member of her rural community, Laura directed the town's Quasquicentennial, organized funding for an exercise center for the town, and serves on the hospital board.

Laura lives in the Midwest, surrounded by her family and friends. She has written nearly two dozen Victorian historicals, thirteen of which have been published by Prairie Muse Publishing and are selling worldwide in English, one in Japanese, and several in German. Two are Scottish historicals.

In October 2012, Laura experienced an amazing day when Amazon's Montlake Romance published not one but three of her newest novels. Two of these have been optioned for publication in Russia and Turkey. Several are also available in German. To date Montlake has published six of Laura's Victorian historicals.

Always beautifully set and with a mysterious twist or bit of suspense, Laura's books average over a million and a half pages a month read by her loyal readers.

LAURA LANDON IS A PRAIRIE MUSE PLATINUM
KINDLE PRESS AND AMAZON MONTLAKE AUTHOR

WWW.LAURALANDON.COM

From Laura Landon
by Prairie Muse Publishing

SHATTERED DREAMS
WHEN LOVE IS ENOUGH
BROKEN PROMISE
A MATTER OF CHOICE
MORE THAN WILLING
NOT MINE TO GIVE
TANGLED: Boxed Set
LOVE UNBIDDEN
THE DARK DUKE

CAST IN SCANDAL Series (2015)
CAST IN SHADOWS
CAST IN RUIN
CAST IN ICE

RANSOMED JEWELS Series (2016)
RANSOMED JEWELS Bk 1 (Montlake Romance)
JADED MOON Bk 2 (Prairie Muse)
DARK RUBY Bk 3 (Kindle Press)

From Laura Landon
by MONTLAKE ROMANCE

SILENT REVENGE
INTIMATE SURRENDER
INTIMATE DECEPTION
THE MOST TO LOSE
A RISK WORTH TAKING
BETRAYED BY YOUR KISS

WHERE THE WOMAN BELONGS
NOVELLA

See all of Laura's books at Amazon.com

www.ingramcontent.com/pod-product-compliance
Lightning Source LLC
Chambersburg PA
CBHW071736190726
48292CB00003B/765